THE WITHDRAWAL METHOD

THE WITHDRAWAL METHOD

STORIES

PASHA MALLA

Soft Skull Press

Published by arrangement with House of Anansi Press, Toronto.

Library of Congress Cataloging-in-Publication Data
is available upon request.

ISBN 978-1-59376-238-4

Cover design by Luke Gerwe
Interior design by Laura Brady
Printed in the United States of America

Soft Skull Press
New York, NY

www.softskull.com

CONTENTS

THE SLOUGH

I

"I SHOULD PROBABLY tell you," she said, swallowing coffee, "that I'm about to lose my skin."

"What? Is that an expression?"

"No, not an expression. People's skin cells rejuvenate every seven years. Usually it's gradual, but I've been using something to make it happen all in one go."

"What?" He put down his knife and fork. There was something suddenly disquieting about the idea of bacon. "How does this work? What do you use?"

"It's a topical cream," she said.

"Topical? Do you mean like up-to-date? Current?"

"What are you talking about?"

"No, but this cream — where do you get it? Do other people do this?"

Her arms, those two pink Ls that began at the sleeves of her T-shirt and ended clutching cutlery on the tabletop, seemed normal enough: not peeling, not cracking, not even dry. "I got it at a specialty store. It's — "

"Is this going to happen like a snake? Like you'll just drop your skin and then it'll be sitting there in the shape of you?"

"I can't believe you're making a big deal of this. It was going to happen anyway."

"Right, so why not make a goddamn spectacle of it? Jesus." The lump of scrambled eggs on his plate was a jaundiced brain. The bacon looked like strips of pig, sliced off and then fried in their own sizzling fat. "When is this going to happen?"

"When?" She shrugged and took a bite of her toast. He waited, watching her jaw work. Nothing flaked away from her chin or cheeks; no skin snowed down onto her empty plate. She stared back at him. "Any day now."

"Like, maybe tomorrow?"

"Like, maybe today."

HE HAD FELT, lately, that his life had become a raisin — if only he'd got to it sooner, when it was ripe from the vine and bursting with juice! But no, it had shrivelled. If he handed out his life to trick-or-treaters at Halloween, a retributive bag of feces would appear flaming on his doorstep. Or maybe someone would pee on his mail.

She, on the other hand, was always up to something new. For the past few months she had been working toward a distance-education master's in film something, film and feminism. So there were countless DVDs that needed viewing. That evening they sat on the couch together to watch the next off the pile. It was a Hitchcock picture, and after some business in a hotel the action moved to a train.

"Oh, I know this one," he said.

"No, you don't," she said, putting on her glasses, getting her notebook ready. "Hush."

"No, I do — it's the one where the one guy kills the other guy's wife or something, and the other guy has to do it too. Kill the first guy's wife, I mean."

"That's *Strangers on a Train*. And you only know it from that Danny DeVito movie."

"Possibly."

"This is different. It's about a woman who goes missing. She's a spy."

"Oh, right," he said, and within minutes was asleep. The dream he had involved Alfred Hitchcock and something about a riding crop, and snakes, everywhere, shedding skin after skin. He had to fight his way through the papery wisps of them hanging like streamers in the air. Was she in it? Maybe. Or maybe he was trying to find her.

When he woke it was to a puddle of drool against his cheek and her undressing.

"What's going on?" He sat up and wiped his face on his shoulder.

"The movie's over. I'm going to take a shower."

"No, not with the movie — with you, with this skin business? What is this about?"

"You're still on about that?" She sighed, standing there in her underwear: the pink of her body banded twice in white cotton. And then she disappeared down the hall and the lock on the bathroom door went *click* and the shower went *whoosh* and he was left alone with what was on the only channel they got on their broke-dick TV: figure skating.

"Why?" he yelled at the bathroom door, the shower hissing back at him. "Why?!"

WHAT WAS THE reason they had moved in together? He couldn't remember. Peer pressure, maybe, from married and responsible friends. Or mutual coercion. Or Catholic guilt, although they weren't Catholic.

At any rate, here they were, and there shouldn't be secrets, not in relationships — wasn't that a basic tenet, like not poisoning each other's smoothies and alternating turns cleaning the oven? What had she been getting up to in the bathroom? In the mornings something would happen in there and she would come out riding the gusts of an expensive smell. In the evenings the shower would come on and fifteen minutes later she would emerge towel-turbaned and otherwise naked. But now there was this business with the cream and the shedding skin — not the life he had signed up for. They'd engaged in talk of "some space," sure, but he also felt a right to know, after seven years together, *what was going on.*

The following night she disappeared into the shower while he sat watching figure skating again. Twenty minutes later here she came, a rosy fakir, all loofahed and nude and clean with steam billowing behind her. She sat on his feet and got out a bruise-coloured nail polish, while on the TV the figure skaters ice-danced and he waited for one of them to fall. He looked down at her feet, up her legs, her stomach and breasts, all the way to her face. From head to toe her skin glowed in one taut, moisturized, perfect piece. Back on the TV, a fellow in a sequined pantsuit was spinning an equine-looking woman by the legs, round and round, to "Devil with a Blue Dress On."

"Come on, fall," he said, slapping the coffee table. "Fall, you fuckers. Fall, fall, fall!"

One by one her toenails went purple. By the time they were dry the skating program was over. Someone had won: there were flowers and a microphone thrust at the winners' weird smiles. He switched the TV off, and unspeaking they clasped hands and stood and went to the bedroom and had sex there, on the bed. He climbed on top and she said, "Plow me, baby!" and he said, "Okay," and plowed her for all he was worth.

But the plowing seemed mechanical. They were doing the right things and making the right noises, but there used to be a time when she'd flip him over and grind away on top and they would come together like champions. Now, not so much: she lay there with her knees in the air and when he finished it was onto her belly with a gasp. She patted his back, twice, and he rolled off and she rolled away, wiping his sperm from her body with a T-shirt.

They lay there side by side in the dark until her breathing slackened and he knew she was asleep. He began sweeping the sheets for flakes of her. Nothing, not even that improbable bed-sand he had experienced with previous lovers, way back when. But who was to say that he wouldn't wake to a husk of a woman beside him, the new version off in the kitchen crafting a morning latte?

He reached over and ran his hand along her thigh, up her stomach, her breasts, shoulders, neck, face, the skin smooth all the way. He felt for a rift from which the whole thing might be beginning to peel away, like cling-wrap from a ham. He would flatten down the loose edge, tuck her back into herself, and there would be no more talk of new anything and that would be that. But there was nothing; she was seamless. Casually, his hand drifted to her crotch, to the soft frizz of her down there. Her chest rose and fell, steady as waves. He lay his palm like so and eased a finger in, just to see: things were damp inside, and warm.

"WHAT I WANT is a record. A document."

Finally, they were getting somewhere. "Explain," he said.

"Think of all you've done in the last seven years."

He thought for a while, and then stopped, because it was depressing.

"Okay, not *you* specifically, but . . . anyone. People."

"You."

"Me, sure."

"I would think of all you've done in the past seven years, but it would involve that yoga instructor who was on the scene for the first few months when we started going around together — before you ditched him, thank Christ — and that makes me sad for you. It makes me want to take you in my arms and kiss you." He shuffled his chair over, leaning toward her, puckering his lips. "Very quickly, and very hard."

She pushed him away. "Shut up. Seven years of your life, just flaking away, gone. This year I'll have all of them, my whole body, in one piece."

"And then what? You'll just keep it around? Are you going to press it like a dried flower or something, make a giant book-mark?"

"I don't *know*. It might not even work like that. I just . . ."

"The thing I don't get is why you'd tell me this now. You've been doing these cream treatments for how long?"

"I got it just before we met. I started pretty much right around our first date."

"Oh god."

"You should be happy! It's like I knew all along that you'd be here for the end." She looked at her watch. "Man, I'm going to be late for work."

"If it happens there, will you bring the skin home? Or just pin it up in your cubicle with coloured tacks?"

But she was already standing with half a waffle wagging from her mouth, and putting on her coat, and now the bike helmet, and removing the waffle to kiss him on the cheek, and out the door, and gone. Left with the buzz of the fridge and his half-eaten grapefruit, he registered what she had said: "For the end." What the hell did that mean?

He went to the bathroom and rooted around in the medicine cabinet for this magical cream, whatever it was. But she had for some reason transferred everything to generic plastic containers. Some of the creams were a mysterious robin's egg blue, others white, others just cream-coloured, the colour of cream. He unscrewed the lid of one and sniffed. And another. And another. They all smelled like her. Or like little fractions of her: coconut + aloe + pink, etc. He crowded all the open bottles together in the sink, took a towel and ducked down and draped it over his head so it formed a sort of cave. With the towel trapping the aromas, he inhaled. Close.

He was late for work. And then, perfect: the fucking subway stalled between stations. After what seemed like ages another train pulled up on the adjacent track and sat there too. He looked in through the lighted windows at the commuters: the frustration on their faces, all those briefcases on all those laps. His own briefcase, on his own lap, had been her idea. "You can't go to work with a plastic bag!" she had told him one day. "But all I take is a sandwich," he had said, to which she had replied, "Well, take your sandwich to work like a man."

But then there was movement. His train was pulling forward. He watched the other train go by, the faces of the passengers sliding past, the lights of the windows fading until they were gone and nothing was left, just an empty track where the train had been. And that was when he realized that he hadn't moved at all. The other train had left. His still sat in the dark of the tunnel, waiting for some signal so it could go.

He thought about this skin business, and about the sex they'd had the night before, purposeful and sterile. He admitted to himself: lately things had gone stale. Maybe something new was just what they needed — a new DVD player, sure, but even better, a new skin. And as the train creaked into motion he began to come around to the idea, and then he was excited, and he was checking and rechecking his cellphone for reception so he could tell her, and was doing this with such fervour that he missed his stop.

By now he was half an hour late for work, so he got out of the subway to call in and let them know — what, that his girlfriend had that morning had an emergency, making implied references to her private parts. That sort of thing worked every time. And then he would call her and say, "Yes, your new skin is just what our relationship needs!" But his phone wasn't working and now the battery was on its last blip of power too.

He was in that part of town where sweaters made from Guatemalan llamas were sold in abundance and everyone smelled like hash. Making his way to street level, he heard music — a song he recognized but couldn't place, played soft and sad nearby.

At the top of the stairs sat a fat man playing the flute. Two CDs bearing the fat man's picture were propped against a yogurt container with a quarter and a penny in it. And now a loonie — *cling!* — and he made his way out, a dollar poorer, into the neighbourhood, acting as though he had somewhere to go, a place where he was needed, someone to see, trying to find somewhere his dying cellphone would work.

A store to his left was selling bongs and bongos. Out front loitered the expected clientele, who eyed him as he slouched by with his briefcase, phone aloft like a compass.

Here was a retailer of used clothes with a rainbow of jeans pinned over the doorway. Here was a place called The Anarchist Bookstore with a sleeping cat in the window. Here was a medical clinic of some description, and here was — hello! — *Your one-stop shop for natural remedies*, and then there was some Chinese writing on the sign.

The door chimes were wooden and knocked against one another like bones. A woman sat working the counter. "Hi!" she yelled, smiling.

"Hi," he said. "Do you sell a skin cream — "

"Skin creams, in the back!"

"Okay!"

"In the back!" She pointed past a rack of soaps that were flecked with what looked like dirt. "*In the back!*"

"Thank you!"

In the back were shampoos made from all sorts of improbable concoctions, remedies for ailments he didn't know could afflict human beings, things that were technically foods but you were meant to rub into your feet. And skin creams. A shelf stretched from the floor of the shop to the ceiling, full of skin creams. "Good Christ," he muttered.

"Need help?!" screamed the woman.

"No!" he screamed back. "Thanks!"

But, yes, he most certainly did. All of the containers were the same: a label featuring a bushel of herbs superimposed over an alpine scene and the brand name, Natür. There was never any explanation of what anything was supposed to *do* — just a list of exotic plants meaningless to anyone except, he imagined, the sorts of people who hugged too long, always.

But then, right at the bottom, wedged into a corner of the shelf, there was one that was different: Formula 7, in a metal jar. He picked it up and was amazed by its weight — as though the container were filled with pennies. He had to put his briefcase down and hold it in two hands. The metal was cool.

At the counter, the woman working eyed him suspiciously when he placed the Formula 7 in front of her. This time she didn't yell but spoke in a hushed, crackling voice that suggested Eastern wisdom, or laryngitis. "You know what that is?"

"I think so. Is it the cream that — "

She waved her hand. "Four hundred dollars."

"Oh," he said, and suddenly realized what song the fat man had been playing on his flute: "The End," by the Doors, whom he loathed.

AT WORK NO one seemed to notice, or care, that he had been missing all morning. From the phone in the stockroom he called her at her office.

"Baby! I found it! The cream!"

"Oh, no. You didn't."

"Of course, I didn't! It's four hundred dollars! But I'm excited. I think it's going to be good. It's going to be great."

"What were you doing out there, anyway? I thought you hated that part of town."

He spoke in a whisper. "Has it started yet?"

"No. No, nothing. I don't think it'll happen at work."

"How do you know? Are there signs?"

"A woman knows these things."

Was she joking? Since when did she talk like that? Since when was she "a woman"? But, he realized, she was right. A woman knew things, all sorts of things. Did she? Probably.

THAT NIGHT HER homework was a Marilyn Monroe picture. He liked Marilyn Monroe — or her bosom, anyway, although he hadn't seen any of her movies.

"Oh, you'll know this one. That scene of her on the subway grate, with her skirt blowing up — 'Isn't it delicious?' That's this one."

"Isn't *what* delicious?"

She gave him a look. "Just put the movie on."

He did. She took up her notebook and sat there in her glasses tapping her teeth with a pen and occasionally jotting something down. After a few minutes, he fetched a notebook of his own, one with a fancy leather cover her mother had given him one Christmas and he'd never used.

If after the skin change she emerged a different person, he figured it would be useful to have a record of how she used to be. This he wanted to seem covert but mysterious, and kept eyeing her at the other end of the couch and saying, "Oh!" and then scribbling something down. But she was watching the movie and working and didn't ask what he was up to.

Stats were first: height, weight, hair colour, birthdate, and so forth. Then he moved into slightly more personal information. Her favourite food was tomato soup, she had lost her virginity at seventeen while watching *The Hunt for Red October*, her desert-island disc was *Graceland*, and she could not abide the squeak of Styrofoam against Styrofoam or the thought, even abstractly, of eels.

And then he wrote this: *I like the way she scrunches her eyes up like a little kid when she eats something she doesn't like.* He wrote, *Sometimes she laughs too loud in public and I complain but really I find it amazing.* He added, *Sometimes I find her amazing.*

YEARS AGO, FOR their second Valentine's Day together, they decided to eat at separate restaurants — the idea being that loneliness would reinforce their love. It worked: he pushed his food around pathetically with an empty chair across the table, the over-attentiveness of his waiter a poor mask for pity.

Later, he clutched her in bed with what could be described only as desperation. It had become a Valentine's Day tradition ever since.

He added this to his list the next night, while she screened something irreverent from France. It required a few pages and an expository style that at first seemed odd beside the point-form notes, but then he liked. He looked up: in the movie one of the characters said, "Je t'aime," to another character, and that character said it back — although there was something Parisian and disaffected about the exchange. The French! They were so mean and great.

Opening his notebook again, he added another little story. The third time they had sex he grunted, "I love you," when he was coming, and afterwards they lay in awkward silence on opposite sides of his futon. "I love having sex with you," he whispered after a few minutes, trying to make it sound like something he'd just covered and was now reiterating, casually.

He was reminded then of this story: one night a few months later they were at a thing for one of their artist friends. Over the crowd of people in complicated shoes they locked eyes and she winked. Something in that wink sang through him, warm. He stumbled beaming (away from some guy detailing his process) across the room and planted one on her, as dumb and happy and slobbery as a puppy. They had pulled away, unspeaking, and for the first time in his life he could see in someone else's eyes exactly how he felt.

On the TV the woman was now wandering morosely around Paris; her lover was nowhere to be seen. Meanwhile, at the far end of the couch, she was making notes.

He kicked her.

"Ow," she said. "Don't."

"Hey," he said, nudging her with his foot.

"Hush, will you? This is for school."

He nudged again and she looked at him, exasperated. "What?"

"I love you," he said.

She stared at him. "And?"

"And do you love me?"

"No, I hate you."

"Really?"

"Yes."

He looked at her. She gazed back, her expression impatient. He looked into those eyes, from one to the other across the beautiful nub of her perfect nose, searching for something. But he couldn't find it, because he wasn't sure exactly what he was supposed to be looking for.

AT NOON THE next day he went into the bathroom at work and locked himself in a stall. He put the lid of the toilet down, kept his pants up and sat. There was someone in the next stall over; he could hear the toilet paper being whisked from its dispenser, the scrub of it between ass cheeks, a cough. He waited until the toilet flushed, the stall creaked open, the taps ran, the hand drier roared, and the bathroom door closed. Left alone, he put his head in his hands and sat there like that, on the toilet lid in the stall in the bathroom, until his lunch break was over.

HE GOT HOME that night and she was still at work. The slick clock above the kitchen table, all chrome and Scandinavian, claimed it was half past six. She was usually home before him and had something happening, food or booze, when he walked in the door. In the fridge he found half a bottle of red wine; it had been there for weeks. He poured himself a glass and drank it, ice-cold and sour, as he wandered around the apartment.

As he made his way from room to room, everything struck him as relics: framed photos of a bike trip through the Maritimes, a table that had belonged to her grandparents, the fern that he had nearly killed and she had revived and that now bloomed green and glorious in the living room — artifacts in a museum, a history of their life in things. What would it all mean when she came home with a different skin? Maybe they'd have to get new stuff.

He sat down at the kitchen table and from his briefcase removed the notebook. What had started as a simple inventory had become something else — notes for a story or a film treatment. Yes, a movie! One of those hipster indie rom-coms, maybe, something quirky starring a hot young actor as him and a hot young actress as her, with lots of talking to the camera and a badass soundtrack. Encouraged, he got out his pen to add another story.

One summer years ago they were doing a shop together, and the woman in front of them in line at the grocery store had a shocking sunburn — the sort that looks as though the skin is still cooking, that it would be gooey to touch.

The woman was middle-aged, a typical July mom in a tank top tucked into khaki shorts, a crotch that stretched impossibly from navel to knees. In certain places the sunburn —

which spread across the mom's back, down her arms, up her neck — had begun to peel. White fractures split the red, the edges dry and ragged. They stood gawking at the sunburn while the mom placed eight boxes of ice cream onto the conveyor belt in a slow, pained way.

And then, before he could stop her, she was reaching out and taking hold of one of the flaps of dead skin on the mom's back and gently pulling it free. The mom watched the cashier ring her ice cream through, oblivious. He was horrified, but amazed. What sort of human being would do such a thing? And then something snapped and, before she could be caught with the evidence, she flicked the little ribbon of mom away.

On the subway ride home, groceries clustered in bags at their feet, he demanded: "Why?"

"I don't know — weren't you tempted to do it? It was just so . . ." She made a noise similar to those she produced during sex.

"No. No, it was absolutely not 'just so' anything. That was sociopathic behaviour. A cannibal might do something similar."

"Oh, come on. Cannibals eat people, not peel them."

"What do you think the first step is?"

"Please."

They would move in together two months later.

He sat there, reading the story over. It came floating up off the page with the milky miasma of a recalled dream. Crap. Had he made the whole thing up? There had been a sunburned lady once at the grocery store, he was sure — but had the peeling attack actually happened, or was it just something they discussed, or he imagined? He poured out the last drips of wine from the bottle, tipped back a sludgy mouthful, and closed the journal. He sat there for a long time with his hand on the cover before he looked up at the clock.

Ten past seven. She was late — very late. She'd never been this late before, not without calling or a plan. Maybe the skin had started to slough away at the office and she'd had to get her colleagues to help with the unwrapping. Or maybe something had gone wrong and she was lying on the floor of her cubicle, strangled to death by the crackling wisps of her old arms.

No, he thought: she was gone. She had shed her old self and life and taken off. Maybe later she would call him from some roadside hacienda in dustiest Mexico, all fresh-skinned and new. A person reborn, free of him and their life together. He imagined her riding her bike along the side of the highway, the skin peeling away from her body, flapping at her heels, as she made her way to somewhere better.

II

SINCE LEE WENT in nearly three weeks ago, I spend my weekends watching movies with her in the ICU. She's got a list of classics she's always wanted to see, so on Friday evening after work I stop by the video shop between the airport and hospital and pick up the next three: *The Lady Vanishes*, *The Seven Year Itch*, and *Cléo from 5 to 7*. We'll watch one a day and then I'll return them all on Monday.

Waiting for me in the hallway outside Lee's room is Dr. Cheung. "Hi, Pasha!" she says, producing a hand to shake, which I shake. Her hand is cold. Her hands are always cold, and her voice is always alarmingly loud — especially for a hospital.

"How are things going?"

"She's doing well!" enthuses Dr. Cheung, beaming. Then she lowers her voice. "We've got the last of the scans back and think we can go ahead with the surgery either tomorrow or the next day."

"That's the Gamma Knife thing?"

"Yes, we'll use it to remove the two remaining metastases from her brain. As I'm sure Dr. Persaud told you, melanoma responds so poorly to traditional radiation that we really think this is the best option."

"And it's safe?"

Dr. Cheung nods. "Absolutely. This in fact has less potential of complication than the surgeries we did to remove the original tumors on her back. Lee has some literature. Why don't you go in and see her?"

"Isn't she sleeping now?" I step away from Lee's room. "Maybe I should wait?"

"No!" Dr. Cheung yells, her hand on my shoulder, urging me forward, voice cranked back up. "She's waiting to see you!"

I pause at the door. Dr. Cheung nods and gives me a shove into the room.

"Hey," Lee whispers. She's propped up in bed with a version of lunch on the tray in front of her: gravy-soaked brown mush, veggies, a lump of potato.

"Hey," I say. I put the newspaper, DVDs, and coffee on the tray, kiss her on the top of her bald head, and sit down.

LEE'S NIGHT NURSE is Olivier, the quiet Congolese guy Lee really likes. If Dr. Cheung is a foghorn, Olivier is a thought. You barely know he is there; he whispers and nods and treats Lee with gentle reverence. Sometimes he mutters softly to her in French, "Ma petite puce," while he is changing her IV.

I sit watching for a bit and then Olivier turns to me and says, "Sir," which is his polite way of asking me to leave. At first I'd been offended by the nurses asking this — after so long together I've seen Lee in every state of compromise you could possibly imagine — but I've realized it's not about me.

"Ten minutes," Olivier whispers, and pulls the curtain around the bed, closing them off. I leave the room, then head down the hall, into the elevator, down four levels, and out of the hospital, where I stand with the smokers, not smoking because I don't smoke.

WE'VE JUST STARTED The Seven Year Itch, headphones clamped over our ears, when Mauricio appears at the curtain, his sideburns two slick daggers on either side of his face.

"Knock, knock," he says.

Lee hits Stop on the remote and swings the screen out of the way. "Bienvenido," she says.

Mauricio and Lee went to school together. I guess he tutored her in Spanish before she went to Mexico for a foreign exchange. They met up down there and travelled around, and then he'd moved home to Buenos Aires. He came back up here a few months ago, maybe because Lee got sick — I'm not sure. I'm not sure if they ever slept together either. There's definitely something. I've always dealt with it by trying to seem okay with the guy, not asking too many questions.

"Hey, man, take my seat," I tell him, standing and offering the chair. "Please."

Mauricio's brought flowers, which he passes to me as we swap places. Shuffling the chair closer to the bed, he takes Lee's hand and runs his thumb over her knuckles.

"How you feeling?" he asks, staring into her eyes.

"Okay," she tells him. "Tired. The pain's not been too bad today."

"Yeah."

Watching Mauricio so close to her, I try to summon up some feeling of jealousy or resentment. But it's hard. My physical contact with Lee has become so perfunctory. Since the diagnosis we've had sex once — and that was six months ago and at Lee's urging, not mine. I capitulated but went about it as though she were something made of glass, the words *skin cancer* rattling around in my brain the entire time. Afterwards she went to get a drink of water and didn't come back to bed. Eventually, I went into the kitchen and found her sitting at the table in the dark.

Mauricio's stroking her arm now, up and down — an arm bruised and scarred from all the lines and ivs constantly being threaded into it. The bruises are purple and yellow blotches. The newest scars are red and wet; the oldest, black scabs. She looks like a junkie. Lee's arms make something sickly rise in my throat and a prickly feeling fizz from my feet to my head. They are nothing I'd want to touch.

But Mauricio doesn't seem to mind. He runs his fingers up and down her arms like the marks aren't even there. They gaze into each other's eyes. Her hair's been gone for ages, but since they stopped the chemo there's a downy sort of fuzz growing in. Mauricio cradles the nape of her neck with his hand, then leans in to scoop her into his arms. He holds her, softly but firmly. She hugs him back. They're this way for a long time, while I stand in the corner of the room, cradling the bouquet of flowers like some sort of caddie or valet.

WHEN VISITING HOURS are over Mauricio and I leave together.

"I'm going to meet some friends to go dancing," he says. "Do you want to come?"

"Dancing? No, man, I'm probably good."

He sambas off into the night and I make my way to the subway station.

Riding home, slumped in my seat as the train roars and squeals its way between stops, I watch a couple at the end of the car making out. They are seventeen, maybe eighteen. Their jaws are really working. At one point the girl climbs up and mounts the guy's thigh and starts grinding into him with her hips. He licks her sloppily from neck to eyebrow, then pulls away, panting. They stare at each other for a bit, then he kisses her on the cheek and tells her, "God, I'm so fucking in love with you. It's fucking crazy."

"Holy fuck," she says, kissing him on the forehead, the cheek, the other cheek, the mouth. "Me fucking too."

AT HOME I POUR myself a glass of cold, sour wine from the refrigerator and take it with me as I move around the apartment. I take an inventory of the things that are technically Lee's — stuff she owned before we moved in together. I try to figure out what I would want to keep if she dies. This is what I settle on: the microwave, the coffee maker, the DVD player, the big soft towel we fought over every time it came out of the laundry. But then I realize that there's no "would"; there's no "if." The doctors have given Lee three months, tops. All these things are already mine.

At ten thirty, I go out to eat. Most nights I do. Lee was the cook. I'm decent with a barbecue, can fry up a burger if need be. But we live in a neighbourhood with plenty of cheap food: Indian, Vietnamese, Mexican. It's late so I head to the burrito joint down the street. I order a beer and sit with it while the guy behind the counter shuffles around getting my food together. I drain the bottle when my order comes up, so I get another one and take it and my tray to sit down.

"Pasha?"

I look over. It's this girl Giselle I went to school with. Back then I had a girlfriend — not Lee, someone else I met through friends — and Giselle had a long-distance thing with some guy she met online. We'd go out for drinks with people from class, and every night would end with just us two left, sitting on stools at the bar together, faces inches apart. We'd stay to last call and have this weird, protracted goodbye before heading our separate ways. I came close to trying something a few times, but never did.

"Hey," I say. It's been eight, nine years, but Giselle looks

good. She was always pretty, but that was never why I was
attracted to her. It was more the way she'd make you feel like
you and her were the only people on the planet, those big
brown eyes staring deep into yours. But right now she's with
some guy in a puffy vest, possibly the Internet boyfriend. I
never met him.

"Come sit with us," she says, so I do, sliding my tray
between theirs.

She introduces the guy she's with as Philippe, a friend of
hers from high school — right away I can tell there's nothing between them. I suggest they grab a beer and stick
around, making sure that it sounds like an invitation to him
as much as to her. Giselle orders a Corona. Philippe doesn't
get anything.

"How are things?" Giselle asks. "Still dating that teacher?"

"No, we broke up years ago," I say. She doesn't ask any
more than that, so I don't offer anything. "What about you?
How's your cyber-man?"

"Ha, right. Him. We broke up," she says, then adds,
"too."

We drink. Philippe has found an *Auto Trader* that seems to
have piqued his interest. I tell Giselle about how I work at the
airport now, in the bookstore. "All my literary ambitions have
at last been realized," I say, and she laughs.

Five minutes later I'm done eating and I've got two beers in
me. "You guys want to go grab another drink?"

Philippe and his puffy vest can't. Giselle looks at him, then
me. "I wouldn't mind, actually," she says and turns back to her
friend. "Can we catch up later?"

At the pub down the street we realize that we both want the same beer, the house pale, so I order a pitcher. Giselle suggests we sit at the bar. "Like old times," she says. The bartender leans in with a candle and our jug and I pay him. Giselle pours and we sit there for a moment, watching the flame distort and refract through our pint glasses.

"Cheers," she says. "Good to see you."

We look each other in the eye as we drink, put the beers down and keep looking.

Our conversation flits between old stories from school and updates on classmates. Neither of us is doing much writing any more — although she's done slightly better, working as a copy editor at some trade magazine. We talk about where we're living. I don't ask if she's got roommates, and she doesn't ask me. I never once need to lie about anything.

Then the pitcher's done.

"Want another?" she asks, giving the empty jug a wiggle. Her face is flushed. "It's on me."

It feels good to be out with someone. "Sure, I say," and pat her leg. "It's nice to see you."

"It's *great* to see you."

We drink, and soon we're drunk, and we're close, and there's a lot more touching: thighs, shoulders, elbows. She gets in so close that my knee slides between hers. Her eyes are heavy-lidded. By the time the third pitcher comes and we're both scrounging for change to pay for it, my face feels like rubber and we're holding hands.

"ISN'T THAT WHAT you were wearing yesterday?"

"This?" I wipe the sweat off my top lip with the back of my hand. "Yeah, laundry day, got a little desperate. Ran out of quarters."

"You reek," she says. "What'd you drink last night?"

Lee's really alert today, sitting up straight. There are days like this every now and then, when it's hard to believe how sick she is. She's her old sharp self, watching me shrewdly. I try to meet her eyes and hold them.

She looks away, out the window. It's been alternating rain and snow all morning. "I'm going in tomorrow morning for the Gamma Knife surgery."

"Why do they call it a knife, anyway? It's not a *knife*, exactly, is it?"

"No, they —" She collapses, coughing. I spring out of my chair to help her but end up just sort of hovering while she hacks and retches. When it's over, she picks her sentence up where she left it. "— do it with a laser sort of thing. You don't feel any pain or anything, and you're usually back to normal within a day. If I was healthy enough I wouldn't even have to stay over. There's some literature there on the side table. Give it a read if you're interested."

My cellphone rings as I pick up one of the pamphlets. It's Giselle. I hit Silence and pocket the phone. "Work," I say.

"On a Saturday?"

"Yeah, Sonya needs me to come in to cover someone's shift tomorrow. And she knows you're her. It's retarded. I should fucking quit."

"I'm 'her'? Who's her?"

"Here."

"You said her."

"No I didn't. *Here.*"

Lee waves the argument away. "You're not allowed cell-phones in the hospital anyway."

"It's fine."

"It's not. It messes with the machinery."

"How?"

"I don't know, it just does."

I pick up the newspaper lying at the foot of her bed. She's done about half the crossword.

"Don't do any clues," she says. "I'm going to do it."

"I wasn't."

"Yeah, right. You always come in here and do them."

"Since when? I hate crossword puzzles."

"You're always doing them. You always come in here and wreck it."

She gets to coughing again. I watch her and try to summon some inkling of compassion, but I can't. All I feel is impatient. I think about waking up that morning in Giselle's bed feeling no guilt, just inconvenienced at having to come to the hospital. When Lee's done coughing I sit there saying nothing. I want to leave.

"Can you get me a coffee?" she says.

"Are you supposed to have coffee?"

"I always have coffee. Just get me one. And don't put cream in it this time; you always put too much in. Just bring me a creamer and let me do it."

I look at her for a minute: the bald head, the gaunt face,

the wreck of a body. But in the eyes is something very much alive. It's anger — not anger at me, specifically; I just happen to be in its path. Lee's not supposed to have coffee, especially less than twenty-four hours before surgery. She knows it and she knows I know it. Her wanting one now is not about coffee. She's letting me know she's given up, she's letting go. She doesn't care any more. And she wants me to be complicit in that.

So I get up and go get Lee a coffee.

"YOU REMEMBER Buster?" I ask Giselle that evening on the phone.

"Oh, right — your parents' dog? You brought him round once. He was cute."

"Yeah. We had to put him down last year."

"Aw."

"He was about sixteen. By the end he got to the point where he was pissing himself, falling down the stairs. So after like six months of him getting worse and worse eventually my mom decided it was time to put the poor guy down — which was, you know, pretty sad. But I guess she let him into the backyard to take a shit before the appointment and he just went for it, bounding around like a puppy. Like, 'Hey, don't kill me! Look, I'm still happy, I can have a good time!'"

I trail off then, trying to remember where this story came from or where it might lead. I'm just lying there on the couch, Lee's Gamma Knife pamphlet unfolded on my chest. "But, you know," I say, "she took him in anyway. My mom's a heartless bitch like that."

Giselle laughs. "I never met your mom, I don't think."

"She'd like you," I say, and then actually wonder if she would. She never liked Lee.

Giselle's quiet. Then, "I want to see you," she says.

"Yeah. Me too."

"I'll come over."

I look around the apartment, at the tastefully framed art, the symmetrical placement of furniture, the knick-knacks. Even if I took the photos of Lee and her family down, it'd be obvious I didn't live here alone. This isn't a single guy's place. "That's okay. Let me come see you," I say.

"Okay."

"Should I come now?"

"Yeah, hurry," says Giselle, and I do.

"I'LL COME BY right after work, okay? It sucks I got called in."

"Hey, someone's got to bring home the bacon," Lee says. But then there's only breathing on the other end of the line, hollow and raspy. She doesn't say anything else.

I hang up the phone and Sonya's standing there staring at me. She's been managing the store since well before I started, a trundling garbage truck of a woman who thinks she's worldly because she works in an airport, despite never actually having been anywhere herself.

"How's Lee?" asks Sonya.

"Oh, you know. Same."

"Sorry, Pasha."

I try to make my face look however it's supposed to. "Thanks," I say.

It's been months since I worked a Sunday. I've forgotten how quiet the terminal gets. The few customers we get are just trying to kill time before their flights, idly browsing the hardcover bestsellers, the magazine racks, the Sudoku books, the travel guides, rarely buying anything. We carry this series of classics bound in fake leather that always draws interest (although few sales). They're classy-looking editions, but expensive, and printed on paper that reminds me of Bibles.

Burying my face in anything is more appealing than dealing with Sonya, so I join the browsers. After a quick pass down the newspaper aisle, in the fiction section I've exhausted most of our selection (from Albom to Sheldon) when I notice one of those fake leather classics called *Adventures in the Skin Trade*. It's up on the top shelf and definitely not one I've seen before.

I reach up for it, but stop. My hand sort of hovers there over the spine while I imagine this skin trade business: people emerging from their outer casings, sloughing them off into rubbery piles at their feet, then donning new ones and heading out into the world. I don't take the book down. Back at the register, Sonya looks at me funny, but her face quickly folds into some puppy-eyed approximation of sympathy.

"You doing okay, bud?" she says, and wraps one of those flabby arms around my shoulder. A customer looks awkwardly up from the copy of *Time* he's reading, then back down at the page. Sonya's so close I can smell the cat odour on her. "Need a hug?" she says and, before I can respond, swallows me into one.

"WHO'S LEE?"

Giselle and I have just got our food when this happens. It's like she's pulled a severed head from underneath the table and dumped it onto my plate.

"Lee," I say. I don't know what is expected of me. I wait.

Except Giselle is waiting too.

"Lee is my girlfriend."

Across the table, Giselle sits staring at me with a clump of salad on the end of her fork. Elsewhere around the restaurant is the tinkle of silverware, the burble of conversation. But between us the air's gone silent and thick.

"She's sick. She's in the hospital." I glance around, then back at Giselle. "Last year she got melanoma. They've given her a few months to live. But you probably know this. Who told you?"

"I'm assuming *she* doesn't know about *me*. She'd be okay with you fucking other people?"

"It's . . . I don't know if it's okay. It's not okay. But we were done months before this happened." I realize that I need to seem more helpless. "I don't know what I'm supposed to be doing," I say, and look into Giselle's eyes in what I hope seems a pleading way.

I'm stunned when she shrugs. "Well, whatever. You're in a shitty spot for sure. But if you just need someone to be with, I get it. I just never thought I'd ever be 'the other woman' — should I feel honoured or something?"

Apparently Giselle doesn't care for an answer. She rifles through her salad for tomatoes, spears two on her fork, pops them in her mouth. I sit in silence, my food untouched in front of me, watching her eat. When the salad's gone she wipes her mouth with her napkin and flips her phone open.

"Shit, quarter to seven. I have to get going. I've got a date tomorrow night, but if you want to hook up later, text me. We're just going to an early movie."

She tries to chip in some money for the bill. I wave it away. And then she's past me, out the door of the restaurant. Through the window I watch her on the sidewalk, flipping her phone open again, checking her messages, moving off down the street.

AFTER DINNER I GO for a walk in the park, down the path to the pond. It's busy there on Sundays usually, but the evening is overcast and gloomy and there are only a few ambitious folks out, young couples pushing strollers or middle-aged women being dragged around by dogs.

I sit on a bench overlooking the pond. There are ducks, a few geese, and a swan. Lee and I used to come for walks down here, back when there used to be two swans. I'm not sure what happened to the other one. No one seems to know. One day it was just gone. We used to joke that the other one had eaten it in a fit of jealous rage, vengeance for a big avian orgy with a couple of the ducks and a horned-up goose.

It was funny because the other birds are such idiots: the ducks flap quacking around and the geese hop about on the shore, pecking at the ground and scattering their bullet-shaped shit. The swan, meanwhile, just glides serenely over the surface of the water, neck like a question mark. A kid chucks a rock at it, shattering the reflection, although the swan looks unperturbed. I check my phone for messages. None.

Behind the swan the water fans out in a rippling V as it swims around and around. I watch it trace its graceful laps and think about taking that neck in my hands, the feathery cord of it, and just twisting. What would it feel like? I imagine the head flopping down, the vertebrae snapping, the swan crumpling and then sinking to the bottom of the pond.

AN HOUR LATER I'm standing in the hallway outside Lee's hospital room, listening to her and Mauricio talking. Olivier is in there too; I can hear him whispering. I picture the three of them, Lee and Mauricio huddled together, Olivier fixing lines and checking levels, soft and calm. I wonder for a moment if he lets Mauricio stay when he pulls the curtain. Maybe right now the three of them are back there behind it babbling at one another in foreign languages. But I don't poke my head into the room to check. I just listen.

My brain registers only the murmur of voices; if it *is* English they're speaking, the volume is too low to make out what's being said. Even so, I wait with a weird mix of dread and anticipation for my name, and at the mention of it for the tone of the conversation to shift from neutral and hushed to something else. But it never happens, and instead of going in I head back down the hall toward the elevators, their conversation fading behind me.

On the way down to the lobby I try to assure myself that Lee's doing fine after her surgery, that it was better not to bust up her little party. The pamphlet made it out to be such a minor thing. She's already back in her room, so she must be okay. But then, thinking this, imagining her lying up there in her hospital bed while I make my way healthily home to our apartment, I feel my stomach turn and the bile rise in my throat. I'm actually going to throw up.

Once the elevator reaches the ground floor I race to the bathroom, stumble into one of the stalls, and fall to my knees. But nothing comes up. I don't even heave, just gasp a little and catch my breath while my stomach settles back down. After a few minutes I lower the toilet lid and sit on it. And I'm like that, perched there on the toilet in the stall in the bathroom, when the announcement comes over the hospital PA that visiting hours are over.

When I see Mauricio leaving the hospital my first thought isn't to follow him. Initially I just hope he doesn't see me, so I duck behind a pillar at the entrance and wait until he's gone past. But once he moves off I let him get about fifty feet ahead and then start trailing him — along the sidewalk, down into the subway, and back up in a part of town frequented mostly by white people with dreadlocks. Once we're at street level I lose him for a moment before I see him through a shop window buying something at the counter. I blow into my hands to warm them, watching from a distance. Then he's away again and I'm back on track, skulking through the shadows of the closed storefronts, off the main strip and down an alleyway lit only by the occasional motion sensor tocking on as he moves past.

At the door to what I assume is his apartment, he stops. I duck under an awning maybe six doors down. The street is otherwise empty. It's so quiet that I can hear the jangle of his keys and the grating sound of one sliding into the lock.

Before he moves inside, his voice comes singing through the silence. "You want to come in, or will you wait there until the shops open tomorrow morning?"

Taking my shoes off inside Mauricio's front door, I don't give an excuse, just act like he's invited me over — and here I am. The place is immaculate, smelling vaguely of omelettes. He doesn't say anything, just hangs his coat and pushes his way through saloon-style doors into the kitchen, whatever he's just bought in his hand.

"Do you want maté?" he asks. "It is like tea. I am making some."

"Sure," I say, and go sit down on the folded futon in the living room — which, I realize, is also his bedroom. The futon is his bed.

While Mauricio clanks around in the kitchen, I look around. Everywhere are musical instruments: guitars, a banjo, little hand-held drums, a keyboard propped in the corner. The only decoration on the walls is a watercolour painting tacked above the futon. Two M-shaped birds flap over a zigzag mountain range snowcapped in white; the perfect red half-circle of a setting sun washes the page in stripes: fuchsia, gold, crimson. It's a terrible painting, something the mother of a proud but untalented child might display only out of parental obligation.

After a while Mauricio emerges from the kitchen carrying a silver tray. On it is a clay teapot and a single, ornately designed, egg-shaped cup with a silver wand sticking out of it. Mauricio sits down cross-legged on the floor and places the tray on the coffee table between us. Without saying anything, he pours hot water slowly into the cup.

"Aren't you having any?" I ask him.

"Yes," he says, and then sits back. "We must let it brew."

A minute passes, maybe two. I watch the steam rise from the cup. Then he takes it in his hands. "At home we would have loose maté," he says. "Here are only teabags."

I watch as he takes a sip from the wand — it's apparently a straw. He sips, then sips again. I wonder if he's going to leave me any. I guess he sees my face, because he laughs. "You have never taken maté before," he says.

"No, I guess not."

"It is like a ceremony. I take the first cup to make sure it is okay for the guest. Maybe it is strange. But, you know, you are away from home and these things become important."

He fills the cup again with hot water and passes it to me. "Do you want sugar?"

I shake my head and put my lips on the straw. The taste is bitter and smoky — somewhere between green tea and eating a cigarette — but not unpleasant. I sip again. There's not much in the little egg-shaped cup, and soon I'm done. "Thanks," I say, placing the cup back on the tray. "This is the life, eh? Couple of dudes, sharing a pot of tea."

Mauricio's looking at me in a funny way. I avoid his eyes. He sighs, so long and heavy that it feels as though he's doing it for both of us, then fills the cup a second time and passes it to me, saying, "You did not come in to see her today." From his tone — not reproachful or accusatory, more restrained — it's obvious that he saw me at the hospital.

"Yeah, I was at work. I've got the day off tomorrow so I'll go by then."

"She thought you were coming. Everyone did." Mauricio pauses for a moment, and when he speaks the words are slow and direct. "But Lee is so strong, isn't she? You of all people must know that."

I don't have an answer for him, so I twist to have a look at the painting above the futon, all Ms and Vs. When I turn back his eyes are trained on me like a pair of high beams. "How did it go?" I ask. "Today, I mean. With the surgery."

"Good. She is doing fine." He gestures at the painting. "This was by my sister. She died in a car accident. I take it everywhere I go."

"Oh," I say. I take a sip from the metal straw. The taste is mellower now, more potable. "That's sad about your sister."

"Of course, she was very small; it is very sad. It has been four years, but still I think of her every day. It is nice to have something of her with me, you know? Some memory. And I like to have a painting because I can think of her making it, putting herself into it. Art is the opposite of death because it is always alive. No?"

Jesus, is he really saying this? But, whatever, I nod. "Yeah, it sure is."

"And what about you?" he asks. "What will you do, after?"

"After what? After Lee's . . . gone?"

"Yes."

I think.

"I will go back to Argentina," he says.

"You will?"

"Yes," he says, and nods. "Unless you need me here."

"Mauricio, just go home."

I catch myself and look over. Kneeling there on the other side of the coffee table, his mouth hangs half open as though he's about to say something. But then he closes it.

"I mean," I add, "you've already done so much. We're really grateful. But you must have your own life to get back to."

Mauricio just lies down, right there on the floor. He doesn't say anything.

I finish what's left in the cup, slurping up the last few drops a little too loudly. Then the room descends back into silence. Mauricio seems to be meditating, or sleeping, his eyes closed, body supine. Meanwhile — and maybe it's the maté — I'm feeling anxious and buzzy. I find myself having to consciously stop my feet from tapping.

After a while, I say, "Well, it's pretty late," and Mauricio jerks to his feet as though he's forgotten I'm there. He walks me to the door, holds it open as I make my way outside. With me standing in the street and him in his apartment, we shake hands, right over the doorstep. It becomes one of those extended shakes — held there, unmoving — that feel like they're going to end with the other guy pulling you in for a hug. Mauricio's face is tired and drawn. I wonder if I look the same way.

"See you at the hospital," I say.

"Hopefully," he says and lets go of my hand to close the door.

OUTSIDE IT'S STARTED raining. Just a light drizzle. I pull my hood up as I make my way back down Mauricio's alleyway, over a few blocks to the subway station to take a train home. Before I head underground, I check for messages on my phone. None.

Using the touchpad, I skip idly through the names, watching Giselle's materialize at the bottom of the screen and slide up, line by line, and then disappear. I stop on the one that says *Lee (hospital)*. I call.

She answers quickly, her voice hoarse.

"Hey," I say. "It's me."

"Hey."

"How you feeling?"

"Tired. I was sort of sleeping." She coughs. "It's late."

"Sorry," I say. "I just wanted to know how the Gamma Knife went."

"Tests back tomorrow."

"I'll call in sick and come in."

"It'll be early. Too early for you. Just go to work and come later." She coughs again.

"No, I want to come in the morning. What time do you get test results?"

"Fuck, Pasha, I don't know. Just come whenever you want."

"I'll come in the morning, okay? First thing."

"Sure, whenever you want."

"Okay." I pause. "Love you."

"Yeah," she says, and hangs up.

AT HOME I DON'T bother with the lights, just track mud through the house in the dark and plop down on the couch in the living room with my shoes on, hair wet. I sit there for a while, the streetlight outside filtering in through the window. On the TV's blank silver face is my own reflection, trapped and distorted somewhere inside the glass. The rain patters away on the roof.

Above the TV in a cabinet are Lee's DVDs, dozens of them in alphabetized stacks. Surrounding them on either side are shelves of our books. Wouldn't it be nice to write your life into one of those? To take everything and filter it into something charming and sweet, take your struggles and make them fun? You could reinvent yourself as someone hapless and amusing, someone whose missteps are enjoyable, not simply wrong. Just slip out of who you are and repackage it all into something new.

I sit there for a few minutes, thinking in the dark.

After a while I get up from the couch and move down the hall, past the bathroom to our bedroom. I turn the closet light on, push my way through the clothes hanging on either side, and, from way in the back, dig out a box. It's stuffed so full of junk that the cardboard is splitting up the sides. I pull out fistfuls of letters, cassette tapes, birthday cards, bills, postcards, receipts — here's one for a pizza delivered two years ago, in case we ever feel like returning it.

A few layers down I find an inch-thick stack of pictures, most of them self-taken of me and Lee, our grinning faces slightly skewed and off-centre in each one. But I'm not browsing; I'm not interested in nostalgia. The photos I pile on the floor of the closet with everything else. What I'm looking for is very specific. I know it's in here; two Christmases ago I got the thing as a gift from Lee's mom and came home laughing.

"What does she think I am, a twelve-year-old girl?" I said, cramming it into the box. "Well, you know," Lee said. "Maybe she thought you'd get inspired."

Amid a clutter of business cards and empty envelopes, I find it: the archetype of a journal, leather-bound and severe. Resisting the urge to blow dust from its cover, I leave everything on the floor and make my way with it back into the bedroom. There's a pen on the bedside table, a remnant of when Lee used to do her crossword puzzles before going to sleep. I sit down on my bed with it and the book, turn on the reading lamp, and sit there for a moment.

It isn't long before I figure out what to write.

BIG CITY GIRLS

NORMALLY ALEX LIKED snow days, when the county buses couldn't make it past RR #2 and school was cancelled. But today Alex and Ginny's mom had invited Ginny's friends over to their house, their house on the quiet empty road with no name with nothing else around, not even cows. The girls were fifth graders, Alex was seven; there were four of them and one of him. When it was just him and his sister, they called each other Dirk — Hi there Dirk, How you doing Dirk. But the one time Alex had called her Dirk around her friends Ginny pretended he wasn't even there.

From the back door of Ginny and Alex's house the snow stretched along the yard to the fence, across the fields, all the way to the wall of trees at the edge of the woods. Then it was the woods and the woods were black and went forever. A girl named Althea had gone in there back in the fall and never come out. She was home-schooled and no one the kids from the county school knew, not really. Althea had either been taken by someone or got lost, it wasn't clear. At one point her footprints just disappeared.

Because of Althea, Ginny and Alex had instructions not under any circumstances to leave the yard — today, the snow day, or any day. Who knows who's out there? Alex's mom said, gesturing toward the woods. Stay where I can see you.

Ginny also had instructions to include her brother, so she and her friends let him help build a snow fort. They put him in charge of rolling up snowballs around the yard, which he did, channelling muddy stripes into the lawn and then dumping his snowballs for Karen and Heather to add to the walls of the fort. Ginny was the packer. Shayna watched.

When the fort was done Alex went to crawl inside but Shayna blocked the entrance. Pretending her breath was ciga-rette smoke she explained that if the walls collapsed someone would need to go alert the rescue crew, and Alex should be that someone. So he wasn't allowed in the fort; he had to stay on guard outside.

Alex was left alone with nothing but a view of the fields piled high with white and perfect and boring all the way to the woods. He tried breathing smoke the way Shayna had, tilting his head back and blasting it upward. The cloud puffed up and evaporated quickly into the sky. It had snowed through the night and stopped that morning but still the sky was low, the grey splitting finally in cracks of blue.

Turning back to the fort Alex pictured the avalanche of it coming down and wondered who the rescue crew was. Was it his father? His father was at work. His mom was upstairs with sherry and *Guiding Light*. Alex wiped snot from his nose with the back of his mitten and laid his hand on the fort. Gently he tested the wall. It seemed solid enough. The girls were quiet. What was going on?

After a while they came out and stood with Alex looking

around the yard for something to do. Shayna pointed to the woods. I don't believe it's too dangerous, she said. When my sisters were our age they played hide-and-seek in there all the time.

No one had a reply to that, which worried Alex. We're not supposed to, he said, and Ginny shot him a quick, sharp look. Everyone stood around not saying anything, gazing off at the black thatch of trees across the field. What was Shayna going to do? The silence and waiting made the air seem icier, whistling up under Alex's toque and needling its way into his ears. But then Shayna just said, Oh, whatever — so it was time to go inside.

The girls followed Shayna and Alex followed the girls into the mudroom. It smelled of laundry. Everyone piled their coats and snowpants onto the washer-dryer and left their Duckies in a grey-brown puddle in a heap on the floor, beside the empty spot where Alex's father's workboots sat at night and two rusty foot-shaped blotches marked the tiles like bloodstains. The room was warm except near the door, where winter light streamed in white through a small window. The window was like a sheet of ice. Outside it was the winter.

In the kitchen Ginny got out the peanut butter and they all went into the den licking spoons. Alex and Ginny sat on the couch, Heather and Karen lay on the floor, and Shayna lounged in Alex's father's chair with her legs draped up over the back of it, head upside down, hair hanging over the footrest. The straps of her overalls slipped to the sides and between them two nubs poked out of her shirt. They made Alex's stomach churn in a gurgling, snaky way. He buried his face into one of the couch cushions and screamed as loud as he could. When he turned back flushed and blinking, the girls were looking at him strangely. What, it's fun, he said.

The den was a brown room; there was a fireplace with fake logs you ignited with a switch. Ginny turned on the fire and brought out Clue. Alex made a grab for Professor Plum. He was always Professor Plum and Ginny was always Miss Scarlet — although this time Shayna took Miss Scarlet and Ginny had to be Colonel Mustard, who was the colour of diarrhea.

With the flames dancing Karen as Mrs. Peacock made her first suggestion, nudging her glasses up onto the bridge of her nose and making notes when she was shown the Billiard Room by Heather. Then it was Shayna's turn: she sighed and made some wild guess at what was in the envelope and, before anyone could stop her, slid down from her chair and checked.

Look, I was wrong, she said, and laid out the cards: Candlestick, Miss Scarlet, Professor Plum. Hey big boy, said Shayna to Alex, that's you and me.

Who did that? demanded Karen. There's supposed to be one person, not two. There's not even a room in there. Now the game's over anyway. Gosh!

Everyone looked around for something to look at that wasn't Karen.

Maybe Miss Scarlet and Professor Plum were having fun with the candlestick, said Shayna, climbing back into her chair. Her nipples puckered. Alex squirmed.

In the Secret Passageway! screamed Heather, whose bedroom was a shrine to the New Kid on the Block Jordan Knight.

Professor Plum and Miss Scarlet in the Secret Passageway with the candlestick!

Alex jumped up and grabbed the little metal candlestick from the board and held it to the zipper of his jeans, made a pissing noise, and waggled his crotch around like a maniac. Candle-dick! Candle-dick! he yelled, and pretended to pee all over everything.

Heather and Karen collapsed and held each other laughing on the rug, tears running down their faces. Ginny looked on anxiously. Shayna watched smirking from her chair.

Then the laughing was over. Alex stood panting with cards and pieces and murderous implements from the Clue game strewn all around him on the floor.

Candle-dick! hollered Alex, but no one responded. He looked at Shayna. Sit down, she said.

Yeah, said Ginny. Sit down Alex.

Alex sat down, right where he was.

It sucks here, said Shayna. It's boring. It's gay.

Ginny looked jerkily around the den. We could watch a video, she said. We've got *Short Circuit 2*. Or play TurboGrafx? Or do a puzzle? Or read YM?

Gay, said Shayna.

If we lived in the city we could go somewhere, said Heather. I bet kids in the city get the day off school for snow days and just go wherever they want.

Yeah, we could take the subway.

We could go to a museum, said Karen, but she was ignored.

We could go shopping.

We could steal a lion from the zoo, suggested Alex.

Or drink coffee in a café. Or a beer!

Wine, corrected Shayna. Or screwdrivers. My sisters *always* drink screwdrivers.

But what if we got stuck there and it was night? said Karen. What if we got trapped?

We'd get raped, said Shayna.

This was exciting, there was murmuring. Alex had a vague idea of what rape meant: it was something dark and wet with a lot of pushing and afterwards a woman knelt crying in the street. It was usually raining. Were there knives? Sometimes there were knives.

Who'd rape us?

A black person, said Heather.

That's racist, said Shayna. Alex nodded. His best friend Richard was a black person.

A homeless person, said Ginny.

Everyone agreed, she had nailed it.

With AIDS! Karen added. Then we'd get AIDS.

And on drugs, said Heather, trying to redeem herself.

And a hook, said Alex, bouncing.

The girls looked at him.

Alex ran up to his room to get his hook. He made a pirate noise as he bounded back downstairs with it sticking out of his sleeve. On his way toward the den he heard Ginny saying his name and something else that sounded tired. He paused for a minute in the hallway and slid the hook into his sleeve before entering quietly. All four girls were sitting in a circle on the rug. Karen was taking notes. Alex stood on the periphery, hook concealed, not sure what to do.

Okay, Karen was saying, writing. Okay, she said.

We'd go to the movies first.

No, to dinner. Dinner, then a movie. Then dancing in a dance club!

What movie?

A rated-R movie. Something with adult situations.

One with Jordan, said Heather. In adult situations.

Heath-er!

Ginny had once told Alex that Heather loved Jordan Knight so much that some nights she would just cry and cry and cry.

Maybe if we were in the city you'd get to *meet* Jordan Knight.

Maybe he'd ask you to *marry* him.

Heather's face flushed. She leaned forward, into the conversation, to envelop herself in its potential. Alex came and sat down just outside the circle of girls. No one seemed to notice him.

Maybe Jordan Knight would rape you, said Shayna.

I'd rape *him*, screamed Heather. She looked around to challenge anyone who might question her. I would, she warbled. I would!

There was a creak and another creak from upstairs and then Alex's mom's face was looming moonlike over the landing. Heather clamped a hand over her mouth.

Everything okay down there? Are you girls being nice to Alex?

Yes Mom, said Ginny.

Alex?

Yes Mom, said Alex.

Did you have lunch? What did you have?

Peanut-butter sandwiches.

Good. There's RC Colas in the fridge but just one each okay?

And then the face was gone. There were two more creaks from upstairs and the wheeze and click of the bedroom door closing.

They sat in silence for a minute. Shayna stood up.

Okay, said Shayna. Let's play a game.

ALEX SAT WAITING in the closet, which was big for a closet but small in the dark. The smell was of must and mothballs and feet. From the crack at the bottom of the door came a thin golden band of light that dissolved a few inches in. Alex's face itched underneath the balaclava the girls had made him wear. He scratched at his ear with the pirate hook. When he'd finally showed it to her, Shayna had said it was a good thing for a rapist to have. She'd touched him on the arm and Alex had felt the warmth of her hand there all the way to the closet where he'd shut himself in. Even now he could still feel it tingling.

From down the hall he could hear whispering. Who would come first?

It took forever. The girls went upstairs and there was some giggling and faintly he heard his mom say, Careful with my things! Then all four girls came clomping back downstairs and they moved into the kitchen and were up to something in there, doing a tour of the house but actually it was the city, with Karen narrating the sights. This ended back in the den, now a nightclub: there was music and dancing, and then the music went off and there was whispering, and then the whispering stopped. Alex strained to hear anything, more talk or footsteps so he'd know that his part of the game had begun. Although maybe the silence meant that Alex should get ready. But how? He straightened the balaclava and raised his hook.

After a minute or so came the whisper of socks along the hall's parquet. Alex waited, waited, and just as the footsteps neared the closet he swung the door open and pounced and grabbed the girl standing there and hauled her back into the closet, slamming the door behind him.

Alex was on top of the girl. He held his hook to her throat.

Can you be Jordan Knight when you rape me? said Heather's voice in the dark.

Okay, what do I say?

Just be slow and nice, she said.

Okay, said Alex. Okay.

But he wasn't sure what came next. Heather lay beneath him, motionless. Alex looked up and, realizing the door was open, went and closed it. He lay back down on top of Heather and began wriggling, slowly and nicely, arms at his sides while Heather held her breath. But there was something. A smell. Alex stopped wriggling. He sniffed. Heather was wearing his mom's perfume, the potpourri and syrup of it thick on her neck.

I think it's done, said Alex.

Heather exhaled a big whoosh of air into the dark.

Alex rolled off her. They lay there in silence for a minute, side by side.

I guess I'm dead now, said Heather. Where do I go?

With his hook, Alex nudged Heather toward the back of the closet where the shoes were lined up. There, he said. Back there.

She sat down with the shoes. Alex stuck his head into the hallway. Who's next?

You dumbshit, yelled Ginny. We're supposed to come looking for her!

Alex went back inside the closet. He sat there for a while, pulling the balaclava up for air, listening to Heather breathe, wondering if they were doing something he might get in crap for. He imagined his father coming home, finding kids in the closet and losing it, smacking his son all the way up to his room and then locking him in.

Footsteps came from the hallway. Alex put his mask back on and readied himself to spring.

It was Shayna. Alex wrapped his arms around her waist and tackled her full force into the closet. As he climbed on top of her he could feel the little blisters of her nipples pushing against his chest. Shayna squirmed beneath his body and Alex struggled to hold her down. Her breaths were deep and the smell of peanut butter came gusting over his face with each one. He'd left the door open and a wedge of light angled into the closet from the hall, right over their faces.

Shayna said nothing, just kept panting and writhing, rippling her hips up and down, her pelvis against his. He pushed against her, hardening. She moaned. He pushed again: his sweatpants, her overalls. She moaned again. He kept going, imagining her nipples, those buds. Alex felt greedy. He stopped pushing and, using his elbows to pin her arms down, ran his thumbs across Shayna's little breasts. She stiffened. Something was wrong.

No no no, yelled Shayna, wriggling away. No!

Alex loosened his grip, and the second he did Shayna bucked and flipped him, pinning him there. Her fingernails dug sharply into his wrists. From the shadows in the back of the closet, Heather gasped.

What are you doing? said Alex.

This, you pervert, said Shayna, and she balled her fists and rained blows at Alex's face, his shoulders, his chest. No no no, she said. Stop, moaned Alex, turtling. Please, stop, please.

Shayna pulled away. Alex relaxed, thankful it was over, but then Shayna screamed, No! again and came down hard with a knee to his crotch. For a moment the closet blazed white, as though a flashbulb had gone off in the dark. Alex wilted. Then the door opened wider and Shayna was pushing through and gone.

I got away, she was telling the other girls, as a dull ache spread from Alex's groin to his stomach. There's a rapist in that alleyway! I think he killed Heather!

Heather crawled out from the back of the closet and climbed over Alex. She stood in the hallway looking unsure where to go.

Let's call the police! Alex heard someone cry, possibly Karen. There was a weird bristly fish in his guts and now it was swimming up his throat. Was he dying? He shut his eyes.

WHEN THE POLICE came Alex had to go to jail. Jail was his room upstairs. The girls collected in the hallway behind Ginny, the tallest, the only one who could reach the lock. In his sister's eyes was a resigned look as she stood there. Put the pervert away, said Shayna. Ginny paused. Sorry Dirk, she mouthed, and then closed the door. The deadbolt rattled into place and the girls' footsteps faded downstairs. No one besides his father had ever locked Alex in his room. Ginny was forbidden to do it. Even his mom had never done it before.

Alex sat on the bed. His balls ached very much. After a few minutes he pulled his Detroit Pistons wastebasket over and barfed a sour peanut-buttery paste into it. He covered the barf with handfuls of Kleenex, then sat back on the bed and stayed there very quietly for a very long time, trying to hear what was going on.

Maybe they were still playing the game, he thought. Maybe his part was to sit here and wait, maybe it wasn't over, maybe there would be a trial. But what was the game? Alex tried to find words for it. He couldn't.

There was no sound of the girls though — nothing from downstairs, just the faint faraway chatter of the TV in his mom's room down the hall. He imagined her in there lying on her bed and lay down then too, on top of his *Star Wars* sheets.

Staring up at the bars of sunlight that played through the blinds onto the ceiling, Alex thought about the moment when he had felt those bumps on Shayna's chest, how softly he had touched them. He hated her. She was mean, a bitch, and she had squared him and then he had puked. And what

sort of sister was Ginny? He punched his pillow hard and
then punched it again. His pillow was Shayna's face, it was
Ginny's face. Alex hit it, he bit it, he screamed into it, he
screamed and roared and screamed.

But then Alex pulled away, hot and itchy. He lay there on
his bed until the light fanning through the blinds began to go
coppery and slow. Soon his mom would head downstairs to
start fixing supper. Soon his father would be home and finding Alex locked into his room. There would be hell to pay, and
Alex would be the one to pay it. Soon the day would be over,
and soon it would be night.

Alex got up and went to his window. He pulled the cord,
the blinds went clattering up. Outside the clouds were gone.
The sky was clear and the sun was dipping below the treeline of
the woods; golden bands filtered through the empty branches.
The tops of the trees were frosted with ice, glimmering silver in
the dusky light, and the shadows of the trees were long purple
scraggles on the snow. But the trees themselves were black.
The trees were the woods and the woods were a cave out there
past the fence. The woods were a dark, grinning mouth.

Why had the girl Althea gone in there? Those first few
weeks in the fall Alex was sure one day he'd be playing in the
yard and she'd come wandering out of the trees and across the
field and stand at the fence, confused and lost. But she would
like him — they were both Als. She would feel safe with Alex
and he would take her inside his house and make her hot
chocolate. He would call her family and tell them she was
okay — or an ambulance, or the cops. But Alex didn't think
those thoughts now. He thought instead of Althea's body,

frozen and blue, appearing under a snowbank when everything thawed in the spring.

Alex's eyes followed the shadows of the trees, stretching
now in the red cleft of sun all the way back across the field,
toward the house, past the fence to the square patch that was
his family's yard. And then he looked down, directly down, to
the space behind the house where the snow fort now lay in
ruins. Beside it were the girls.

With the light deepening they seemed too defined, too
real, as though someone had cut their pictures from a magazine and laid them down there, one by one, side by side. Their
faces were turned up toward the house although they couldn't
see Alex, he knew, framed in his bedroom window. It was still
too light outside and too dark in his room. So Alex stood
there watching them, unseen: four girls on their backs in a
line, making angels in the snow.

THE FILM WE MADE
ABOUT DADS

IN THE FIRST scene of the film we made about dads, we caught them as children, well before they became dads themselves, when their own dads were full-on capital-D Dads-with-moustaches who had been in the war. We got some great shots of the dads at age eight swinging from the monkey bars in the schoolyard playground. Afterwards, we interviewed them about their goals. The answers: astronaut, fireman, psychiatrist, florist, psycho killer, Oscar Robertson. We asked them, "Describe your dad in one word." The unanimous response was: "Mean."

NEXT WE FOUND the dads at sixteen, getting hand jobs on the couch. The cameras were rolling. The dads were oblivious and said nothing, just rolled over on top of their lovers and, fully clothed, humped away until something damp oozed through their jeans. "Can you edit that so I look better?" wondered the dads, wiping themselves down in the bathroom. We smiled, keeping our distance, and told them we'd see what we could do.

IN COLLEGE THE dads grew beards. They bought cars and one night tried acid. We had run out of funding and couldn't shoot. "Remember this," we encouraged the dads, who were giggling at rain.

A FEW YEARS LATER, we received a grant and resumed filming. By then the dads were done college and had found wives to marry. At the altars, the dads said, "I do," and the wives said, "I do," and the dads kissed their new wives and the wives kissed back and then they ran out of the church while people threw rice at them and cheered. The dads and their wives went to Niagara Falls, where they stared silently into all that water and thought, Hmm, and later fell asleep with their shoes on. "Maybe edit in some love," we told the post-production crew. "Okay," they said.

THE DADS AND wives bought houses. The wives taught grade school and brought home children's drawings that they pinned to their fridges with magnetic fruit. The wives looked at the drawings and said, "Aw," in a pointed way. The dads were stuck in middle management; they built workshops in their garages. "That's my workshop in there," they told the wives. "That's my space." We went out into the garages and panned over the workshops, over the workbenches in the workshops, and the tools that would rarely get used. "This is golden stuff," we said to one another. We were making a film about dads.

THERE WERE MOMENTS we didn't get. The dads told us about nights of laughter with their wives; they told us about moments of tenderness, shared joy, or sorrow, a walk in the park and ducks. But the cinematographers' union allowed us a cameraman only for a certain number of hours. We would show up in the morning and the dads would say, "You should have seen us last night," but we could only shrug and say, "Sorry."

THEN THE WIVES got pregnant. The dads inseminated the wives with their sperm, which shot out of a dad's penis and into the corresponding wife's vagina, etc., and nine months later a baby plopped out like a prize. We had to find some stock footage for the delivery, because the doctors wouldn't let the crew into the delivery room. The result was a beautiful montage with flowers blooming and shots of the universe and the emergence into the world of living things, hippos and such, all set to a specially commissioned soundtrack of synthesized brass and drum machine. At the hospital, the dads stood in the hallway with unlit cigars wagging from their mouths, talking to anyone who would listen. "My wife is having a baby!" they hollered, thrusting a cigar in whoever's direction. The person, usually no one the dads knew, would decline the cigar and back away nervously, as if from a bear.

WHEN THE DADS saw the babies, shrivelled and purple in their wives' arms, they declared, "That's the most beautiful thing I've ever seen in my life," and then cupped the babies' skulls in their hands as though they were testing fruit. The babies cooed and gurgled and so did the dads; it was unclear who was imitating whom.

TWO YEARS LATER there was a plan for another baby, and the process repeated itself: the sperm, the vagina, the cigars, the unintelligible exchange of sounds. We used different stock footage this time, crosscut with scenes of the first child, confused and alone in a field of lavender (this we staged using a blue screen).

NOW, WITH TWO kids, the dads were really cooking. Along with the children, they had gas barbecues, station wagons, digital cable. They were no longer stuck in middle management; they were somewhere better. The kids got older, and the dads coached their soccer teams. The dads drank beer on Sunday afternoons and watched football. But the dads might add something incongruous. "I also have season's tickets to the opera," they might say. Or: "It's fine if one of the kids turns out gay." These things, we decided, would best be snipped right out of the film.

WHEN IT WAS time for the children to move away from home, the dads were strong. The wives wept in the driveways as the children pulled away in cars with couches strapped to the roofs, and the dads held the wives and stroked their hair. It would later be easy for us to erase the tears that ran down the dads' faces. We have computer programs for that sort of business.

THEN THE DADS became granddads. Their sons were now dads. In minivans the sons brought grandchildren, and the dads crouched in front of the babies among them and produced noises as they had at babies they themselves had once sired. For older grandchildren small change was produced from unlikely places, behind the grandchildren's ears or the couch, and then displayed magically. "Grandpa!" the grandchildren said. When it was time to go, the dads hugged their sons and their grandchildren and marvelled in the driveway that the boys among them, although they had their shoes on the wrong feet, would one day also, somehow, be dads.

AFTER SOME TIME, it became difficult for the dads to sit down, nearly impossible to urinate. The dads' pee came in a dribble. There was some putting off and some more putting off, but at the wives' insistence a medical examination confirmed it: the dads had very advanced-stage cancer of the prostate. There was no hope, the cancer was everywhere, they would be dead in six months, said the doctors, with their hands on the dads' shoulders and a look of caring in their eyes. We scored this segment of the film with a single cello sawing away, sad and lonely. Back at home, we took long, long takes of the dads standing at the window, watching cars pass by on the street. The wives hovered nearby and drank sherry.

WHEN THE DADS DIED, no one knew quite what to say. At the funerals, former co-workers made speeches about dedication that left everyone feeling empty. This we recognized would be impossible to convey in our film, unless we resorted to voice-over. But we shot what we could: the mourners and flowers and the open coffins with the dads lying inside, silent and still. People walked by, peering in, some of them sniffling back tears. "It was time," declared the wives, sensibly. They left and went back home to stand in the parlours of their houses, where they nibbled triangular sandwiches and accepted the condolences of family and strangers with polite nods, whispering, "Thank you, thank you. Thank you, everyone."

WHEN IT WAS ALL over, when the wives were left alone in their houses, when even their children had driven away in minivans, we rushed back to the studio to put together a rough cut of our film about dads. We had spent years making a film about dads, and now the dads were gone, and our financial backers had expectations. Our crew had been there for all the critical moments: we had captured everything in the dads' lives, from the formative years to the golden, deformative years. Now it was time to make some art. And there were reels and reels of film piled around us in the studio, but we just sat there, looking around — at the computers, at the rushes, at one another — not quite knowing where to begin.

PUSHING OCEANS IN AND PULLING OCEANS OUT

IT'S APRIL AND the world is opening up like a hand with something secret in it. The world is all, Hey I've got something to show you, so you lean in and go, What? You go, Show me! And you look and the fingers peel back and then whammo there it is, green and muddy and fresh and dripping wet with rain.

The world is melting but it's almost all water anyway. The world is like 75 percent water. It's a ball made of water and some mountains and other stuff, some trees and hills and deserts. Buildings and roads. People walk around on it and we're like 75 percent water too. My dad Greg is 236 pounds, which makes him 177 pounds of water, like a hundred thousand glasses of water, maybe more. He's a bathtub full of water — bigger than a bathtub, a kiddie pool. Anyway, my dad Greg is a whole lot of water. And Mom is the moon.

You learn all this water stuff in grade five science. The units are called The Earth and The Human Body. And in The Human Body we learned about vaginas and wangs. Big whoop though, right? Vaginas and wangs, big whoop.

It's springtime and you've got to make sure that Brian wears his rubber boots because of all the mud. Like Granny says, Brian's slow and only seven, and my dad Greg'll forget if I don't do it. But my dad Greg calls me Big Gal or BG for short because I'm responsible and mature for my age (nine).

Brian crapped his pants four times in class already this year so one of his teachers called home to see if maybe he needs diapers and my dad Greg said no so they said well okay make sure he wears pants with elastics around the ankles. Get it?

But one time he came home with a diaper on anyway and my dad lost it. He called them up at Brian's school and said fuck and everything, I heard him. He said, Are you telling me how to raise my fucking kid? And then after, he went and sat on his bike in the garage for like thirty hours or something.

My dad Greg won't let us talk about Mom. He took all the pictures of her that were around the house away and hid them somewhere. One time we were having lasagna for dinner and I tried asking him if he could remember if Mom's favourite food was lasagna because mine is but my dad's is burgers. I had to get it from somewhere! But he didn't say anything, just kept eating. And when I asked again he gave me a long quiet look that I could tell meant: stop.

TODAY'S WEDNESDAY, April 8. That's the first thing you do when you get to school, write the date in your workbook at the top of the page. You're supposed to do cursive but I print because cursive looks messy and in my printing all the letters are the same size, it looks like a typewriter if I do say so myself. Then I sit for a bit and start to pinch my eyelashes and pull away, and sometimes you get a few little curls of eyelash and you sprinkle those down onto your book. You keep doing that and eventually you have a little pile of black eyelashes, and you organize that into a perfect square on the empty page. But I hide it with my hand when Mrs. Mills comes walking by.

There are some things you just have to keep secret. Like for my birthday last year my dad Greg bought me a diary with a lock and everything, and he told me I could write whatever I wanted in it, about my day or if I was mad or whatever, and I could lock it up and they would be my secrets. But you write things down and they can get found. People can read it and know everything. It's better to keep your thoughts in your own head, you have them there for a second and then they're gone and you're the only person who will ever know what they were. You think things to yourself and they're safe.

So anyway it's the last day before Easter weekend. Because it's the last day I haven't done too much work, just wrote the date in each of my workbooks (le 8 Avril en français) and did the eyelash stuff and then didn't do anything else because this year I'm going to help hide the eggs. I've been planning all day where I'm going to hide them — places that are easy for Brian but not too easy. This year it's me in charge of the egg hunt because last year SOMEBODY forgot where he put them and then like a month later all this chocolate melted into our TV.

Easter's about Jesus or something? We don't do religion at my school.

Oh — anyone calls Brian a retard, I'll kick their ass.

Another thing we learned in The Human Body was about

periods. Girls get their period and blood comes out of their vagina. Not me though, even though it can happen as young as ten. I've been making sure to keep my legs tight together or cross them so nothing's getting out. If I have to pee I hold it to make the muscles stronger so my vagina will never let out any blood. It'll be the toughest vagina in town, not like all those other wimpy vaginas, dripping all over the place like one of Jared Wein's nosebleeds.

You get your period and you also get boobs. Some of the girls in grade six have boobs. Like Kelly Sanchez (she's already twelve, though). They stick out of her shirt, she looks like she's hiding Easter eggs, ha ha ha.

What I remember most about Mom was when she came back from the hospital and only had one boob. They cut off the other one and gave her a special bra to make it look like she had two boobs, but sometimes around the house she didn't wear it and her shirt just sagged on the one side. But that's just what I remember, I was only four. She was tired and they'd shaved her hair off. She just lay in bed and my dad Greg made me be quiet around the house, all the time, right until she went back to the hospital and then it was the end.

FINALLY AT THREE fifteen the bell rings. Everyone goes running out into the hall and it's Easter. I get my bag at the rack and I'm putting on my jacket and Jared Wein comes up and goes, Wanna walk home? Jared's okay, he wears glasses that are always falling down his face and he has to scrunch his nose to move them back up. I go, Yeah. Also he usually gets a nosebleed.

On the way home from school Jared and I go down to our fort in the woods to check if it's okay. There's a path with trees that grow over from each side and make a tunnel, the branches bend in and touch over top and you have to duck when you're walking along. Then it opens up and that's where our fort is. We call it The Inner Sanctum, and it always needs fixing because teenagers come down and drink beer and light fires and mess everything up.

It's been raining so today The Inner Sanctum is wet and sort of cool, and dark, and it smells like worms. There's a log to sit on so Jared goes and sits there and he pats the log beside him like he wants me to sit down too, but I get a stick and I start whacking the ground until it breaks. It breaks into a smaller piece, and then I whack that on the log, and it breaks even smaller, and I throw that piece into the woods. There's a beer cap on the ground so I pick it up and sniff it: pennies and sugar.

If we stayed late enough it'd get dark and we could lie back and look up at the sky and see the moon up there through the space in the treetops, white as bones, full or half or waxing or waning (part of The Earth was to learn about the moon) and we'd lie back and I'd maybe let Jared put his head on my tummy and we'd both look up at the moon and I might tell him, That's my Mom, Jared, that's Mom looking down. Then I'd wave at the moon: Hello, goodnight! But I wouldn't cry. I wouldn't cry or anything.

But we can't stay that late because I have to get home for Brian. Besides, if Jared Wein gets a nosebleed we don't have any Kleenex.

We fix up The Inner Sanctum and Jared goes to his house

and I come home but Brian's not there yet. My dad Greg usually gets in at five thirty from his job at the parking garage. If he's not home for dinner you got to make hot dogs, one for you and one for Brian. Sometimes my dad Greg'll leave you a note and sometimes he won't.

INGREDIENTS TO MAKE HOT DOGS FOR DINNER:
2 hot-dog wieners (in freezer)
2 pieces of Wonder Bread
2 Kraft Singles slices
French's mustard
Heinz ketchup
2 paper towels
1 microwave

Okay. You take the hot-dog wieners out of the freezer. You take a paper towel. You put one of the hot dogs on the paper towel and you put it in the microwave and you microwave it for 1:10. You take the other hot dog and other paper towel: repeat. Then you put the hot dogs in the bread and a piece of cheese on the wieners and you can even do them together at the same time, and you microwave them on a paper towel for forty-five seconds. I put mustard on mine, and ketchup, in two straight even lines. Brian has them plain. If they're too hot make Brian wait because if not he'll just stuff them in his mouth and burn himself and he'll cry and then you have to hug him and rub his hair and stuff.

Oh, I forgot to say to WASH YOUR HANDS. Before and after making hot dogs, with hot water and soap. There are germs everywhere and if you get them in your mouth you could maybe get, I don't know, cancer or leukemia? Not really, I'm not an idiot. But kids get leukemia all the time and then they have to get bones from their brothers or sisters. I'd have to get bones from Brian. Or give him some of mine.

IT'S 4:06 AND I'm washing my hands when the bus pulls up outside. It's always the same: it sounds like Granny when she gets all wheezy, then the doors open and you can hear all the kids screaming inside the bus, and then the doors close and it roars and goes away, and then it's quiet. Brian comes in the front door with his backpack and he sees me and yells, Hi! and he gives me this big hug and yells, Hi! again, and then I tell him to wash his hands.

Sometimes Granny comes by to see if we're okay before my dad Greg gets home. She's his mom and smells like cigarettes and old people. He doesn't have a dad.

But today it's just me and Brian. We play Trouble. We eat Fruit Roll-Ups — me: grape, Brian: orange. Sometimes I let Brian win Trouble, sometimes I don't. I have to help him move his men. He's always red. I'm always blue. Today though he wins by himself.

I let Brian watch TV at five, but only for half an hour. After last Easter when the TV got ruined my dad Greg bought a new big-screen one and put a satellite dish on the roof. There are lots of satellite channels that are inappropriate for kids. We're only allowed to watch channel 2 — my dad Greg's rule. He watches TV a lot now. Not me. TV ROTS YOUR BRAIN!

I clean up. I make sure the games are all square on the

shelf. The edges have to be even and matched up equally, which is called symmetry. We learned it in math.

And then I wash my hands. Sometimes I wash them too long and they get all pink and sore, but that just means they're clean.

Hey, I almost forgot: it's Easter, almost. Moron!

AT 5:34 THE GARAGE door goes up and the bike comes growling inside like always, and then my dad Greg is in the kitchen in his security guard uniform and he picks me up under one arm and Brian under the other and spins us around. I sometimes forget how big my dad Greg is: he's like four of me, maybe more.

We sit at the table in the kitchen while he makes beans and toast and eggs for dinner. He sings, Beans, beans, the magical fruit and makes fart noises and stomps around like he's crazy, and the whole house shakes. Brian laughs but then he does that thing where he starts rubbing his face with his knuckles, so my dad Greg has to come over and put Brian on his lap and hold his hands for a bit. Wanna stir the beans, BG? he says to me, so I go over and do it.

When everything's ready my dad Greg puts the beans out on plates with the toast and eggs. He puts mine down and he points at it to show me the toast is cut in triangles and there's an egg on one side and the beans in a little neat pile on the other, how I like it. Symmetry.

After dinner he tells me to go do my homework while he gets Brian ready for bed, but I don't have any homework (because it's Easter) so I go up and clean my room, make sure

everything's straight and lined up and there's no dust anywhere. I have my own Handyvac but I'm only allowed to use it
once a week and I already used it on Sunday.

Then it's almost bedtime. I put on my pajamas and go
brush my teeth and wash my hands. After, I go into Brian's
room to say goodnight, but he's already asleep with this big
smile on his face, so I lean over the railing and whisper-yell,
Goodnight Greg! to my dad Greg who's watching TV and he
turns down the volume and whisper-yells, Goodnight BG!
and I go into my room and wait until it's exactly 9:00 so I can
get in bed.

For a bit I lie there thinking about Brian's Easter egg hunt
and running my hand over the pillow, feeling for feathers
sticking out. I pull them out with my fingernails and drop
them behind the bed. One time my dad Greg moved my bed
to put up a shelf for my books and he found a big pile of
feathers and asked me, Are you taking feathers out of your
pillow? I said no. It felt weird, but my dad Greg just smiled
and said okay.

Lying in bed, through the window I can see the moon. It's
just a sliver but it's still there. Soon there'll be no moon at all
for a few days, a new moon, and then the moon will come
back like it's just been hiding or taking a break, slowly, bit by
bit, until it's full and as big and round in the sky as the sun.

I started thinking Mom was the moon when I was little. It
was a secret from my dad Greg. I could talk to her and stuff,
every night. I know it's dumb now. But it's like tradition and
there's nowhere else she can be. Sometimes you can see her
and sometimes you can't but every night all around the world

Mom the moon is busy pushing oceans in and pulling oceans out. Tides. And all us people are basically water too and at night the moon pushes us into sleep.

11:38. I'VE BEEN lying staring at the moon and planning the egg hunt for like three hours. I'm going to have to make a list, write it down so I don't forget, so nothing happens like choco-late getting into the TV again. I keep thinking about Easter, imagining Brian going around with his little basket and find-ing eggs, all smiles and laughing and happy.

But maybe I have insomnia? Insomnia is when you can't sleep, my dad Greg has it sometimes. You just stay awake for-ever. You can die from not sleeping. Yeah, I think I have insomnia. I should count sheep.

One two three four five six seven eight nine ten eleven twelve thirteen fourteen fifteen sixteen seventeen eighteen nineteen twenty twenty-one twenty-two twenty-three twenty-four twenty-five twenty-six twenty-seven twenty-eight twenty-nine thirty thirty-one thirty-two thirty-three thirty-four thirty-five thirty-six thirty-seven thirty-eight thirty-nine forty forty-one forty-two forty-three forty-four forty-five forty-six forty-seven forty-eight forty-nine fifty fifty-one fifty-two fifty-three fifty-four fifty-five fifty-six fifty-seven fifty-eight fifty-nine sixty.

Nothing. Sixty seconds is a minute. Sixty minutes in an hour times sixty seconds = three thousand six hundred sec-onds. Twenty-four hours in a day = ?

Hold on, I need to write this down. I just have to turn on the light and find a paper and pen.

24 hours in a day = 1440 minutes = 86,400 seconds. And that makes . . . 604,800 seconds in a week. How many seconds in a year? Whoa, hold on.

31,339,600.

The other thing you can do if you can't sleep is have some warm milk. So I wait until exactly 12:00 midnight and get up to go down to the kitchen. I stop on the stairs. My dad Greg is still up. I can hear the TV. I lean over the banister and look into the den, all quiet. Like a spy.

The TV's on. There's a lady moaning, like she's being hurt or something? My dad Greg has the sound way down, but I can hear it. He's sitting on the couch — I can see him, with his feet sticking out from under a blanket. He's sort of twitching or something and the couch is going *creak creak*, and the lady on the TV is going *uh! uh!* and he's making noises too, like grunting. *Creak creak, uh uh, grunt grunt.*

I take another step down on the stairs and lean even more over the banister so I can see the TV and there's a lady with her boobs shaking and flopping around, like slapping up against herself, and now there's a man on her too with his butt in the air and I realize he's humping her, and the blanket on the couch is shaking in time with the boobs and the butt and I can see my dad's face and his face is different, it's like a secret side of him I've never seen, mean and hungry and weird, and the couch goes *creak creak* and the lady with the floppy boobs goes *uh uh* and my dad Greg goes *grunt grunt*. But then something in my tummy goes *gloop* and I have to pull away from the banister because my head is all funny, and I turn away and run upstairs to the bathroom.

And then I'm washing my hands. I didn't even turn the lights on, so now I'm washing my hands in the dark with hot water and lots of soap, hard, and the water's too hot and it hurts and I can already feel my hands burning from it, I know they're going pink but I don't care.

I hear someone behind me but I don't look. I hear my dad Greg go, BG. He leaves the lights off and comes over, so he's right behind me. I still don't look.

He reaches over and turns off the tap. My hands are sore, my stomach still feels weird and like gurgly. BG, he says again. I don't turn around. We stand there in the dark. Then he reaches out to put his arms around me but he sort of stops and just stands there, and then he pulls a towel off the rack and holds it out to me, but I don't take it. I just want him to go away.

PENIS: DINK DICK wang schlong dong winky wiener cock peter rod pud monkey johnson prick willy member purple-helmeted-warrior tackle twig-and-berries banana sausage meat doodle noodle package privates one-eyed-monster rocket hard-on boner steamer stiffy erection.

THE NEXT MORNING I wake up at 7:47 but it's not really waking up because I didn't sleep very much, obviously. I have to wait until exactly 8:00 to get out of bed, so I just lie there for thirteen minutes thinking. The curtains are closed now, my dad Greg must have come in during the night and closed them, and that makes me feel weird — the idea of him being in my room when I'm sleeping, looking at me, standing over me, being there.

Through the curtains the light comes in grey, and I can hear the rain hissing outside. I decide it'll have to be an indoor day, which means games, so at 8:00 I get out of bed and go into Brian's room, and he's just lying there with his eyes open like he's been waiting for me. He looks at me and smiles and goes, Hi! I lift the covers and crawl under. Brian hugs me. He's warm.

Brian it's almost Easter, I go. Are you excited for the Easter Bunny?

He kicks his legs and goes, Yes! Yes!

That's cute, how he still believes in the Easter Bunny? I put my arm around his chest and I can feel his heart beating. *Bub bub, bub bub,* says his heart. I rub my hand on his chest and he kind of purrs like a cat. And then I slap him on the tummy and he laughs, so I do it again. I leave my hand on his tummy and it's like round and I can feel the dent where his bellybutton is. And then, sort of quick, I move my hand down a bit and touch his wang, just to see: it's small and weird, a little rubber tube.

Brian's gone all still. I smack him again on the belly. Wanna get up? I say, and he goes, Yes! Yes! and nods his head so hard he nearly shakes me out of the bed.

TOP SECRET LIST OF EASTER EGG HIDING PLACES! (SO FAR)
Kitchen — between the Wheaties and Sugar Crisp boxes
Kitchen — in the handle of the silverware drawer
Kitchen — on top of the breadbox
Kitchen — in the fruit bowl
Kitchen — under the kitchen table (stuck with tape!)
Den — between the couch cushions

Den — on top of the VCR

Den — under the lampshade

Hallway — on the frame of the picture of me and Brian

Stairs — one egg on every stair, in the corners

MY DAD GREG spends the whole morning in the garage working on his bike, which is good, because after me and Brian play like a hundred games of Trouble, at lunch (1:24) when he comes in to heat up some Chunky for us he's weird and doesn't look at me really. He puts our bowls of soup down and coughs and just stands there for a minute. Then he grabs an apple and goes back into the garage. Then at precisely 4:09 he sticks his head into the kitchen where I'm reading *Harriet the Spy* and Brian's colouring and he says, Hey, stopped raining, taking the bike for a spin. The way he says it is too happy, like he's trying to be happy, and he's got this fake smile. I just nod okay. He's quiet for a bit, then he goes, You okay holding down the fort? So I nod again and then he's just gone.

Granny's coming tomorrow to make us Easter dinner. At 5:14 she calls and says, Happy Easter! and tells me about the great ham she got. Ham? Grody. But I don't say that. I say, Yum. I say, Sounds good Granny. I tell her my dad Greg is out on his bike but should be back soon and she asks if we're okay. I say, Sure. Then she wants to talk to Brian. He gets all excited and takes the phone and yells, Hi! and Yes! and then just laughs a lot.

When Brian hangs up I notice something sort of smells so I get down and sniff his bum. Yup. He crapped himself. This is one thing I can't handle: crap. So I tell him to just stand in the middle of the kitchen until our dad Greg gets home, not to touch anything. I open the window and sit there watching him, glad he's wearing pants with elastic ankles.

My dad Greg gets home at 5:58 and smells Brian right away and goes, Woo-wee buddy! He picks Brian up over one shoulder like a fireman and carries him upstairs. The tub goes on. I can hear them both laughing from my spot at the kitchen table and the water splashing around while my dad Greg washes the crap off my brother.

After dinner (fried baloney, Tater Tots, hot V8) we watch a movie on satellite. My dad Greg tries to get us to all sit on the couch together with the blanket overtop like usual. I tell him I'm okay and sit on the floor. The opening credits come on and I can feel someone like nudging me in the back with their toe. I just stare at the TV as if I don't notice but it's hard to focus on the TV, it's like I can see the pictures but my brain can't figure out what they are.

The movie we watch is *The Parent Trap*. My dad Greg is all excited because it's a movie that was out when he was a kid. At dinner he told me, It's more for girls than boys — you'll like it, BG. When he said the name I thought, Cool, a parent trap, what an awesome idea. You'd dig a hole and cover it with sticks and leaves, maybe put a case of beer on the other side for dads. Something else for moms? Then dads would come along and be like, Oh great, beer! and when they went to go for it they'd fall through and into the hole. A parent trap. Then you could study them and stuff, poke them with sticks, do experiments and tests.

But it turns out to be Disney! The worst! There's this girl

and she's got a twin sister but she doesn't know or something, and then they try to get their parents married. There's no trap really, just a plan, and not even a good one. I squirm around on the floor a lot and my dad Greg keeps going, You want to come up here with us? But I don't say anything to that.

The movie gets done at 8:58, kind of late, so my dad Greg hustles us off to bed. And then goes back downstairs, so I'm left lying there wide awake, thinking about what he's maybe doing down there under the blanket with the groaning ladies on the TV. But I guess I'm tired from the night before so after not too long I forget about my dad Greg King of the Perverts and start to get really sleepy and before I can even check out the window to see the moon I fall asleep.

I WAKE UP and I feel swampy and slow but I have this idea there's something I should be doing. It's — 4:17 a.m. There's something, but everything feels cloudy and my brain is only just winding up, still maybe half asleep. I roll over and then I'm drifting off to sleep again, when it hits me.

Easter.

The egg hunt.

In like three hours Brian is going to get up and go hunting for eggs and I forgot to even finish my list, let alone hide any eggs. I wait until 4:20 (which isn't perfect, but this is an emergency) and swing my legs over the side, get out of bed and it's like slow motion, all heavy and weird, and in the dark my room is sort of blue from the moonlight through the window.

Moving out into the hall I still feel underwater, swimming, looking around, trying to adjust my eyes to the dark. Wait.

There's an egg on the floor outside Brian's room, a little dark lump against the carpet. I lean down and it's like I can't believe it and for a second I think maybe the Easter Bunny really did come. But then I realize who would have put it there, who knew it was my job and went and did it himself anyway.

I pick up the egg. The foil around the chocolate is starting to peel so I smooth it down and put it in the pocket of my pajamas. I look at my dad Greg's bedroom door which is closed with only black showing from the crack underneath, and then I start to tiptoe down the stairs, slow.

Guess what? There are eggs lined up in the corners of each stair JUST LIKE I WROTE ON MY SECRET LIST. The eggs go into my pockets and it's like I'm doing a weird kind of front crawl or something, down one step and reaching, then the next, eggs into my pockets, but feeling I'm maybe sinking, maybe drowning, and the house is dark and still with only the hum of the fridge from the kitchen to prove the world is even alive.

I move around the house, silent, leaving the lights off, looking in all the spots I wrote down, taking the eggs and loading up. Between the cereal boxes: check. On top of the VCR: check. All of them. He's put them in other places too, stupid places like lined up on the kitchen counter. Way too easy. But even finding eggs in places I didn't have on my list makes me feel weird — my hands go prickly for a second, I feel my face hot. Once the egg disappears into my pocket the feeling goes away.

Around 4:50 my pockets start to get heavy — they're sagging and bulging with eggs. I look around one more time but

I'm pretty sure I've got all of them. So I go to the back door and put on my shoes.

Outside it's still dark. The sky is navy blue, almost purple, all clouds left over from yesterday's rain. There's no stars. Only the moon glowing in a little white fingernail behind the night. I shiver a bit in my pajamas, and it's hard to walk with my pockets full of eggs, the way they swing heavy at my sides. I have to hold my pants up by the waist to keep them from falling. I close the back door quietly and drop a single egg there. The porch light shines off the silver wrapper. It twinkles.

I go out across the lawn all wet from a day of rain, soaking the bottoms of my pants and cold on my ankles, and then onto the street where my footsteps echo a bit, *tap tap tap* in my runners on the pavement. Every twenty steps exactly I drop an egg. I count twenty and duck and put one down, then twenty and duck and put one down, again and again all along the curb of the street. I put one right in front of Jared Wein's house and think about knocking on his window, getting him to help, but I decide no, this is something I have to do on my own. Then at the end where there's the path I look back and there they are, all in a line lit up by the streetlights.

Down the hill at the end of our street, along the path, into the woods. Eggs dropped all the way. It's dark because tonight the moon's not enough but I know the way by heart: where to step, where to duck. When I come to the entrance to the tunnel that leads to The Inner Sanctum, I stop. I've only got two eggs left, but I made it. From way up above, Mom the moon is looking down. She's faint and out of focus, just the corner of her face like she's turning away and every now and then little wisps of darker cloud go past like smoke. All around her the night sky is a big murky sea but she shines out of it far away and watching, up there.

I haven't brought anything to dig with, nothing to make the hole for my Parent Trap. There's a broken beer bottle behind the log so I use that, holding it by the neck and using the jagged edge to carve into the mud. I use my feet too and my hands — dirt gets up underneath my fingernails and sticks there. I go down on my knees and can feel the earth cool and wet through my pajamas. But I keep digging, I dig and dig and I'm sweating even though it's cold out and I'm shivering and digging and covered in muck.

As the hole gets deeper and deeper the earth gets wetter and once I'm a ways down there's water at the bottom collecting in a little pool. I stop for a second and think maybe it's from the ocean, that this is water that flows in a river all the way from the coast underneath the surface of the world and I've tapped into it. An underground seaway, linking all the water on the planet.

In The Human Body we learned a little about all the tubes you've got inside you — Fallopian tubes and whatever, all those tubes like canals and rivers carrying stuff back and forth around your vagina, or wang — depending on what you've got. And right then, right when I'm thinking that — I swear — the clouds break up a bit and even though she's gone so tiny Mom the moon comes smiling down into the water at the bottom of the hole, lighting the puddle up silver.

From my pocket I take the two last eggs and open my

fingers to plop them one at a time into the water at the bottom of my Parent Trap. But I don't. I look down and the water's gone black again. The hole's not big enough for a parent. It's barely big enough to trap a cat. I'd need like a digger and a crew of a thousand Jared Weins to make a Parent Trap big enough for my dad Greg, to trap him there and keep him for a while and teach him a lesson.

So I put the eggs back in my pocket and I squat there beside the stupid useless hole in my pajamas in the mud, kind of cold and it's five in the morning and for other people tomorrow will be Easter but not us. This year there won't be any Easter. There's nothing that makes my dad Greg sadder than seeing Brian sad, and if there's no chocolate for Easter Brian'll be the saddest he's ever been ever, and my dad Greg will be even sadder. But I'll have saved two eggs. Later I'll give my brother one in secret and I'll have one too and no one will ever know.

Right then I hear a voice go, Hey, and nearly fall over. I have to put my hands down in the mud to stop myself.

It's my dad Greg. He's standing at the entrance to The Inner Sanctum. The branches are low so he has to duck and it's still dark so he's like a black hunched-up shadow but it's definitely him. Hey, he says again. But he doesn't come in.

My heart's going crazy. I wait for it to slow squatting there in the mud, seeing what my dad Greg's going to do. He doesn't move and I don't either. We both just wait for something to happen. It's like in Trouble when you've got one guy left and Brian's got one guy left but they're both in their homes and you're just popping the popper and popping, trying to get out.

We wait for a long time, me and my dad Greg. Both our breath comes in clouds. He sits down after a while in the mud but still doesn't say anything. I don't either. My hands are covered in mud, and I can feel mud stuck up under my nails and drying in streaks up my arms but I don't really care. I'm tired.

After a while the sky starts to lighten a little, going greyish up through the branches of the trees. The moon's fading. Soon it'll be morning and the moon will be gone for the day, and then the next night she probably won't be there at all.

I start thinking maybe if the world is like a person and underground seaways are the tubes, making the world go on, then when the tides go in and out it's like the world having its period. Like the blood of the world rushing in and out and making everything grow. It's a big thought like the kind you have to say out loud when you think them and it kind of makes me go whoa a little bit. But I can't tell my dad Greg about it, about periods and stuff. Not him. Even though he's over there just waiting for something, I'm not sure what.

So then he goes, Hey, in a weird sad tired voice.

By now the light is morning light. It came so quick, it's pale and thin but it's washing over the night, erasing the night.

And my dad Greg goes, Hey, again, and that's when I realize he's showing me something. He's holding out his hands, cupped together. I can't see so I have to get up and take a step closer. It's the eggs. They're all there in his big hands, like twenty of them, maybe thirty. I found them, he tells me, like he's proud.

And I say, Yeah. I look at his hands, my trail of chocolate eggs collected in there together like grapes. I put my hand in my pocket to make sure I've still got the two extras.

You found them, I tell my dad Greg. You found them all, I say.

**LONG SHORT
SHORT LONG**

IN A SCHOOL in London, Canada, there was a classroom. In it: a teacher, Miss, weary in her skirt but standing, and twenty-eight fourth graders silent as the sky in rows at their desks. Miss clapped her hands four times and said, "Ta, tee-tee, ta," one clap to each syllable. Then a translation: "Long, short-short, long." And the students all died.

With laughter, like a cloudburst.

Why so funny? Miss didn't understand, fresh from Althouse and already of waning hope, B.A. History with a minor in Music also. She held up her hand in a gesture that meant: silence. It took a while; the laughs were a downpour, a drizzle, the occasional drip from a drainpipe. "Shhh," the one named Trish encouraged them, though Miss was sure she had been the first to laugh. Then, okay, quiet enough.

Miss tried again. *Clap, clap-clap, clap.* "Long, short-short, long."

Boom. Down rained hilarity.

Miss threw up her hands and retreated behind her desk. When her students had settled she decreed, "Work period," and from her book bag got out some marking, set to it, trying not to think about the basement bachelor apartment she rented with the towels for drapes, her life.

IF MISS HAD been watching Bogdan, the pale boy by the door, when the words *short* and *long* had come from her mouth, she would have seen him tense. And after, if she had looked up from her marking, she would have seen him sitting there staring straight ahead, paralytic, while the rest of the class lifted the lids on their desks and went rustling around inside for work.

But Miss didn't notice Bogdan, the thin one with the dark, sunken eyes and hair cut short on top and left long in the back, the one who huddled with that tiny first grader, Farid, in quiet corners of the playground, the one Trish had run by one day pointing and screamed, "Short-Long!" And Miss didn't know that "Short-Long" was what they all called Bogdan now. What she did know was that the week before during lunch hour she had discovered Farid lashed to the baseball backstop with his own belt, Bogdan commanding him, "Talk, you filthy cur!" and smacking him in the face with a catcher's mitt. Miss freed Farid, who went bounding so happily off across the playground that she didn't feel the need to punish Bogdan. Besides, he had such a cute accent and sang so sweetly.

But yes. A short-long haircut and Bogdan lived in The Co-op and wore Zips, brought his lunch of weird leftovers to school in an A&P bag, had sported high blue socks since coming to London at six years old. Suddenly in the fourth grade high blue socks were *not* okay — but that was all he had, seven pairs! So then sneaking his mother's tennis socks from her dresser and with the pink bobbles popping up over the tops of his Zips during phys. ed. volleyball it was worse, even worse than before. Trish had bumped Bogdan's serve into the ceiling, and when he grinned at her through the net she pointed at his feet: "Short-Long's got girl socks!" Bogdan's next serve rocketed by so close to Trish's little blonde head that it ruffled a few curls. All the other kids went, "Ooo-ooo," and Bogdan had been asked to sit out the rest of the class.

What Miss could not have known was that in that quick empty moment after she said, "Short-long" and before the class lost it, something electric zipped up Bogdan's arms and exploded burning in his face: the music teacher he liked was with them too. And their laughter had risen like a wave and crashed down over him, leaving Bogdan wilted and lonely and lost.

MISS WAS A NOMAD in the school; she didn't have a classroom of her own. At the end of each period she transferred herself down the hall for another forty-five minutes of autoharp and scales. She was teaching her students the music of different cultures — Indian, Japanese, Australian Aboriginal, Dutch — and wanted to show them how, while the melodies and song structures were different, the rhythms were often the same. "Syn-co, pa, ta, ta," she could have said to illustrate this, or "Tiri-tiri ta" or "Ta-ah-ah-ah." But she chose "Ta, tee-tee, ta" because it was easy and she was tired. Miss didn't know what it meant.

She didn't know that in Morse code, "Ta, tee-tee, ta" (long, short-short, long) is noted like this: − . . − Or that in Morse code, − . . − signifies the letter X. Miss didn't know this, but Bogdan did. When Bogdan's father had still been alive he had taught his son Morse code — for emergencies, if the house were raided — tapped out on the floorboards or flashed in the dark from a lantern. Sitting there Bogdan realized that the rhythm "ta, tee-tee, ta" was − . . − or X. And X represented an unexplained variable, a mystery, an unknown.

These were the things that Bogdan thought, staring up at the front of the room at Miss marking behind her desk. He tried to understand what she had done. It had been like torture, like punishment, like how Bogdan would track The Arab down at recess, pin him to the ground, and spit at him through clenched teeth, "I am going to break your glutinous maximums, you filthy Muslim dog," bending the small boy's arm behind his back.

One time Bogdan had pushed his arm too far; The Arab began to cry, the quivering lip and then the whimpering. Bogdan felt a sudden emptiness in his stomach and pulled away. "What kind of friend are you?" The Arab asked, rubbing his arm, tears streaming down flushed cheeks. "We are not friends," Bogdan said. "You are the enemy."

The Arab stiffened, looked at Bogdan's face as though searching for something, then turned and sprinted across the playground. He spent the rest of lunch watching kids play King's Court from the portable steps while Bogdan dug a trench around the climbers with a stick in the mud. But the next day, as always, The Arab returned.

Thinking this, Bogdan stared at Miss. Back and to his left was Trish, who he didn't want to look at. When he did she would mouth "Short-Long," lips pursing as if for a kiss on the SHOR, teeth bared on the T, tongue lolling for the L, the open mouth of ON, the final sneer of G. Trish always did that to him in class, the stealth of it exasperating. And Bogdan would spin around in a sweat. Even thinking of it, his palms grew damp.

A SHORT-LONG was how his mother cut his hair. And hairdresser was her job!

She cut her son's hair in the shop she had set up in their duplex, before the mirror with the combs and scissors in blue jars of antiseptic juice. On the turntable in the corner of the room she would play the only album she had brought with her on the move to London, Canada: the *Sticky Fingers* LP with the actual zippered trousers on the cover, which Bogdan occasionally fingered but never dared unzip.

Every two weeks when the haircut was done Bogdan's mother stepped back and told him, "There, you look like Mick Taylor," which meant that Bogdan looked like his father, who had looked like the Rolling Stone Mick Taylor. And the wistful smile on his mother's face in the mirror made him feel nice, sad but nice, closer to something in a country that no longer existed and every day he felt sliding even farther away.

MISS WASN'T REALLY marking. Sort of, but more she was waiting to look up sharply and order some loud kid: "Out!" She hoped it was Trish. Trish in those stirrup pants like an acrobat, prissy, too eager with her head of perfect blonde curls and private voice training and hand shooting up fluttering to correct Miss on something Trish had learned at the Conserva-tree (like the Queen, she said it). "Miss, Miss!" and then, "Actually . . ." Doing harmonies when the class sung "Happy Birthday" even.

When Miss told her friend Lindsay back home in Newmarket about Trish late nights on the cordless phone under the covers in her basement bachelor, her futon in the den, the den in the kitchen, she resorted to the second person. "You little bitch!" she screamed into the receiver at Lindsay, who became a proxy for Trish, such were the intensity of Miss's feelings.

Bogdan wiped a dribble of sweat from the front of his short-long and stared at Miss. She was so small and pretty and nice — why did the kids torment her so? While the rest of the class murmured to one another in an effort to make her yell, Bogdan sat demurely. Not working, but at least silent. He stared at Miss and a thought began forming somewhere faint in the back of his mind, way out back where short became long.

THE SHORT-LONG took Bogdan's mother exactly three minutes and fifty-two seconds to style. Bogdan knew this because she timed it to the first song on the second side of *Sticky Fingers*. It was a game — the rush of scissors and both of them laughing as the music began to fade and there was still more snipping to be done. On this song Mick Jagger's singing was garbled. The only words that Bogdan could make out were, "When you call my name," which were then followed by something like, "I sell a bite like a padlocked hog." This he imagined: a pig in a cage, grudgingly hawking bacon from its own hide.

BOGDAN ONCE CALLED Miss "Mother." He said it in line at the pencil sharpener, and even before Trish, behind him, announced it to the class and the class screamed, his face blazed. Why had he called his teacher that, he wondered now. She did not look like his mother. She was too young, too thin and nervous. He liked Miss plenty but still it made him feel weird — and especially weird around his own mother that night at home, as though he'd betrayed her.

Thinking about this really got Bogdan sweating. Temples, armpits, hands — feet, even, squelching around sockless inside his Zips. He watched Miss. He knew she was waiting for the whispers of the class to rise above a trickle, to burble up into a running stream, and he knew the class knew this and were flirting with that line, testing her like swells against a levee.

Bogdan felt that he should hate Miss, or something. How could she be so dumb? But his anger dissolved into pity. Look how she floundered about at the front of the classroom, how easily she gave up. And so tense! Whenever he got his own work back from Miss, Bogdan could feel the bulge of curlicues on the back of the page, so hard she pressed with her red pen a loopy sort of Braille pushed through to the other side.

Around the classroom the other kids whispered. Part of him felt glad they had for the moment forgotten about him, felt Miss deserved it for provoking them, and another part of him felt like screaming, "Shut up, shut up, shut up!" But that would be impossible. Still, in his brain something was beginning to take shape, the particles of it collecting into a thought, an idea.

ON THE OTHER side of *Sticky Fingers* was a song Bogdan knew the words to better. Mick Jagger sang clearly and sometimes his mother would sing along and so would Bogdan. But this song opened with something Bogdan didn't think was true: "Childhood living is easy to do." What? Sorry? For people like Trish, maybe. For people with thermally regulated lunch bags and Nike Airs and ankle socks; people who got good, curly, cute haircuts at proper salons, not one owned by their mothers with all middle-aged women for clients except one kid, her son.

WHAT MUSIC DID Miss listen to, at home alone in the basement where she lived? Not the music of many cultures: whatever was playing from the radio-alarm clock beside her futon (U2, The Eagles, Cher). On nights her calls to Lindsay went unanswered Miss poured herself a glass of pink wine and cranked the volume and the music came out tinny and faraway from the clock radio's speaker while around her one-room apartment she twirled and sipped and spun.

At the front of the classroom Miss sat with her pen hovering over a test on the various dances of the Spanish-speaking world and suddenly missed very much playing her trumpet in the free-jazz band she and some other students had formed — was it already five years ago now? But then she had been robbed of her trumpet (as well as all her CDs, her stereo, her VCR, and a very expensive knife) by a roommate with a coke problem. Something inside her left with that trumpet. It had never come back.

She should buy a proper stereo. By the monophonic rattle

of a clock radio, that was no way to live. Miss marked the test
B = ¡Bueno!, the pen carving down through the paper and into
the enamel of the desk below. Bogdan watched, imagined the
tip of the pen etching some sort of secret message on the
other side.

The students kept up their whispering. Miss flipped to
another test, Trish's, always a struggle not to give an A+. She
stared at the test, but instead of marking it laid her head on the
desk, forehead first. And then, seeing this, it came: Bogdan
had an answer, a crazy answer. Miss had been giving him a signal. She had been using a code. She had been sending him a
message. He knew now what it was. Long, short-short, long:
Mission X.

IF SHE GOT HER haircut done in time, Bogdan's mother
whisked off the apron and pulled her son down from the chair
and danced with him in waltz-time to the next song on the
record. They swung each other around, *one-two-three, one-two-three*, and though it was fast and fun, Bogdan couldn't help but
think slow thoughts of his father and mother doing the very
same dance to the very same song in the kitchen of their old
apartment. "Ta, tee-tee, ta," "Long, short-short, long," − . . − —
these were all waltz-time too: *one-two-three, one-two-three.*
Bogdan and his mother laughed and waltzed while the guitar
jangled and the drums drummed and Mick Jagger sang, "I'm
gonna tear my hair out just for you."

HIS FIRST GRADE four math test Bogdan had (a) got back,
(b) seen his result (14/45), and (c) eaten. It was on fractions. The

other students were eyeing one another's papers, comment-ing on the marks — "Trish got perfect!" — and out of fear that someone would see his, in a panic Bogdan tore into little pieces which he popped in his mouth, chewed to mush, and swallowed down. The test was one page, double-sided, not too much to eat, but Trish noticed what he was doing and started screaming.

"Why?" Admin asked when Bogdan was sent down with the ragged page as evidence. After three years in Canada Bogdan's English was good, but on occasions when he needed it most, it failed him. So he sat there in silence. Admin sent him back to class, but instead he went home. And at home he sat with his mother and cried and cried and cried.

The next day he came to school and kneeled on The Arab's chest and spat in his face. Miss again found him doing it and this time took him down the hill and watched him cry, and although spitting on someone was a horrible thing she said nothing, just sat there. After a while The Arab came over and sat with them too. The Arab put his hand on Bogdan's back and said, "It's okay." When the bell rang the three of them waited a long time, well after everyone else had disappeared into the school, to go back inside.

Sitting in the classroom surrounded by whispers, watching Miss with her head down on her desk, Bogdan knew it was time. He accepted his mission, Mission X. He knew what he had to do.

He opened his desk. The contents were ordered neatly into piles: textbooks on the right, workbooks on the left, a nifty row of ruler, pens, pencils, and a math-set in between. And the scissors. He slid his thumb and forefinger into the two loops and removed them slowly, opening and closing the blades as he did, and the sound of metal sliding against metal sent a shiver through him. They came together with an icy snick. And he opened them again so he could see how, yes, they formed a cross. Or the letter X.

THE LAST SONG ON *Sticky Fingers* was Bogdan's favourite. Sometimes his mother had another client coming in for a haircut and they couldn't make it to the end; other times her afternoon was free and they would get there. She took Bogdan in her arms, held him close, and he laid his head against her chest and closed his eyes. They swayed gently in place like that as the song rose up slowly from the turntable: pretty guitar and piano and singing from somewhere faraway. Bogdan nuzzled into his mother, the two of them wobbling there amid clumps of hair strewn all over the floor, and for a minute that was all there was in the universe: the two of them, and the song.

BOGDAN STOOD. The whispers continued. If any of his classmates noticed him it was in passing. They were mostly watching Miss, her face buried in her marking. Bogdan looked around, back at Trish. She regarded him at first with disdain, as usual, and seemed to be readying herself to mouth his nickname, but then noticing the scissors in his hand Trish's face changed. It took a moment for Bogdan to realize what that look was, her mouth parting slightly, the eyes widening: fear. For once, Trish had nothing to say. Bogdan slid out from behind his desk.

The scissors in his hand felt light; his body seemed distant. It was as though part of him were there in the classroom and part of him were moving through his life leading to that moment: now tapping out Morse code back home with his father, now lying down with his mother on a mattress on the floor of their new duplex in The Co-op in London, now dancing, now eating a math test, now from across the playground watching The Arab sitting alone on the portable steps, now here. And through it all he heard that song, the last one before the needle would lift and leave them in silence: the cymbals crashed like waves and the drums came rumbling — and, oh, the violins! They were saddest of all.

Bogdan stepped toward Trish. The class went quiet, snapped off like a radio. Bogdan raised the scissors, now at Trish's desk. Miss looked up blearily. It took a moment for her eyes to focus. What she saw was a shaggy-haired boy standing there in the middle of the classroom with a pair of scissors in his hand, and the girl at her desk beneath him staring wide-eyed at the blades, and every face in the classroom turned toward them in wonder.

"Bogdan," said Miss. "What are you doing?"

It was Mission X, he wanted to say. But he was elsewhere. In his head he heard the song at the end of the record, the one he and his mother would dance to, and things were rising up and rising up and it was all cymbals crashing and the music became thunder.

He moved in. His thumbs worked the hinge and opened the blades of the scissors. Trish's hair was a perfect little nest of golden curls. He reached out with one hand and grabbed a fistful. Everything seemed to happen at the same time: Trish screamed and he snipped, and a big clump of sand-coloured ringlets went spiralling down and landed on the floor beneath her desk.

Miss put her hand to her mouth. But she didn't do anything else. She made no move to stop him. She said nothing, just watched Bogdan looking down at the little blonde twists lying between his Zips. Trish had gone white. She sat there staring up at Bogdan with her mouth a perfect round O. No sounds came out. Bogdan grabbed more hair and cut again, snipping away another chunk from the top of Trish's head. "Short-long," mouthed Bogdan. "Short-long."

But then he was tackled. Someone hit him from behind in the lower back and took him down, hard, onto the classroom floor. "You freak," came the voice of a boy pinning him to the tiles, and then there were hands wrestling the scissors from his fingers. He heard Mick Jagger singing softly, "Let it go, now," and then, "Yeah, let it go." So he let it go.

Lying there on the floor Bogdan had a perfect view up the row of desks to Miss, sitting there at the front of the classroom covering her mouth. The song in his head was fading: the end was just like the beginning, with the guitar light as air and piano sprinkled over top like bits of glass. Bogdan's eyes met his teacher's. Was she smiling behind her hand? In her eyes was something.

As one boy crushed his face into the floor and another twisted his arm behind his back, the song in Bogdan's head disappeared. In its place, with the wisps of Trish's hair scattered all around him, Bogdan could hear whimpering, and the whimpering became weeping, and Bogdan smiled, because the weeping was desperate, wailing and lost, and it was the most beautiful music he'd ever heard in his life.

**DIZZY WHEN YOU
LOOK DOWN IN**

AFTER ABOUT TEN minutes of me catching him stealing looks across the waiting room, the big guy finally speaks. "I know you," he says, wagging a rolled-up *Sports Illustrated* in my direction. "Northern, right?"

"Yeah, Northern." I still can't place him.

"Point guard."

"These days?" I laugh. "Thursday nights at the Y, sure."

"But in high school you played point, right? For Northern?"

"Wow — that's, what? Ten years ago?"

He nods, that big head bobbing slow like its batteries are dying out. "I went to St. Paul's."

He comes over, sits down with a seat between us. The magazine gets dropped and then there's this slab of a hand coming at me. Shaking it feels like sticking my arm inside a turkey.

"Brad Bettis," he says. "You're Dizzy Calder's big brother, right?"

"Yeah, that's right." I remember Bettis now, a monster of a four-man who'd bang away at our guys in the paint, knocking them down and then offering a hand to help them back up. A brute, all power, but classy — a yeti with a Catholic conscience.

He's gained about sixty pounds, most of it under his chin. I don't ask him why he's here.

Bettis grins. "Dizzy Calder. Man, that kid could *play*."

I wait it out. The announcement for Dr. Singh comes on the PA again, the nurse starting to sound flustered. A little brown guy in scrubs rushes by flipping pages on a clipboard. His footsteps go clopping down the hall and then I'm left with Bettis, still grinning.

"Dizzy Calder," Bettis says again, shaking his head. "Whatever happened to him? They were asking for him all over the country, I heard."

"He went to Guelph for a semester."

"I heard that!"

"Yeah. Didn't play. Well, he was on the team but never saw the floor. They said he was too small to play three, and didn't have the outside game for a shooting guard."

"So, what? He dropped out?" Bettis has this look like I popped his favourite balloon.

Above Bettis's head, the clock on the wall reads a quarter to two. The anesthesia should be taking hold. They'll be starting now with the saws and blades and whatever else. But Bettis is leaning in, ready for some gossip. I can hear his breath coming in puffs. I tell him what he wants to hear. "He quit the team, finished the year at school, and then went down to Cuba."

"What, to play ball?"

"No." The PA crackles to life and it's the same nurse, sounding tired now. Bettis is waiting for more. "To build houses. He worked on some community project, building houses and pipelines and whatever. Ended up staying down there for six years."

Bettis sits back, all three hundred pounds of him slumping against the plastic chair. "Oh, yeah," he says, eyes narrowed, considering. You can almost hear the squeak of the hamster turning its wheel. After a moment, he picks up his *Sports Illustrated* from the floor, unrolls it, and smooths out the cover. Opening it, looking down, he says, "Too bad. That kid could *play*."

WHEN I GOT BACK to my folks' place, my mom had put together a box of Dizzy's basketball memorabilia for me to look through. Almost lost in that mess of offers from various schools on Athletic Department letterhead and MVP awards was a postcard that Dizzy kept tucked into the frame of his locker back in high school. Now, sitting here with the fluorescents buzzing overhead, Bettis beside me flipping through his magazine, I take it out from my jacket pocket and give it another look.

I don't know where he picked the thing up. It wasn't addressed or anything, it wasn't like anybody had sent it to him. Just a blank postcard, no postage. The picture is from a Celtics-Bulls game at Boston Garden, taken from high in the stands, up in the nosebleeds. Way, way down on the court you can make out ten players: the white and green of the Celtics' jerseys, the Bulls in their road red. Bill Cartwright and Horace Grant are out wide on the baseline, with Kevin McHale and Robert Parish hedging inside, and Larry Bird's sagging off Scottie Pippen down to the elbow. And over on the other wing, on the guy with the ball, is Danny Ainge. Poor Danny Ainge with his hands up, knees bent, feet shoulder-width apart — all fundamentals, all hope. In front of him, mid-dribble, casual, like he's playing a game of pickup with some buddies and afterwards they'll all go out for a beer and wings or whatever, is Michael Jordan.

The Celtics are frozen, waiting, and the Chicago guys are like that too, standing there, no one with their hands up, no one looking for a pass. The rest of the Bulls are out for the show — best seats in the house. Maybe John Paxson's up there at the top of the key thinking about all the times in practice he's been left ducking while Jordan's up swinging on the rim over top of him, and he's thinking, All right, Danny Ainge — good fucking luck.

Before games, Dizzy took that postcard down from his locker and stared at it, finishing off the highlight reel in his head. In his mind he'd be way up there with his head scraping the roof of the Garden, bouncing around in that crowd of lunatics splashing whisky into big cups of fountain soda, leaning forward to see what the hell law of physics Jordan was going to break this time.

"WHAT YOU GOT there?" This is Bettis, curling and uncurling the *Sports Illustrated* in his hands.

I hold the postcard up so he can see it. Bettis squints. "What's that? Celts-Bulls?"

"Yeah," I say, "from Boston Garden."

Bettis nods. He's sweating now — dark circles around the armpits of his shirt and hair slick at the sides. And he's looking at me, all intent, and I know what's coming; he's opened up a door and he's on the other side ready with that question certain people who don't have any good sense ask one another in places like this. I put the postcard back in my pocket.

"So," he says, puffing, "who you here for?"

DIZZY WASN'T REALLY a huge Michael Jordan fan. He went through phases, obsessed with a whole bunch of different players, copying their moves in the driveway. Isiah Thomas used to drive him crazy with his dribbling. Dizzy's handle was good, sure, just never enough to run point. But we'd watch Pistons games on TV and Zeke'd be down there low to the ground, ball *parump*ing off the floor like a drumroll, between the legs and behind the back and spin-dribbles, socks halfway up his calves — and smooth. And Dizzy'd be all over those moves, all winter working the ball in the garage until it was warm enough to get a good bounce going, and from inside the house we'd hear him through the wall, dribbling away, then after a while inside, all sheepish and bashful like he'd been beating off to the Sears catalogue out there or something.

But the one thing he never had was a favourite player. Back when we were kids, all of us would call who we were on the playground. I'd be Kevin Johnson, Mark Price, Tim Hardaway. Big guys were Ewing, Olajuwon, Mutombo. You'd usually get six or seven kids arguing over who was Michael Jordan. But Dizzy was just Dizzy. It was like he thought of the pros as just regular guys and pretending to be them was about as weird as pretending to be your favourite scientist when you wrote a biology test. He borrowed bits from here and there, certain moves — but everything he took he made his own.

Like his routine from the line. It was a weird mishmash he'd put together from guys he liked in college or the pros. He'd line up with the hoop, then take a half-step right — just off-centre, his feet right together. Then he'd get that shock of blond hair that hung in front of his face out of the way with a flick of his head, take a couple dribbles, and pull the ball up to his mouth — he either kissed it or said something, a little message, maybe. Guys lined up around the key would beak him for that, but usually they'd shut up once they checked the score sheet and saw he'd accounted for half our points. Then a knee bend and another dribble and a pause, and the ball would come up just over from his forehead, another pause, then that sweet left hand, all wrist: his shot would trace an arc you could teach math with before landing with a *thock*, the mesh catching the ball like a pair of hands and releasing it bouncing on the baseline.

BUT HERE'S BETTIS, staring at me, mouth hanging open like he's waiting to be fed. What do I tell this guy? I can just imagine him backtracking, all apologies with his big chubby arms around me. When I finally answer, I make sure to turn away a bit to show him that I want this conversation to go only so far. "Waiting for someone in surgery. You?"

"Yeah, me too. My wife." He holds up his ring finger, a sausage wrapped in a strip of gold, as proof. "She's having an operation for endometrial cancer. Know what that is?"

"I work in pharma. We practically had to go through med school our first year." Then, almost as an afterthought, I add,

"Sorry to hear that," and surprise myself when, thinking about Jen, back home in Oakville, I realize I actually am. "Yeah. She'll be okay." Bettis nods at this to reassure himself. And just when I think the conversation's over, he goes on. "So you're in sales?"

"That's right. Four years now. Regional manager, Peel-Halton." By reflex, I find myself going to my wallet to hand over a business card, but then think better of it.

"Right," he says, rubbing sweat from his hands down his pants. "I'm articling here in town, myself."

"A lawyer?" I hope I don't sound as blown away by this as I feel.

"Almost," Bettis says, "but I've had to take a few weeks off because of, you know, stuff?"

There's something in his voice when he says this that forces me to really look at him for the first time, and it's like someone's kicked my legs out from under me. I see bags the size of teacups under the poor guy's eyes, a week's worth of stubble peppering his jowly face. Here's someone reaching out, his wife dying, for all I know, and I'm closing down. I swivel around to face him, take a big breath before I speak. "Actually, I'm here for my brother," I say. "I'm here for Dizzy."

BEFORE BASKETBALL took over his life, Dizzy was always the kid off on his own, the kid who'd eat dinner in total silence while me and Mom and Dad joked with one another about whatever, and then we'd turn around and his plate would be empty with the chair pushed back from the table and he'd just be gone, off wherever, down to the ravine or up to his room.

Dizzy drove Mom crazy, especially with how careless he was with his health. He usually had his insulin on him, he'd just forget. Before we ate Mom always asked him, "Did you take your meds?" and Dizzy would nod, hiding behind all that hair in his face. Then I'd watch him sneak a needle out of his hip-sack, stab himself through his T-shirt under the table, then stash it and move right to his knife and fork and dinner. But he hated it, always did — not so much the needles or the diet, but the dependence, relying on something just to stay alive.

He's been Dizzy for so long that when Mom called me up at home in Oakville last week and said, "Derek's coming home," it took me a minute before I realized who she meant. Even in the few emails we kicked back and forth I never read the D he signed off with as his real name. Of course those weren't ever much more than him telling me how his Spanish was getting better, or me giving updates about the NBA. It felt more like checking in than real communication, and often his messages would sit unanswered for weeks before I could think what to write back — and, considering the lag between replies, I assume he had the same problem with mine.

Dad came up with his nickname one day down at the Pinery. I'd shown my little brother how spinning in place could make the world swim up and away from you. He'd loved it. Mom and Dad and I watched him all afternoon twirling circles with his arms out until he couldn't twirl any more, staggering down the beach and trying to make the water before he fell down. I'd been seven, he'd been five, and all the way home in the back seat he was Dizzy, and then it came to school with him that Monday, and that's who he's been ever since.

While I was happy as a kid to sit down with the TV, maybe play Trouble with Mom or Dad, Dizzy couldn't stay inside. It's funny, because he was always so quiet, not your average hyperactive kid bouncing off the walls and shrieking and starting fights. Just restless. First chance he got from about age eight to twelve, he was right down to the ravine behind the housing complex, building forts to shut himself away in. First the ravine, then the basketball court: places he'd escape to, passing in and out of them, sly and silent, like a ghost through walls.

"DIZZY?" SAYS BETTIS.

"Yeah. It's a complication from his diabetes." I pause. "You knew he was diabetic?"

Bettis shakes his head.

"No, why would you. Sorry. Anyway" — I breathe here, deep — "he's got some problems with his feet. Pretty serious."

"Oh, that's terrible."

"Yeah. They're amputating one for sure, but they're going to try to save the other one. The right foot." His jumping foot, I think, but I don't say it.

"Amputating? Oh, god. That's — that's terrible."

"He didn't take care of his feet down in Cuba, was the thing. Trucking around construction sites in flip-flops or whatever. After so many years it started to take its toll."

"Man," says Bettis. "Well, I hope everything turns out as good as it can."

"Yeah. I mean, he's not going to die or anything."

I realize what I've said as soon as it comes out, but Bettis is just nodding, slow and thoughtful. If, for a second, he's forgotten about his wife, I can guess the one thing he's thinking is that Dizzy's ballplaying days are now officially over. But he can't say that. And neither can I.

DIZZY AND I FIRST played together when he was in grade ten and I was in grade twelve. He'd averaged something stupid in midget ball the year before, thirty-some points a game, half a dozen triple-doubles over the season, forty-two in a city semi-final his team won by twenty. I stayed back for a second year of junior, so I was captain on a team that lost twelve of fourteen in league play, but I made it to the all-star game, where I missed the only shot I took and got dunked on twice. Dizzy had fourteen as the midget MVP, passed up a few layups, air-balled a three-pointer and jogged back down the court grinning like he'd just done the grandest thing in the history of the sport.

The following year I moved up to the senior team and Dizzy went out for the juniors. The senior coach, Mr. McGowan, this shrivelled-up old guy who'd been coaching senior ball at Northern since, Dad joked, they made the switch from peach baskets, showed up at the first junior practice and grabbed Dizzy when he came in the gym and wheezed something at him like, "How'd you like to play up in senior with your brother?" I can just imagine what Dizzy might have done: shook the hair out of his eyes, shrugged, given McGowan that funny little half-smile of his, said, "Sure, okay," and left the gym without another word.

So Dizzy was the coveted recruit and I was backing up this kid, Raul, who'd come back for grade fourteen — the victory lap, he called it. It pissed me off a bit, because otherwise I would have started, and in practice the guy was a real cock, giving you titty-twisters when he came off screens, bringing his knee up into your balls if you guarded him too close. He had this scraggly little goatee like pubes on his chin and a bald slash through his eyebrow he told everyone was a knife wound but I heard he'd shaved there himself and never grew back.

For our rookie initiations Raul made me and this other kid, a big gangly stringbean of a redhead called Clark, run suicides with a hard-boiled egg between our ass cheeks. If it fell out you had to eat it. Clark got going too fast right away, only made it to half-court before his came *plop* out of his shorts, bounced once, and rolled right into the tip-off circle. Raul came over shaking his head and watched Clark chew his way through the egg while I waddled up and down the court — foul line, baseline, three-point, baseline, half-court, baseline — until Raul decided I'd had enough.

For his initiation, Dizzy got his head shaved. They buzzed everything right off, starting with that flop of bangs in the front. He sat on a bench in the change room while they did it, almost patient, waiting until the last of it was lying on the floor between his feet. Afterwards he even offered to sweep up, dumped all that hair into the trash by the sinks and came into the gym looking like a Navy SEAL.

First drill of practice he had Raul on him and did some crazy crossover I'd never seen before, and Raul went for it, diving one way and then stumbling back the other, and his one leg buckled and he was over on the ground hollering like he'd been shot. Dizzy didn't say anything, even helped Raul limp off the court, then came right back into the next drill on defence, first senior practice of the year, this scrawny little kid, fifteen years old. While he didn't start a game that season, he was usually off the bench for ten, easy, with a handful of boards and a few dimes and a couple of steals in there too.

BETTIS WANTS MORE. And, shit, I guess I owe it to him. "So he's been back from Cuba for a while?" he asks, and I start to feel like I'm Dizzy's agent doing press or something.

"No, not long at all. My parents flew him back a few days ago, basically right after he called and explained what the doctors in Havana had told him."

"And he's been in hospital ever since?"

"Pretty much, yeah." I pause. "But I haven't seen him yet."

"How come?"

"Well, I've been working," I say, knowing it sounds weak. "I live in Oakville, so I just thought I'd come down today, for the surgery."

"You talked to him since he's been home?"

"Not exactly." Bettis is looking at me funny, trying to figure this out. "He — he doesn't exactly love what I do for a living, to be honest."

"What, sales?"

"No, not the sales part."

"Then?"

I consider this, not really sure I could even answer in

specific terms if I wanted to. Instead, I reach into my pocket and pull out the postcard. "You should check this out, actually," I tell Bettis, passing it to him. "It was his."

THE NEXT YEAR, my last year of high school, we both made the starting rotation. And, to be honest, we were magic together — all those years of two-on-two on the driveway at home finally paid off.

We had a system if McGowan's flex offence broke down, which it often did. I'd call for a reset, and while everyone was shifting around I'd drive the lane, go up among the trees, turn in the air all desperate, and there Dizzy'd be like a saviour open on the wing, rolling off a screen, hands up and ready. I'd kick it out and he'd catch and shoot, that jumper like a silk handkerchief pulled loose from a shirt pocket.

If a defender stepped up from the weak side he'd throw one of those killer head-fakes — he'd grown his hair back, so that shock in the front would go flopping up and send whoever sailing by, and he'd put it on the floor and come swooping down the lane, lay it in, his hand on the glass not a slap so much as letting the basket know he'd been there.

"HE USED TO STARE at that thing for hours," I tell Bettis.

"It's great," he says, smiling, handing it back to me.

"I brought it for him. When he comes out. I thought" — What did I think? — "I thought he'd like to see it, for old times."

Bettis's smile widens. "Old times. They are old times, aren't they?"

I look down at the postcard, at that frozen moment in history. I realize for the first time how faded the picture is — the parquet yellowing, Jordan's jersey a washed-out pink. I look up at Bettis. He's still grinning at me, putting on a good show despite whatever's going on with his wife. I drop the postcard into my pocket and do my best to force a smile to match his.

DIZZY LOVED basketball but could never watch it on TV for longer than a few minutes — he'd get all antsy and be up with a little Nerf ball, doing post-moves against the doorframe in the TV room, a drop-step and then baby-hooking into the kitchen. And when he got bored of that he'd just disappear, like when he was a kid. I'd turn around from my spot on the couch and he'd be gone — maybe out in the garage, dribbling away, or taking free throws in the driveway with his mitts on in the snow. I might go out there and we'd play some post-up, slipping around on the ice and Dizzy dropping lazy fadeaways over me with either hand.

But that year things started to change. Right around the start of the season he got this girlfriend, this mousy little thing with dreadlocks and a hoop through her nose, and he'd be out in the garage less — more often she'd swing by in her parents' Golf and pick him up. They'd be off somewhere, and when he'd trudge back in that night, shaking the hair out of eyes red and bleary from weed, Mom'd ask where he'd been and he'd tell her, "Out," showing that little half-smile that was the citizenship card to whatever world he lived in.

Still, the second year of senior ball we played together, our team was magic. Big carrot-top Clark hit the weights and put on about forty pounds, turned into a real force down low. We got a new kid, a transfer named Healey, a comedian, and dead-eye from outside. He'd come off screens down low and pop out for threes, and make us howl doing Marv Albert all through practice, with McGowan barking at us to "Shut up and do it right," totally baffled as to what was so funny.

Regardless of whatever else he was getting into, Dizzy was the star. Grade eleven and already one of the most dominant players in the county, maybe the entire region. He was off on weekends with the under-21 rep team — at sixteen! — for tournaments all over the place, down to the States for training camps and clinics, playing against prep-school guys with NBA deals waiting for them like presents wrapped under the tree. But more and more often basketball was taking a back seat to whatever else: the girlfriend, the Grateful Dead, weed. Every chance he got he was reading *The Catcher in the Rye* or that motorcycle repair guide, whatever it was, and then at Christmas his girl got him the Che Guevara biography, and after that you'd never see him without it.

I remember playing against Bettis and his St. Paul's Panthers that year in the playoffs, how they threw a box-and-one at Dizzy. McGowan called a time out right off the tip, took us into the huddle, and rasped at us to run the zone offence, four-on-four, and to take the open shots as we got them. We worked possessions for minutes on end, swinging the ball from one side of the court to the other, watching their box shift left and right, and Dizzy running the odd cut through the key to keep his man moving. We wore them down, let the ball do the work, and ended up pulling away in the second half before taking the game 36–24. We'd never scored less than seventy points all season, and here we were finishing with a combined sixty. Dizzy had eight, a season low, but he didn't seem to care. In the change room Clark stood naked except for his high-tops and tried to get us going on some lame team cheer before Healey came slinking up behind him and dumped the ice bucket over his head.

I MENTION THIS to Bettis now. "You remember that year in the playoffs when you guys tried the box-and-one on us?"

He's not biting. The high-school talk isn't reeling him in like it was minutes ago. He's twisting his wedding band around his finger. He's looking at the clock. "She'll be coming out of surgery now," he tells me. "It'll all be over soon."

Dizzy should be done too, and I start to wonder why a nurse hasn't come out to tell me anything. And here's when I realize that I'm not sure I want him to come out, that I want the surgery to go on until Mom and Dad show up so I don't have to see him by myself. I imagine him with bloody stumps disappearing into bandages, lying in a hospital cot like a bomb victim. And me walking up, not knowing what to say. I can picture myself standing there, him looking at me, waiting, and then eventually I'd fish the postcard out of my pocket, hand it over. Maybe he'd take it even, that sad little piece of cardboard nostalgia — not even close to enough, so far from enough it might as well crumble to dust in his hands.

MY LAST GAME of high-school basketball was the city finals. We played a school from across town that had snuck its way through the playoffs, the Richmond Heights Golden Bears. They'd finished sixth in the regular season, then made a run, taking out the third-place team in overtime in the first round, rode the win into the semis and blew out the two-seed, then met us, who were seeded first, in the finals. They played this crazy three-quarter-court press that some schools never quite got the hang of breaking. If you rushed, they'd trap you at half-court and you'd either throw the ball away or turn it over on the ten-second call.

Before the game Dizzy sat there in the corner of the change room with that Che Guevara book open on his lap, warm-ups on, shoes untied. He was using the Jordan postcard as a bookmark but wasn't looking at it, instead totally sucked into whatever the hell revolution he was reading about. When McGowan came in Dizzy dropped the book into his gym bag and sat back, ready for the predictably inane pep talk the old man had planned.

The game started and the stands were packed with half our fans, half theirs, both sides going crazy with banners and cheers and a few nuts from both schools with trombones and bass drums. But we got down fast. We were caving to their press, offering stupid cross-court passes like gifts, dribbling right into their traps and getting stripped, rushing our offence and forcing dumb shots. Down our end they were hitting everything, and by the end of the first quarter were up 17–2, capped at the buzzer with a bomb from half by their shooting guard.

Second quarter, Dizzy took over. He started dropping into the backcourt when we inbounded, taking the ball himself and dribbling through the pressure, pulling up in their end and looking for me to run the offence. We started hitting shots. First possession, I nailed a three on a botched pick-and-roll, and then it was all Dizzy. He got the ball on the wing against their zone and found holes, weaved through it like a needle through cloth. He hit layups and jump shots, collected other people's misses and put them back for two. He drove and dished to Clark, who powered it up strong, both hands on the glass. At half-time we were down five, 31–26.

A NURSE COMES out then. Bettis and I sit up like something's stung us both. She looks at me and smiles — trying to seem nice, I guess. Then she turns to Bettis. "You can go in and see your wife now, Mr. Bettis."

He stands up and the *Sports Illustrated* slides off his lap to the floor, lies there glossy and glistening in the waiting-room lights. "How is she?"

"Recovering fine. The surgery couldn't have gone more smoothly."

"Oh, thank you." Bettis lays one of those paws on the nurse's shoulder. "Thank you."

He turns to me, bowing his head. "Good to see you," he says. "And good luck." And then he's gone, and by the determined way he lopes after the nurse, I have to wonder if he's already forgotten about me.

SO WE CAME OUT for the second half, and both teams started slow. We turned the ball over to their press; they couldn't hit a shot. The crowd got less rowdy, then quiet, then just bored.

The game was sloppy — passes off guys' hands out of bounds, power moves fired straight off the backboard and out to the foul line. Four minutes in, with the score barely changed at 34–28, I dribbled the ball off my own foot and McGowan called a time out. On our way over to the huddle, Healey muttered in his Marv Albert voice, "Neither team looking confident out there."

McGowan was waiting. "Christ almighty," he spat at us and then went nuts with the marker on his clipboard, all squiggles and Xs and Os in the craziest game of tic-tac-toe you've ever seen in your life. When he was done Clark stepped up and started yelling, "Let's do this! Let's fucking do this!" and we actually sort of got into it and the other guys were up off the bench and the crowd went crazy and we stuck our hands together and "One-two-three: Northern!"

Both teams came out of the time out fired up. First possession, their big man threw down a huge dunk in traffic, and back the other way we broke their press into a three-point play by Dizzy. Then we got a steal of our own, a few more unanswered baskets, and by the end of the quarter we were tied at 47.

ALONE IN THE waiting room, I sit with the clock ticking up over my head, getting on three o'clock, and I start to think I should maybe go see if anyone's got any updates at the nurse's station down the hall.

But I'm paralyzed, stuck there sitting in my chair, Dizzy's postcard stiff and awkward in my jacket pocket. I think about the few times I came back home from school once I moved out and went away to university, sometimes a day early on holidays just to watch Dizzy's games. He dominated the league, scoring at will, but seemed casual about it, only driving to the hoop when games were close enough that he needed to.

His hair was long everywhere, not just the front, and he played with it tied up in a bun, looking like a skinny blond Buddha out there. In grade thirteen he started showing up to practice stoned, and then to games all pie-eyed and bleary, even dopier than usual. He'd still be in charge, but just a step slower than usual, just a bit off the pace of his former self. Even so, the letters kept pouring in from schools — UBC, Western, StFX.

When I'd come back for Thanksgiving or Christmas he'd be out all day and night with that same girlfriend and a bunch of kids just like her, all dreadlocks and tie-dye and bloodshot eyes from dope. He missed a tournament one weekend to go to Ottawa for some rally, some protest against something happening halfway across the world. And when he graduated, instead of taking schools up on any of the tryout offers, he headed to Guelph with his lady, lasted a semester before calling university quits forever.

There was one dinner, though, right at the end of June before high-school graduation, that seems now to mark the end of the Dizzy I thought I knew. The basketball season was a distant memory, and I'd brought Jen to meet Mom and Dad for the first time. They liked her right away, and everyone was getting along and we were talking about moving in together for the summer while we did internships at companies in

Toronto. Dizzy sat at the end of the table sneering at us and pushing his food around, barely acknowledging Jen was even there. When I talked about trying to get into drug sales and he muttered something like, "That's ethical," I finally lost it.

"What the fuck's your problem?"

Mom and Dad froze. We've always been a calm family — fights happen to people on TV, not us, and suddenly it was like someone had stepped out of a soap opera and, one by one, slapped us all across the faces. Dizzy shook his hair out of his face, staring at me, and for the first time I saw that the sleepiness in his eyes was gone. He started going off about corporations and the American FDA and unreleased side effects, slapping the table. No one could believe it. He shook his head at me, then turned to Mom and excused himself from the table. "I have to go take my *insulin*," he said, getting up, then disappearing down the hall.

It's past three now, by the waiting-room clock, and to shake the memory from my head, I take out the postcard again. Sitting there looking at it, I start to wonder how things changed for Dizzy after all those years creating stories to go with the picture. Was there a point where he ran out of possibilities? Was there a day when he looked at it and didn't see anything, a time when everything that had been hope and glory and a whole universe of fantasy faded, and, just like that, when that image of the greatest player to ever play the game became nothing more than a bookmark?

THE FOURTH QUARTER of that city final was tight. We traded baskets back and forth, Dizzy on his game, driving to the hole, scooping up their misses under our basket and going coast-to-coast, picking passes off, working their press. But Heights came hard too. They were pounding us inside, knocking down open shots, their pressure throwing us off our half-court set, making us overly careful, nervous.

With under a minute to go we were down two, 60–58, and they had the ball, running a weave up top to knock as much time off the clock as they could. Me and Healey were trapping and recovering, trying to force a turnover, waiting for McGowan to holler at us to foul.

Then something happened. Heights' point guard jab-stepped one way and came hurtling down the lane. As he picked up the ball on the hop-step, one of our rookies, a good, solid kid named Leeman, came with the help and got a hand in, tied him up. The refs called it a jump — our possession. McGowan yelled for time and got us in a huddle to figure out a last shot. Not that we had a play. Everyone knew to get one guy the ball and sit back and let him do his thing.

We took our time off the inbounds with their pressure, working the ball back and forth in the back-court before we crossed half and set up our zone offence. Thirty seconds on the clock, and everybody in the gym knew who we were going to. I had it up top, dribbling over to the wing where I knew Dizzy would come swinging through for the pass. Heights were playing us tight, though, and he got the ball farther out than he usually liked — right up near the hash mark. The rest of us spread the floor, and Dizzy squared up, triple-threat, with one of their guys right in his face. The clock was counting down — twenty-six, twenty-five, twenty-four —

and right before the five-second call he put the ball down, hair in his face, and started to move in.

We waited. No one wanted a pass. Their zone was laid flat out, waiting for Dizzy to go outside so they could bring the trap and he'd have to swing it back around to someone else. And, for whatever reason, my little brother gave them exactly that — he brought the guy up the sideline, into the corner, and then there were two on him, and the rest of us realized we had better rotate around to give him another option.

I came off a screen from Healey, wide open at the top of the key. Dizzy looked at me, still working his dribble with two defenders closing in on him. His eyes met mine. My hands went up. Eighteen seconds on the clock, seventeen. And then he went around the back, split the trap, and he was at his sweet spot, a step in from three, right where he'd made a living all season.

But, for whatever reason, he didn't shoot. He looked at me again quickly and then took a step *backwards* so he was beyond the arc. And then, like he'd been a bomber from out there all his life, he let fly for the win.

I heard McGowan yell, "No!" and then there was just silence as the ball made its way to the hoop, my teammates and I just watching, no one crashing the boards. It came down off the front of the rim, bounced up off the backboard, rim again, before falling out. One of the Heights guys nabbed the rebound, but we were so dazed we didn't even think to foul, and it was one quick outlet pass, and another, and their point guard was up for two at our end to put it at 62–58 and out of reach.

"MR. CALDER?"

I look up and it's the little doctor with the clipboard, slight and brown and sort of bowing at me, like he's a butler or something.

"Yes?"

"I'm Dr. Singh."

I stand up and we shake hands.

"I've got some good news," he says. "We were able to save your brother's right foot. Just some pustules, some minor infection."

"Oh, good." Right away, this seems a dumb thing to say.

"He's in recovery, a bit disoriented, but otherwise doing fine."

"Yeah?"

"We told him you're here," Dr. Singh says. "He said he'd like to see you."

Dr. Singh bows again and then he's off down the hall at a decent clip, and I have to hurry to catch up. I've still got the postcard in my hand, although now I realize that it's bent and folded like Bettis's magazine.

AFTER THE GAME I sat in the locker room with my shoes off and uniform still on. Clark was crying a bit, and McGowan put his arm around our big man and told him he was proud of how far he'd come, and to the other guys he said they did a great job and that he was looking forward to next year.

But I sat there, remembering that look Dizzy had given me before he shot, almost apologetic, but something in it that seemed cocky, superior — like, "This one's mine. Sorry." And then the miss and he'd gone shuffling off the court while the clock ran out on our season.

He'd got changed and was sitting there in jeans and a hoodie, reading Che across the change room. Eventually he looked up and I caught his eye. He slung his gym bag over his shoulder, stuck his thumb in the book to keep his page, and came across to where I was, sitting beside the door.

"Good game," he said to me, his palm out for five or a handshake.

I just sat there, offering nothing.

Dizzy smiled then, that one side of his mouth turned up at the corner. He flipped his hair out of his face. "It's just basketball, man," he said. Then, as he opened the door to head outside, my brother looked back at me with the same expression as the one he'd given me on the court — not arrogance, I'd misread it before. This was a look of distance. Once, when we were kids, I'd been sent to fetch Dizzy from the ravine. I'd stood up top, looking down, watching him pile branches on top of one another in the valley, whispering to himself, pointing here and there as though he were directing other people. When I'd finally called out, "Dinner!" he'd gazed up at me with the same look he gave me then in the change room, like I was part of a world he didn't care about belonging to. Just as I had back then, I couldn't take it. I had to look away. Dizzy waited for a moment in silence like he was going to say something else, but instead just shrugged, then ducked out the door and was gone.

WALKING DOWN THE hospital hallway, Dr. Singh bopping ahead of me in the dim light, that's not the way I want to remember my brother, not now. I want all those moments I can tell other people about, those moments when I was there and so close to being a part of his life — our post-up games in the driveway, running pick-and-rolls to perfection, me driving and dishing to him for the spot-up jumper. I want the kid at the beach, spinning and giddy and tumbling in the sand.

Dr. Singh stops at a door and peeks in through the little window. I'm still a few paces down the hall. When he starts to open the door, I pause. By now Dizzy's postcard is little more than a crumpled, papery mush in my hand.

I look to my right, into another room just like the one I'm sure my brother's in. Sitting on a chair with his back to me is Bettis, and lying in the bed in front of him is a pale, pretty woman with a bald head. He's got both of her hands in his, held up to his mouth, and his big shoulders are heaving, shuddering like a glacier run ashore. He's weeping, but his wife's looking at him with a smile on her face — the tired, sad smile of someone saved.

I turn away and Dr. Singh has disappeared. The door to Dizzy's room hangs open, an invitation, with a triangle of pale yellow light slanting into the hallway from inside.

But I don't move, not yet. I stand thinking about my brother, lying there in bed. In my mind the image starts to play out as a film. I see myself going in, sitting down in an uncomfortable chair at the foot of his cot, saying hello, not much else. My parents arrive. After some discussion, I end up staying the night. Dizzy and I don't talk much — he fades in and out of sleep, I huddle under a blanket in the chair; a breakfast comes he doesn't eat, then a lunch. I call Jen and we talk and decide that I should stay out here for a while. The days go by. Some nights I stay at the hospital; others, I sleep in my old bed at my parents'.

Meanwhile, Dizzy would be getting better, but our conversations would still be minimal — me asking if he needed anything, if he was feeling okay, whatever. Maybe I'd even bring in tapes of old NBA games, although I can't imagine we'd watch them. They'd probably just lie in a pile on the side table between a few vases of flowers, him never acknowledging them, me never suggesting we put them on. The nurses would come in and I'd look away while they changed the bandages where his foot used to be; if he was sleeping they'd ask me how he was doing and I'd nod and say, "Good." But mostly I'd just sit there with him. And sitting with him, I feel myself hoping, might just be enough.

I start to move down the hallway, toward Dizzy's room, toward the light shining out of it and the soft murmur of Dr. Singh talking to my brother. I'm thinking now about how, eventually, Dr. Singh is going to say that Dizzy is okay to leave. I see myself collecting his things, and through the window of his room a winter morning — sky like a white curtain, bright. I see me and Dr. Singh easing Dizzy into a wheelchair, some paperwork filed, some talk of prosthetics, good luck. And then I'm wheeling my brother down the hall, through the doors of the hospital, into the light, outside, where the snow's just starting to fall.

BEING LIKE BULLS

IT TOOK THREE weeks in a row of no one coming in before the place really got to me. My parents' old shop had always been full of stuff that, even back when we still got tourists through, I couldn't imagine anyone would ever want. Junk. Everywhere, piled up on shelves or hanging from display racks, all with more or less the same tacky logo splashed across the front in neon script: *Niagara Falls, Ontario*. It might have been gradual, building up over time, or it might have just been that something snapped. But suddenly everything my eyes landed on — the coffee mugs, the key chains and pencils and snow globes, the T-shirts and sweatshirts and jackets and hats, the daytime postcards with the water flowing green and frothing white over the edge, the sunset postcards burning orange, the nighttime postcards all purple and blue — came needling back into my brain. Simply put, the place was a museum of crap. So I got my jacket on, closed up, and drove over to CanAm Tower.

Dave and a new girl I hadn't seen before were out in the parking lot having a smoke. They both had their uniforms on, navy blue jumpsuits stamped with the CanAm logo: the stars and stripes and maple leaf styled into a yin-yang sort of thing.

Cross-border solutions, it said along the bottom. Their belts dangled various paraphernalia: flashlight, walkie-talkie, nightstick.

The nightsticks Dave and I used to joke about — until one morning just before dawn he caught some pickers trying to drag an old fridge out of the pit and bashed one of them into a coma. The guy had been from one of the camps out in wine country and for a while things got pretty dicey: while Dave's victim was still in hospital a few of his pals snuck into town one night and beat two American pit workers to near death. CanAm responded by equipping its night security with tasers and instructions to zap first and ask questions later. But the picker came out of the coma and things settled down. Instead of being reprimanded, Dave was just put on the day shift at the top of the tower, told to radio in if he saw anything suspicious.

I came across the lot, waving. Dave nodded back. "Busy day?"

"Right," I said. "Something like that."

The girl — her nametag read *Kaede* — was plugging her nose with one hand and smoking with the other. She was young, mid-twenties or so, and when she grinned at me I was surprised to find myself grinning back. Looking away, I scratched at my elbow through my jacket. "Cold out today," I said.

Dave turned toward me and I could smell the liquor coming off him in waves. Nine thirty in the morning, so this was probably remnants of the night before. Lately I'd been staying in, reading magazines and falling asleep by ten. "Kaede," he said, in a weird, slow voice, "this is my good friend Aagyapal."

"Paul's fine," I told her, eyeing Dave.

"Hi, Paul," she said, fingers still pinching her nose, breathing smoke through her mouth.

Then she checked her watch, took one last drag, smiled again at both of us, and wandered off down the street, flicking her butt over her shoulder. It spun there on the pavement in the wind, sparking orange, until a bigger gust snuffed it out.

"Cheery girl," I said.

"Japanese," Dave whispered. He punched my shoulder, seemed like he was about to say something else, paused, and eventually added, "But totally speaks English fine." Kaede moved off in the direction of Rainbow Bridge until she was out of sight.

I shivered. "Mind if I come up? Some October. Feels more like January."

We shot up the tower in the elevator, the view spreading out beneath us. In the observation room Dave sprawled on the couch in the corner while I gazed through the south-facing windows over that end of town. It was empty, nearly derelict. Nobody along any of the little avenues that used to be so full of tourists, nobody down the end of the boardwalk where folks would line up to watch the river come crashing down over the edge, nobody at the coin-op viewfinders tilted on haphazard angles from the last time — months ago, now — that anyone had fed a loonie in to spy on what was happening below.

"Those fuckers were hogging the pool table again last night," Dave said, stretching. Then he laughed. "I feel like my old man — 'Send them back to their own country.'"

Way down below, two bulldozers plowed their way through

a heap of trash. A group of workers followed, shovels at the ready. "It's not like it's their choice to be up here, man," I said.

"What do you mean?"

"I mean, they work for the same company you do; they get stationed wherever they're told. Even you, right? They could have you over on the American side. But you're here."

"Thank Christ for that," Dave grunted. "Pauly, you should try to get on with security. They're looking for people right now — I guess the pickers on both sides are getting pretty out of control again. But a little guy like you they'd never make work nights. You'd be on days like me and Kaede and you wouldn't have to do shit."

"And I'd do what with the shop? Sell it?"

"Oh, fuck. Here we go. How long have we been going through this shit with you, man? There's got to be a point where you just let go. And what about money?"

"Don't worry about me and money." Dave didn't need to know that my parents had stashed enough of their income away that I could go right through to a doctorate without a dollar in loans. He'd have thought "trust fund" and then I would have heard it — especially now that I was living off their hard work and not going to school.

The diggers and bulldozers kept working, shifting the garbage around, moving it into the compactors. The sounds drifted up: the grumble and growls, the grinding of trash packed into neat little squares, the buzz of generators, and the steady drone of trucks moving single file in and out of the pit, dumping their loads and then heading out to fetch more garbage.

THE NEXT DAY I drove down to the store, pulled up into that familiar spot out front. Above loomed our sign, paint flaking; the G of Gold had peeled off in the past year and I'd never bothered to replace it — so now the family business was called Canada _old Souvenirs. I caught myself sighing as I got out of the car, my standard reaction to thinking about the day ahead: sitting there, waiting in vain for the chime of the doors opening.

Leaving the Closed sign turned out, I took my spot behind the counter. Dust had settled over everything, the gleam of figurines and paperweights hidden under greyish fluff. I thought about cleaning it off, going around with one of those feather things. But what was the point? Quickly the feelings from the day before began to rear up again, as sickly and shame-soaked as a hangover.

I looked at the photograph of my parents taped to the cash register, something that usually kept me going. It'd been taken the day they opened the store and stuck up there shortly thereafter. In the picture the two of them stood out front, my mom in a sari and my dad in his turban, the new sign shiny and bright above. Later they laughed at how arbitrarily they'd named it, the naive, immigrant enthusiasm of Gold, and the photo captured exactly that in their faces: eagerness, trepidation, hope.

I'd been born a few years later. We never had many problems. Mostly people found us charming, maybe a little perplexing, this polite Sikh family hawking Canadiana. The honeymooners would come and *ooh* and *ahh* at our shop full of kitsch, or there were the tour groups who went nuts for our novelty T-shirts. You could just imagine them parading around back home in their new duds like they were something special, someone worldly. But we sold the same things to everyone. Each tourist who came to the Falls had the same experience: pay too much for parking, look at the water, buy something shitty, load back onto your chartered bus, and go home. There was nothing special about it.

The register itself was an old, clunky thing. We'd never modernized to digital for some reason, and whenever we rang up a sale — as I remember *sales*, anyway — the thing dinged and clunked as we filed the cash away. Without a second thought, I punched the drawer open, peeled the picture of my folks off the register, and stashed it in the cash drawer, banging it closed. Maybe Dave was right, I thought. Maybe it was time to call it quits, sell the land to CanAm, finish school with the money.

There was a knocking sound then — I had this crazy idea that it was my folks from inside the register, begging to be set free, before I realized someone was at the front door of the shop. I hopped the counter and saw that it was the new girl, Kaede, uniform on, looking very official.

"We're actually open," I said. "Just haven't turned the sign around yet."

She nodded, that big goofy smile splashing across her face. I'm not a big guy, but I had to look down at her: she was maybe five feet tall, with broad cheekbones and a little bob haircut streaked with gold. Her grin exuded a warmth that I'd nearly forgotten could exist in people.

Kaede stepped past me, started moving through the store. She had a camera strapped around her neck.

"Any trouble?" I asked. "With security, I mean?"

"Hardly," she said, and kept looking around. Was she actually shopping?

From one of the racks, she picked up a pen with a little *Maid of the Mist* boat that went sliding up and down the stem when you tilted it. She pointed it at me like a sword, cocked her head in an inquisitive way. "How much?"

"Honestly, when they closed, every tourist shop in town unloaded their stock on us. We've got a warehouse full of this crap. Take it. Take whatever you want."

Kaede shot me a quizzical look. "Yeah? How about if I take some pictures?"

"What? Of this place?" I laughed. "Knock yourself out."

The lens cap came off and she was at it, snapping away, doing little knee bends and leaning back to get certain angles. When she turned toward me, though, I put my hand up. "Whoa."

"Oh, sorry. I didn't —"

I forced a smile. "No, you know. Just didn't have a chance to do my hair."

She capped the camera. "Gotcha."

"Hey, can I ask you something? What the hell are you doing here? In Niagara Falls, I mean. I know you're in our shop because it's totally amazing. But to come all the way from Japan to work guarding a garbage dump — I don't know, seems a little weird."

"Paul," said Kaede. "I'm from Calgary. My parents are Japanese, and I taught English in Tokyo for a bit, but — no, anyway, I'm here mainly for a project." She held up the camera. "I'm a photographer. Back when the Falls were here, people took thousands of pictures, but they're all the same — the water, the boat-ride, whatever. I want to document the way it is now, for an entire year. The people who live here, their homes, their jobs, and what's become of all the old sites — Marineland, especially."

"Marineland? There's nothing there."

"Exactly. And CanAm gives me a place for free, and I can shoot on the job, so . . ."

"So you'll be here for a year?"

I felt like I should add that I'd be around, that I could take her out to Marineland sometime, whatever. But I'd forgotten how to do this sort of thing. My last attempt at romance ended with me humiliating myself with some German back-packer, a big horsy woman down for one night from Toronto. We'd met at Dooley's and gone back to her hotel. But it'd been a bust. The machinery didn't work, I guess you'd say; I ended up sneaking off as soon as she passed out. And that had been months ago now.

Kaede was making for the door. "Hey, Paul — can I ask *you* something?"

"Um. Sure."

"Am I ever going to get used to the smell? It's awful."

"Ha, yeah," I said. "Give it a couple months."

She shook her head, said something about getting back to work. At the door of the shop, she paused. "Your friend Dave said something about a bar? Do you ever go there?"

"Dooley's?" I thought of the German. "I used to. Not so much any more."

"Dave invited me tomorrow night. You should come. I

haven't got a phone yet, but why don't you drop by my place beforehand? We'll go together."

AFTER SPENDING AN hour trying to find my going-out shirt, I headed up to Kaede's apartment off Lundy's Lane, in the back of the old Econo Lodge. She was waiting on the steps, cycling through the images in her camera. On the walk down to Dooley's we went around to some of the old tourist stops so she could take a few pictures in the dusky light. Most of them were boarded up; the few that still had their windows intact had been converted to housing or CanAm offices.

"Find it depressing?" I asked.

"No," she said. *Click, click.* "More interesting."

We took a little detour to Clifton Hill, stopping in front of what used to be the old Guinness Museum. While Kaede snapped away I explained how, at first, the place had been turned into a nostalgic retrospective. "They filled it with inter-active displays and old videos about the nutbars who went over in barrels, and there was a little working model with water rushing over the side and a pair of headphones to listen to the actual sound of it, recorded way back when."

"And what was that like?"

"The real sound? It's weird, I can't really tell you. I mean, I know what noise waterfalls make, I just can't remember exactly what it was like *here* — like if we were standing in this spot, what we'd be listening to. Or if we could hear anything at all."

She stood looking at me with the camera in her hands, waiting for more. But I just said, "Let's go," and started walking again, leading us through Victoria Park. With the overcast sky darkening, the shadows of the trees stretched and deepened.

"Is it true I shouldn't walk around here alone at night?" she said.

"Well, after dark you get garbage pickers coming down from Welland or Fort Erie and that. There have been some problems."

"But I'm security, Paul." Her hand brushed mine, sending a ripple of heat up my arm. "If I was working nights these are the people I'd have to deal with, right?"

DOOLEY'S WAS RUN by its namesake, a salmon-coloured, tubby little Newfie who had opened the place back in the days of happy tourism. When asked about keeping it going while everyone else went under, Dooley would shrug and give his standard answer: "Folks gotta drink."

The place was split into two gloomy rooms: one featured a pool table ringed with stools; the other side had the bar and a few booths. The clientele practised a similar division. Guys like me and Dave, locals from way back, stuck together, while anyone else — especially the Americans who'd been stationed up here — went to the side of the bar where we weren't. Every now and then one of our guys would get a few drinks in him and start to feel sore, "accidentally" spill a beer on someone's lap and have to take it outside. Not me, though. I've never been a fighter.

Dave and everyone else were set up in the booths, empty pitchers lined up on the table. Our crowd were folks who went to high school together and had stuck around, most either working public service or jobs with CanAm. Dooley had sold the jukebox since it only caused fights, so there was no music, just the clicks and clacks of pool balls being knocked around in the adjoining room, subdued conversations filtering through wafts of blue smoke from Camels or Marlboros bought at the duty-free.

Kaede and I got chairs and added them to the end of the table. I started going through introductions when Dave slammed his beer down and stood up. His eyes blazed. "I don't know what the fuck you think you're doing, Pauly. I mean, nice of you to honour us with your presence for once, but if anyone was invited here tonight it sure wasn't you, you fucking sellout."

"Dave," I said, my hands raising in defence. "Easy, man, I'm just — "

Then the rage was swept away with a wink. "Shit, man, I'm just pulling your chain. Nice shirt." He turned toward the bar. "Shots for my man Pauly here, Dooley! Line 'em up!"

Dooley came around with beakers of Canadian Club for me and Kaede: cheers and down the hatch. And right into the beer, mugs filled and pushed sloppily in our direction, half of it splashing onto the floor.

"To new friends!" screamed Dave, and everyone clinked glasses and drank.

Getting drunk at Dooley's was purposeful, steady. Conversations were two or three lines traded between big swallows of Moosehead or Blue. Dave's cousin Lisa asked me, "How are things at the store, Pauly?" and I said, "Shitty," and everyone took a big gulp of their pints. But then there was Kaede, right beside me. I turned to her while everyone else sat working away at their beers in silence, wondering how she'd fit in.

"So," I said.

Kaede lit a cigarette. "In Japanese 'so' means once, before, ever, never."

"So?"

"So what," she said, blasting smoke out the corner of her mouth. "Let's get wasted."

Within an hour we had managed just that, chatting, trading drinking stories from our school days. We got closer, her leg against mine. "Are you glad you came out?" she asked.

"Sure. It'd be better if the bar wasn't in Niagara Falls, but whatever."

"You've been back here how long?"

"Six years. Since my mom passed away. My dad and I ran the store for a year, and then one day at work about a year later a blood vessel popped in his brain. Right in front of me."

"Oh, Paul," said Kaede. Then, slowly, "Your parents never saw the Falls dry, then."

I shook my head.

"Would they have stayed, do you think?"

I wasn't ready for this question. I picked up my beer, then put it down. Kaede just sat there waiting for a reply as if she'd asked for the time or directions. Finally I just said, "I don't know."

Then we heard a shout. Dave was in the face of some guy at the bar with a full pitcher in either hand. I didn't recognize him, but he had about four inches on Dave, and the guy beside him, whom I'd also never seen before, was even bigger.

"I heard you, asshole," Dave was saying. "You called my buddy a coon."

"Koontz, dickwad. I said *Koontz.*"

"Dude, we've got a friend named Koontz," said the other guy, stepping in. "He's in the other room if you want to meet him."

Dave kept staring at the first guy. "Pauly!" he yelled. "This guy called you a coon."

"A what?" I had to stop myself from laughing.

Kaede grabbed my leg. "Did he just say 'coon'? Does that even apply to you?"

Dooley came flapping out from behind the bar. "Outside, lads, outside!" he hollered, and shooed them out the door — the two bewildered strangers first, and then Dave, already rolling up his sleeves. A bunch of our guys followed. The pool room went silent and then a crowd poured out the door as well.

"Jesus," I said, turning to Kaede. "Sorry you have to see this."

But she was already standing. "Come on, Paul! Fight!"

Out in the parking lot the bigger guy was pointing to a Jeep with New York plates. "Dude, look at the fucking tags." Dave wouldn't, but I did: KOONTZ. "This is his car. Can you see?"

Dave stood face to face with the other guy. "I don't know who the fuck you think you are, coming up here and acting like you own the place."

There was some sort of idiotic retort, something in response from Dave, and then they were swinging at each other. Our buddies circled around to hold the other

Americans back, saying, "Let them go, just let them go," while Kaede, a foot shorter than everyone else, was hopping on tiptoes and craning her neck. "I can't see! Paul, what's happening? I can't see!"

Dave got a few shots in, but the other guy was just too big for him. A few seconds later he grabbed one of Dave's punches out of the air, like picking fruit from a tree, and hauled him in. Dave took a solid elbow to the chops and then a big left hook came swinging around, the crack of his jaw releasing an empathetic gasp from the crowd. Then our guys were diving in — although now the Americans were holding *them* back to let their buddy go for it.

"You didn't miss anything," I told Kaede. "It's over."

Kaeded slumped beside me. "Why didn't you tell me what was going on?"

"Oh, come on. I hate this bullshit. You want to get out of here?"

"I guess so," she said, turning to me. "But where do you want to go?"

IF DURING THE daytime it was a ghost town, N.F. at night was more of a graveyard. We tottered through the empty streets, Kaede clinging to my arm with her nose buried in my shoulder, the world swimming up underneath our feet. Those buildings that weren't boarded up loomed, their windows black and empty, on either side of the street. Drunkenly I tried to focus on the road ahead, one step after the next. Everything was a muddy fuzz. But when something went scuttling by in the shadows, my brain snapped to attention.

"What?" Kaede said. "What was that?"

"Nothing. Just keep moving."

"Paul," she said.

I looked straight ahead and took her hand. "Let's go," I said. But there was someone following us. I could hear whispering from the shadows: up front, then behind, off to the left, then the right. I thought about Dave, losing it on that picker on the American side, smashing the poor guy's skull in with his nightstick. Over a broken fridge.

We stumbled along a little faster, the clopping of our footsteps echoing all the way to the end of the street. "It's not far," I said. "Maybe you should get your keys out now."

At the door to her housing block, Kaede struggled with the deadbolt while I watched the street and listened. The shadows seemed to shift and ripple. I strained to tell if the wisps of voices I heard were real or imagined. And then I saw something that looked like a child rise up from the ground at the end of street, as though it were getting to its legs from all fours. Kaede's keys clattered on the lock. The shape stood there, facing me, unmoving — a dark blot hovering in the shadows of the next block.

When the door finally opened, I nearly pushed Kaede over to get inside.

"Is it one of the pickers?" she asked.

Her eyes were red from booze, that usually perfect bob all askew and wild. I didn't say anything, just put my hand on the small of her back. She reached up and wrapped her arm around my shoulder. Together, we wobbled our way down the hall to her apartment.

"You should stay here," she said, letting me into her place. "You know, just in case."

"Sure," I told her. "What, on the couch?"

"No," she said, reaching past me and locking the door. Her arms looped around my waist, her face turned up at mine so I could smell the sweetness of booze on her breath. When she spoke again the words were slow. "My bed's much more comfortable."

THE NEXT MORNING, while I was struggling to ignore a pounding headache and find my socks amid the mess on her bedroom floor, Kaede lay in bed piecing together the night before.

"There was a fight, right? Did you start it? I feel like it was your fault, for some reason."

I threw a pile of shirts to one side, only to discover a pile of pants.

"Or was it because of something you did? Man, I was so drunk."

"That's what happens when you drink, I guess. Imagine that."

She was silent for a minute. I could feel her watching me as I went rifling through her stuff. "Paul, do your friends always fight for you?"

"Jesus, Kaede," I said, kicking my way through laundry and books. "You've got no idea what you're talking about. And I don't know how you expect to get any sort of project done when you can't even keep your bedroom in order either. Look at this place. It's like a twelve-year-old got her own apartment."

She sat up in bed. "Get my project done? Excuse me?"

"Yeah, you know, the one where you come rolling into town, taking pictures of people's homes — like we're animals in a zoo or something. These are real lives, Kaede. We're not just something for you to leech off."

"Oh, give me a break. At least I'm doing something, Paul. Look at you, rushing around to get your stuff together so you can go sit in your parents' store where no one ever comes."

I froze. A million things went through my head to scream back at her for this. I pictured myself grabbing fistfuls of her stuff and whipping them around the room. But I was not the type of guy to lose it. I breathed, looking away. Very calmly, I peeled my jacket off the back of her desk chair, made my way in silence down the hall, and quietly closed the front door on my way out, walking sockless in my shoes all the way across town to work.

Maybe half an hour later Kaede showed up in her uniform, breezing in through the front door while I was going through some paperwork. She browsed absently through the postcards, moved a few things around on the shelves, not acknowledging me until she held up a maroon and gold Canada sweatshirt to her body. "What do you think?"

I had no reply, just made a note on the page I was working on and turned to the next.

"You guys are so tense."

I flipped through the pages as though I were looking for something.

"In Japan they have places for people like you, for businessmen."

I glanced up from the files. I was a businessman now?

"To blow off some steam," she said, coming toward me. "Shops where people buy a ticket and they can smash things."

"Shouldn't you be at work?"

"People go nuts for it. Apparently it's a huge release, destroying all these delicate things — china, crystal, glass. They just smash the shit out of everything."

"What do they use?"

She clasped her hands together and swung them, whistling.

"Baseball bats?"

Kaede nodded. "And whatever else — tire irons, swords, you name it."

"Swords?" I struggled not to laugh. "People pay to do this?"

"Lots."

I stood there looking around the shop at my stock, wondering. But Kaede acted first. She grabbed a snow globe from the shelf. "Let's smash this."

"Whoa."

"Come on, aren't you mad at me?" She winked. "Won't this be a good release?"

I paused, she let out a frustrated huff, and before I knew what was happening, she hurled the thing against the tiled floor. It shattered, sending its contents — an igloo, a snowman, a couple of evergreens, a handful of white confetti — flooding outwards on a wave of murky water and broken glass, leaving half the cracked globe rocking back and forth on its side.

"What the fuck are you doing? That's our stock!"

But she just handed me another one, giving me a look like, *Come on.*

"Kaede."

That look again. I took the globe from her hand, felt the dust that had accumulated on the smooth glass, weighed it, then dropped it beside the other one. It bounced harmlessly, rolled a bit, and came to rest against the counter. Kaede picked it up, looked at me with a frustrated expression.

I sighed, took it from her. "Okay," I said, "fine."

When the globe exploded I honestly felt something, a rush, as though a floodgate inside me opened up when the glass bulb split and spewed its contents all over the store. I looked up at Kaede. She smiled, already handing me a paperweight in the shape of Horseshoe Falls. This I hurled at the ground, laughing, screaming, "Motherfucker!" Ceramic shrapnel sprayed up as it hit. My body was buzzing. I put my hand out, greedy for more.

Kaede took another paperweight from the shelf, juggled it from one hand to the other, then put it back. "We need to save things for other people."

THAT NIGHT KAEDE made me spaghetti at her place. Over dinner we planned the whole thing, settling on twenty dollars a person — all my friends could afford, I figured — and decided that a week would give us enough time to get everything ready. Kaede made it clear that we had to be very specific in the area we allotted each participant. Otherwise, she advised me, there would be mayhem. "In Japan there are very strict rules. Do you think we need to do the same?"

I thought of Dave. "Yeah, that's probably a good plan."

When dinner was done I offered to clean up, but I'd only washed two dishes before we were peeling each other's clothes off right there on the kitchen floor. She pushed me down and climbed on top, hands running up my chest. In the light I noticed her face: a weird half-smile played at the corners of her lips, as though she were trying not to laugh. I scooped her up and flipped her around, wedging myself between her legs.

She went rigid.

"Kaede — is something wrong?" My pulse quickened. I'd been too rough, too creepy.

"Um, sort of." She looked uncomfortable. "It's just that — well, these tiles are really cold. I know it's boring, but can we just go to my room?"

After we'd finished, chatted each other to sleep, and then rolled away to opposite sides of the bed, I woke up in the middle of the night freezing. In need of clothing, I stumbled in the dark into the kitchen to retrieve my boxers and T-shirt. On the walk back to the bedroom I stopped at the living-room window. I'd forgotten that strange shape, that kid, whom I'd seen the night before. I stood for a while gazing out into the night. But there was nothing, no sign of any movement or anyone skulking around in the shadows, no kids or adults or anyone to speak of.

Back in bed I lay there on top of the sheets staring at Kaede's back, curled away from me. I spooned up behind her, wrapping an arm around. Whether she was asleep or not she looped her fingers through mine and pulled me even closer. It was good, comfortable, but every time I started fading into sleep I'd hear noises from outside. I'd snap awake and lie there, hugging Kaede, imagining that little shape scuttling around the building, bursting up out of the night with its face pressed to the window. I didn't fall asleep until the first light of dawn began to crack its way through the curtains.

I SPENT THE NEXT day going around telling my friends about Kaede's idea — *our* idea, I suppose. At first they just raised their eyebrows and laughed, but when they realized that the invitation was serious they were quick to sign up. Lisa and Colin were a bit more reticent; there was almost something sympathetic in the way they agreed to come.

"Are you sure this is something you want to do, Pauly?" Lisa said.

"Sure as sure. Just go nuts. Like bulls in a china shop. It'll be fun."

Colin shook his head. His folks had been friends with mine; I wondered if he was thinking about what they'd make of the store smashed to bits. But then he just smacked me on the back and said, "Well, Dave'll be happy. At least a paperweight won't fight back."

Eight people confirmed, all old friends. A hundred and sixty bucks isn't exactly a fortune, but it was a lot more than I'd make trying to sell the stuff. And everyone seemed to be genuinely excited — both for themselves and for me.

Until the big day a week later, Kaede and I spent every night together; if she could work her security patrol so it swung past the store, she would, hanging out until she thought the CanAm folks might wonder where she'd got to.

She had the day before the big smash-up off work, so I surprised her with an impromptu trip to Marineland. Nearby was the warehouse space where I kept everything the other souvenir shops had passed along to me, so we decided to go by there as well.

We parked on the main road about halfway between the two places and hit the warehouse first. The place was like an airplane hangar, full of junk. Kaede poked around taking photos, kneeling to snap the boxes full of knick-knacks, getting up close to shoot the postcard racks and shelving units teeming with relics of a place that no longer existed.

"After we get through everything you've got in the shop, we'll restock it with this stuff."

"For who?"

But she just raised the camera to her face and took my picture.

Then we walked back past the car and on to Marineland, where we hopped the wall by the front gate. It was another chilly, grey day, and the few trees that still sprouted from the cement walkways were leafless and lonely-looking. I took Kaede down to the old killer whale tank, where we crossed over to the stage and sat, dangling our legs above the empty pool. Everywhere the blue paint was flaking, the muck of rotten leaves clinging to the corners in brown clots.

"So what did this used to be like?" she asked, shooting the tank with the flash on, then off.

"I used to come here every summer with my parents. The whales were the best, the way they splashed around, how it looked like they were smiling. We always sat up close on purpose, because the orcas would do these backwards flops that'd spray up into the crowd. Then we'd walk around, get cotton candy or something, and dry off in the sun."

Kaede pulled out a pack of cigarettes from her purse and put them down between us, took one for herself and lit up. After a few drags, she took the cigarette out of her mouth, leaned in, and kissed me on the cheek. "Paul, this is going to be so good. You feeling okay?"

I nodded at her cigarette. "You smoke the way my mom used to, like every drag is the first one you've ever taken in your life."

"Shut up!"

I faltered for a second, looking at her face — the incredulous expression in her eyes, faking hurt — and then went in. Her mouth parted and I felt her tongue. Then she was at my neck, I was at hers, our hands were everywhere. After a while I started laughing. "Man, this is the sort of shit I used to do in high school: sneak into abandoned parks and make out."

"Is it good?"

"Yeah," I said, leaning into her. "It's good."

ON THE WALK back to the car, I took Kaede's hand, swung it happily. The sun had started setting, but there was no sunset — no colours, no light. The clouds just started shifting to darker shades of grey and the world under them began to fade in their shadows.

We reached the gate and, holding her camera, I helped boost Kaede up. She straddled the top of the wall and then dropped down, out of sight, on the other side. While I was draping the camera around my neck I heard her call out, "Paul! Paul, there's someone over here."

I thought instantly of that dark shape in the street our first night together, rising from the ground like something feral. "Hold on," I said. My hands were shaking as I scaled the wall. "Kaede, where is it? Kaede?"

"It's in the trees. There — there, I saw it move again."

Perched on the top of the wall, I looked down at Kaede, standing there at the bottom. Across the parking lot were the woods, the evergreens thick and dark, the maples and birches bare with their empty branches clawing in the wind at the darkening sky.

I scanned the trees. "Where is it?"

"It was there," Kaede said, pointing. "I saw it move between the trees. I think it's watching us. Who is it, Paul?"

I dropped down from the top of the wall. My knees had turned to jelly and I crumpled on landing, turning my ankle. "Fuck," I said, wincing when I stood. "Come on, let's go."

With Kaede supporting me, we made our way toward the car parked around the bend. Both of us kept our eyes on the line of trees on the far side of the road. I couldn't see anything. "Are you sure there was someone in there?"

"Yeah, of course I'm sure. There was someone watching me."

Then the car was in view, up on the soft shoulder where we'd left it. My ankle was killing me; I moved stilt-legged on it at a trot while Kaede hoisted up my weak side. "If there was something in the woods, it's gone. We probably scared it off."

Kaede just kept scanning the trees. "It was small," she said, "like a kid."

We got to the car and, leaning against the door, I struggled with the keys. I was so focused that I almost didn't notice what someone had scratched into the paint on the hood, the letters two feet high. My stomach did a backflip. I slammed my fist into the windshield.

"What?" Kaede said, but then saw where I was looking. "Oh, Jesus. Who would do that?"

Shaking, I opened the door and got in. Kaede hopped across to the other side. The word had been written facing inward, so I had to read it from the driver's seat. I hit the power-locks, then sat breathing behind the steering wheel. "Okay," I said, and started the engine.

Just as we were pulling away there was movement up ahead in the woods. With all the streetlights out it was hard to tell, but it looked like something was coming thrashing toward the road through the trees.

"There!" called Kaede, pointing through the windshield.

Then it was out of the woods, a small shape scampering along the gravel shoulder. A kid. In a panic, I pressed down on the accelerator and laid on the horn. But the kid kept coming, and instead of fleeing back into the woods it burst onto the road, hands up as though to stop the car. I honked and sped up, the motor roaring.

"What are you doing?" Kaede screamed.

At the last second I tried to veer out of the way, the tires screeching as I cranked the wheel, but it was too late. The fender hit the kid at the waist, flinging him up onto the hood.

He smashed against the windshield and, as I slammed the brakes, rolled back down into the street. At the moment of impact my headlights shone right into the kid's face: he was maybe ten years old, the eyes not so much wide in terror as they were with something enraged, something desperate.

I STOOD OUTSIDE the hospital with Kaede, watching her smoke. It was close to three in the morning, but I felt almost unnaturally alert. Kaede, meanwhile, had withdrawn. She wouldn't look at me. Every time I tried to touch her she shrugged my hand away. And as soon as each cigarette was done, she lit another — now on to her second pack of the evening.

"He's going to be okay," I tried again. "You heard the doctor."

Kaede shook her head, ashing onto the ground.

"They'll find his family. These people all live around here, they all know one another."

Nothing. Not even a glance in my direction. I wondered if she could sense in my voice the doubt that, even if they could track the parents down, they'd care enough to come in to pick up their son. I'd heard about the way the pickers lived — like animals, apparently. And these were people with decent jobs only three years ago. It's amazing how quickly human beings can degenerate. I looked back at Kaede, standing there shaking her head. I'd had enough.

"Oh, come on, would you? He ran right into the road. What was I supposed to do? You think I wanted to hit him? You think this is how I wanted to spend my night, at the fucking hospital, talking to cops and doctors and nurses and whoever? Jesus Christ."

"Right," she said.

"Listen, there's no sense hanging around here. Do you want a ride home?"

"No," she said. "I'm going to stay for a while. I need my camera from your car."

I left Kaede standing at the door of the boy's room. He'd been shifted from the ICU to a regular bed. Luckily, all the accident had resulted in was a broken leg, a dislocated shoulder, and bruised ribs. Other than a nasty black eye he hadn't done any damage to his head, which was their main concern.

Even so, the doctors wanted to keep him in for observation for the night. "Still trying to track his parents down," I heard a nurse telling Kaede as I moved away down the hall. "With these cases it can be tricky, though. Could be a runaway or abandoned, just living off garbage and staying in empty buildings. You never know."

THE NEXT MORNING I called the hospital, explaining who I was. By some miracle they had found the boy's parents, part of some sort of squatting commune in an old winery off the 420. With my car in the shop to fix the windshield and buff the scratches out of the hood, I hobbled up to Kaede's place that afternoon to let her know, but there was no answer. As I turned to go home, I nearly ran into a woman coming up the walkway. She wore the CanAm security uniform, seemed to be in her mid-thirties, sort of pudgy; her nametag

read, *Carol*. I guessed that she was American: Dave claims all
the women wear white tennis shoes, and Carol sported a pair
of gleaming Reeboks.

"You looking for someone?" Carol asked, pulling out her
keys. "I'm the super."

"Kaede?"

"The Japanese girl? Pretty sure she didn't come home last
night. You her boyfriend?"

"Didn't come home?"

"Listen, pal, she might be gone for good. It happens all the
time — you get these foreigners over here looking for work,
then they don't like it and bail." Carol looked me over. "You in
the market for a job?"

I shook my head. Carol excused herself, moved past me,
and began unlocking the door. Watching her fumbling with
the keys, my body felt heavy, as though I'd gone swimming in
my clothes and was now trudging back onto land. I turned
and dragged myself down the steps.

I HEADED DOWN to the store about an hour before everyone
was scheduled to show up — it was just gone seven, right
around dusk. I hadn't slept the night before and other than my
one trip out, I'd spent the entire day at home waiting for the
phone to ring. It hadn't.

With my ankle still badly swollen, the walk down there
took about three times longer than it normally would. In the
parking lot I had a good long look at the shop: the chipped
paint, the sagging foundation, the stain of where the G had
once been above the door.

As I went to let myself in I noticed a letter tucked into the mailbox. As I pulled it out, a lump collected in my throat, hard as a stone. Inside the store I ran a souvenir letter opener up the side of the envelope and shook it open. All that came out was a photo — no note, no indication of who it was from. Although that much was obvious.

The photograph was of the boy I'd hit, lying in his hospital bed. It was a close-up. Kaede must have gone into his room to take it. He was in rough shape: torso wrapped in bandages, right arm in a sling, left leg up in traction. He was asleep, one of his eyes ringed with a deep purple bruise.

I was furious. My foot bearing down on the accelerator had been an accident, the wrong reaction to the situation for sure, but certainly not purposeful. Forget what he'd scratched onto my car. I didn't get angry. I wasn't that kind of guy. What kind of monster would try to kill a kid?

I went to throw the picture out, but then reconsidered, instead stashing it in the cash register underneath the one of my parents. At some point I'd look Kaede up in Calgary and send the thing right back to her: fuck you.

A few minutes later the first of my pals arrived with their respective smashing tools — two baseball bats and a shovel. As more people began to show up, I got busy administrating the ensuing chaos and forgot what had happened the night before. But then, once things were set up, my friends stationed in their various assigned positions around the store, it all came back. I wondered if the kid had gone home yet — or to whatever approximation of a home his parents kept. And I wondered where Kaede had gone to: maybe she'd moved into the pickers' commune out of solidarity, or maybe she was already sitting on a plane over the Prairies, looking out the window thinking what a monster I was and what a mistake she'd made with me.

Dave was the last to arrive. He seemed fidgety, eyes darting back and forth, obviously anxious to get going. "This is where you'll be," I told him. "From those figurines down to the ashtrays — see how it's taped off? Try to stick to your area."

"Gotcha." The guy had found a cricket bat somewhere, and he was weighing it in one hand against one of the CanAm security nightsticks. Finally he tossed me the bat. "Going with old faithful. But you can use that, if you want."

With everyone there, my friends had gone quiet. Gone was the bemusement that had greeted my invitation; even Lisa and Colin seemed resolute and focused. As per the instructions Kaede had helped draft, each person had on long pants and a shirt, eye protection (interpreted as everything from swimming goggles to an Itech hockey helmet), and gloves. People had exactly one minute to destroy anything they wanted in their allotted space. That was it. After sixty seconds they had to stop.

I rested Dave's cricket bat against the wall.

"Let's start this thing!" yelled Lisa. People laughed, which was good.

"What's the deal, Pauly?" said Dave. "Are we gonna bust your store up, or what?"

Everyone laughed again, but there was impatience in it. My thoughts kept zipping between Kaede, the boy, my parents, and back to Kaede. And my car, what had been written there — why had a little kid wanted to do something like that?

Dave caught my eye, and I could tell he knew that something was up. "We don't have to do this, Pauly," he said. There was a murmur of agreement from around the room. "No," I said, nodding. "I'm good," I said.

PRETTY MUCH THE entire store was destroyed. The minute rule went right out the window as soon as the first display of figurines smashed against the floor. Even from where I gazed on from the periphery, it was impossible not to get caught up in things — the explosions of crystal and glass, the cracking of wood, the shelves crashing down in an avalanche of kitsch. But beyond the vague, vicarious thrill of voyeurism, I didn't feel anything. I'd expected to be flooded with sadness, or relief, or nostalgia, or catharsis. Instead, all I did was watch.

At one point I guess everyone must have caught themselves: there was a sudden pause, clouds of dust rising all around, and eight people were left looking at one another in an almost bashful way, catching their breath. I'd like to think some sort of mercy instinct kicked in, although I guess there just wasn't anything left to smash.

Dave spoke before I could. "Think that's enough?"

People offered to help clean up, but I wasn't having any of it; they'd paid and I was offering a service. On their way out, everyone shook my hand and told me how great it had been, apologizing if they'd got out of control, offering to pay extra if I needed it. Colin paused at the door and said, "Jesus, Pauly, everyone in the whole town is going to want in on this. Totally amazing. Can I buy shares?"

I was left sweeping up, collecting shards of glass and ceramic and plastic and tin on the big wide broom and clearing everything down the aisles. While my hands trembled and the sweat cooled on my back, I still wasn't sure what to *think* about the whole business.

I'd been at it for maybe an hour when I heard a car pull up out front. I froze, broom in hand, wondering if one of my pals had forgotten something. Three doors slammed, I heard some muffled conversation from the parking lot, and someone knocked on the door. Through the window, I could see Kaede — with two or three other people clustered there too.

Standing on my step beside Kaede were the kid from the hospital and two other scruffy-looking adults. The man wore sweatpants, the elastics hiked well over his ankles, an old Ontario Hydro parka, and deck shoes. The woman had on an identical parka and a pair of tattered grey leggings. Between them was the kid. He teetered on a single crutch, leaning against his dad. Just like the photo: one black eye, one leg in a cast, and an arm in a sling. The other bandages were gone — or hidden under his clothes.

"Hey," I said.

"Hey," said Kaede. "Can we come in?"

Behind them a taxi idled in the parking lot. The night was cold and their breath came puffing at me out of the dark in clouds. I looked at the man's face, and the woman's, and the kid's, glowing golden in the light from the shop. The smell of cigarettes hung over them like a shroud. All three regarded me with the same expression: a sort of exhausted rage, like caged animals with very little fight left.

"Careful," I said, stepping over the splintered remains of a stack of ashtrays. "We had a bit of a party earlier."

"We know what went on here," said the man, lifting his son. "We want in."

"Bronco wants in," said the woman.

"Bronco?"

"That's me," said the kid.

I looked down at him. While his face seemed tired and gaunt, something in his eyes burned.

The dad strode across the shop and grabbed Dave's cricket bat, still leaning against the wall. "This'll do. Help him over here."

I realized he was talking to me, so I moved beside his son. Kaede nodded at me. Bronco wrapped his arm around my waist and leaned in.

"Careful," said his mom. "He's still real sore."

I moved slowly with the boy across the shop, around the occasional bit of stray trash, both of us with a gimpy leg, one step at a time. With the crutch working on one side and me on the other, Bronco limped along, wincing occasionally, toward his dad. When we got there he placed the bat into his son's hands and stepped away. "Okay," he said.

"What do you want to break, baby?" asked the mother, scanning the aisles. She saw what we all did: empty shelves, debris cluttering the floor, clothing racks smashed to pieces and their contents strewn about and covered in dust. At the back of the shop sat four huge piles of refuse.

"There's nothing left," Bronco said.

My eyes were on the cash register, sitting there untouched

on the counter beside the dad — who, apparently, noticed it too. "There's this," he said, tapping it with his fingertips.

"Whoa," I said. "I need that. And it's an antique."

"Look what you did to my son," said the mother, her voice like ice. "Everything else is ruined. What does it matter?"

"No," I said. "It matters."

"Fuck you," said the dad. "Bron, do this one, buddy."

"No," I said. "I said no."

"After what you've done?" yelled the mother.

I was surprised when Kaede stepped forward. "After what he's done? Do you know what your son scratched onto his car?"

The parents looked at each other, then the son. Bronco tapped the bat in his hand.

"Just do it, Bron. Smash this thing." The dad pushed the register onto the floor. The bell dinged and the drawer clattered open wildly as it hit; one of the sides split and the Enter key popped loose, skittering off under a shelf.

The kid hobbled forward. Some response in me clicked and I grabbed the bat from his hand, lifting it above my head and out of reach. "Forget it," I said.

Things seemed to slow down. I breathed, turning to Kaede. The expression on her face was drawn, the lips tight — but in her eyes was something softer, something like an apology. Then they flashed. "Paul!" she cried.

I spun around and realized that the dad was on the move, wordlessly barrelling toward me from behind the counter. In his eyes was the same look that had been in his son's eyes when I'd smashed into him with my car: hunger, fury.

He was on me then, screaming into my face: I saw a mouth jawing away and felt a spray of spittle, the heat of breath, was aware of sounds but not words, not what was being said. Then a hand came flying out of somewhere, smacked me in the shoulder and knocked me reeling backward — right onto my bad ankle. Pain shot up my leg. I tensed, regained my balance, and then stood sure-footed, waiting.

The dad was coming at me again, fists up, and from somewhere I heard other voices — Kaede's, maybe the kid's and the mom's. Something, though, had caught hold of me. I stopped trying to make sense of what was going on. With the dad set to fight I stepped forward, oblivious to the flare of pain in my foot, and cocked the cricket bat, eyes trained on the flat smooth plane of the dad's cheekbone, hearing the crunch of splintering bones even before I started to swing.

THE LOVE LIFE OF
THE AUTOMATON TURK

VIENNA, 1755

ALTHOUGH HE FANCIED himself one, it would have been a stretch to consider Wolfgang von Kempelen much of a wolf, regardless of whether he was going by his Hungarian birth name, Farkas, or the Wolfgang it became when the empire's official language was changed to German. Kempelen was a haughty, blue-eyed fellow with sandy hair and whiskers resembling more those of a kitten than anything lupine. Yet even the feline comparison was limited to moments of inertia: born with a sort of defect in one of his feet, when forced into motion Kempelen staggered precariously from one place to the next, compromising anything that might have been taken for catlike charm.

At the age of twenty-one, Kempelen was introduced to Empress Maria Theresa at the suggestion of his father, a retired civil servant who had been a favourite of the former king. The monarch was immediately taken with this beguiling youth from Pressburg: having easily bested all the top chess players in the land, the empress had long been in search of a worthy opponent, and she found exactly that in young Wolfgang.

Their first match, Kempelen took Maria Theresa's offered hand, bowed slightly, and sat down behind the other side of the board, blue eyes sparkling, that half-smile almost playful, almost cocky.

"So you are the young genius everyone's talking about." The empress was thirty-seven at the time, with a frizzy poof of orange hair, bulging eyes that suggested a thyroid malfunction, and pale, sallow skin.

Kempelen shrugged. "Genius? Such a relative term."

The game commenced with Kempelen adopting a classic French opening and ended four hours later in a stalemate. A rematch a few days later produced the same result. Finally, after six games, Kempelen took Maria Theresa's queen during a gruelling endgame and, with her remaining pawn and knight gone astray across the board, winked and said, "I believe that's checkmate."

"I believe it is." Maria Theresa gestured and from somewhere appeared a dark, pretty girl with a thick dossier in her hands. "Now, chess is all fine and good, but if you're up to it, we would like to present to you a true test of your intellectual prowess."

As the empress's maidservant handed Kempelen the dossier, his fingers lingered for a moment against the young girl's. "Hello," he said. "What's your name?"

The girl froze. Kempelen's hand snaked up to her wrist.

"That's Franciscka," interrupted the empress. "She's dumb."

"Dumb?"

"Mute. She hears fine, but can't — or *won't* — say a word."

"Ah," said Kempelen, and at this Franciscka withdrew, scampering into the shadows. Kempelen watched her for a moment, then returned his attention to Maria Theresa.

"This, Wolfgang, is the Hungarian civil code, written in Latin, which needs translating into German. We hear you are quite gifted in both."

"When do you want it by?" asked Kempelen, weighing the papers in his hands.

"No rush," said the empress, "but we're looking forward to seeing your work."

Kempelen bowed. "Pleased to be of service."

DAYS LATER A translation appeared of such sophistication that it sent rumours rippling through the empire of a mysterious crippled prodigy who had turned the empire's archaic charter into Germanic magnificence.

Asked about his process by Maria Theresa, Kempelen shrugged. "Languages are just equations of one another — it's all a matter of figuring out what best equals what."

The empress loved this, the precision of it, and waited for more.

"Now tell me," he asked, looking around. "This Franciscka — she's not married?"

"No, Wolfgang, not that I know of."

"Interesting."

ON THE STRENGTH of this translation, Wolfgang von Kempelen earned a permanent position in the Austro-Hungarian court. Gossip persisted about the nature of his relationship with

Maria Theresa, exacerbated by public speculation as to the sexual orientation of Maria's husband, Francis Stephen, Duke of Lorraine. (The duke's imperial role could be best defined as secretarial, and he also delighted in the hobby of amateur florist — admittedly, his bouquets were among the most stunning in the land.)

But civilian conjecture remained just that. Neither Kempelen nor Maria Theresa had anything in mind beyond a strictly platonic relationship: they played chess; she saw his intellect as a tool of the empire, something that would lead them forward; he delighted in having a venue in which to exercise his ideas.

His first day on the job, the empress took Kempelen on a walk about the palace grounds, slowing her pace to match the counsellor's limp. Having spent most of their time together seated on either side of a chessboard, Maria Theresa was surprised at his gimpy leg trailing stiffly along — the fragility it suggested unnerved her. She preferred to think of this fellow as a pillar on which the edifice of a new Austria-Hungary would be built, rather than some pathetic cripple stumbling from one place to the next.

Kempelen halted before a team of gardeners watering the manicured lawns and hedgerows.

"Have you ever thought," he said, eyes narrowed, "that a single machine might be able to do the work of a dozen of these men?"

The empress watched him, trying to imagine what he saw, what plans and schematics were already being sketched in his mind's eye. "A machine?" she asked.

"Yes. A machine."

That afternoon Kempelen retreated to his court-appointed villa in the woods. Days later, unshaven and sleep-deprived, he re-emerged with elaborate plans for a sprinkler system to irrigate the entire grounds of the palace. It was quickly built, widely considered a stroke of genius, and, while failing to endear him to the gardeners who lost their jobs, raised his stock even higher with the empress, who promoted him immediately to senior counsellor.

The accolades were fine, but it was more the thrill of creation that pleased Kempelen: here was something that he had conceived and given life to, something that was inarguably superior to its human counterpart. He stood proudly before the court as they applauded him, chest puffed out like a peacock, lame leg hidden behind the podium, and in his speech promised even more impressive inventions to come.

That evening's feast ended with Kempelen drunk and in bed with one of his fellow counsellors' daughters, something that quickly became a trend over the months to follow. While he systematically redesigned the palace's irrigation, waste disposal, and archival systems, Kempelen just as systematically made his way through the palace's female courtiers and maidservants, luring them to his villa in the woods, only to shoo them out the door the following morning like mice discovered in the larder.

Soon Kempelen had had them all — that is, with the exception of the elusive Franciscka, who fled any room he entered, always with a flirtatious glance over her shoulder before retreating to some distant corner of the palace. During a chess match that saw the empress taking Kempelen's pieces at will, he confided to Maria Theresa that Franciscka seemed to represent the final variable in the equation of his life, and that without her he felt things sprawling infinitely, with no end in sight.

"So even your love life you reduce to science?" wondered the empress.

Kempelen frowned at her, and it was the frown of one who, hearing his own philosophy spoken aloud by another, was forced to bring it into question.

"You've always told me everything is science. Even chess, you've said, relies on logic so precise that a machine could play it."

Kempelen shrugged. "Maybe I'm in love with her."

"Oh, Wolfgang!" exclaimed the empress, shaking her head. "Be careful. There's something suspicious about that girl — always lurking around, silent, popping up in places she shouldn't be. I'd stay away from her, if I were you."

After a restless, sleepless night, Kempelen lay in bed staring at the ceiling. He pictured Franciscka's face: those big, brown eyes, that little nub of a nose, the lips thin and tightly drawn, as though hiding something forbidden within. Thoughts of her made his head swim, unable to rest on anything definite or absolute; formless images and ideas went caroming off one another, colliding and spiralling away. Kempelen closed his eyes and, one by one, methodically, he pulled the fragments in and laid them out as pieces to a puzzle. With systematic precision he went through, organizing, arranging, and as he did, something conclusive began to take shape.

Kempelen swept the bedclothes aside and, ignoring the matter of dressing, limped briskly out to the maidservants' quarters in his nightshirt, where he pounded on the door, dropped to one knee, and, when a startled Franciscka appeared, promised to renounce his licentious ways if she would agree to marry him.

Franciscka looked down at the man grovelling at her feet, eyes reflecting sky. She felt very little, other than a vague satisfaction that she had played her cards right for the past two years, not like those other tarts around the palace. After six years as a maidservant, Franciscka was fed up with being bossed around by the capricious Maria Theresa and knew that as a counsellor's wife she would be excused from her position.

Extending her hand to Kempelen, who took it and pressed it to his forehead, Franciscka thought fondly of this impending freedom. Kempelen looked up, saw her smiling, and mistook it for lover's joy. His heart raced: he finally felt something that defied his wealth of knowledge, a deep, booming sense of uncertainty that brought him to his feet. He swept his bride into his arms and hollered, "I love you!"

AT THE WEDDING, Maria Theresa appeared ambivalent, yawning openly as the vows were read. Beside her sat Francis Stephen, gloating at the magnificence of his floral arrangements, bright and glorious around the palace chapel. The benediction ended, Kempelen beamed at his bride, and then plunged at her for a nuptial kiss vigorous enough that the priest had to step in and pry him away. The place erupted with cheers — most enthusiastically from Kempelen's colleagues, relieved that the palace's most coveted bachelor was finally off the market. Maria Theresa clapped wanly, a thin smile on her lips, while her husband blew kisses to the newlyweds as they made their way under a shower of rice out of the chapel.

The marriage was consummated purposefully, with Franciscka bent over and staring out the window while Kempelen grunted and thrust from behind. When he finished with a mighty holler, she pulled away, squatted, and Wolfgang watched while his ejaculate was emptied on a stream of urine into the chamber pot beside their bed.

Franciscka's royal duties relinquished, she moved into the counsellor's villa. For the first time in his life, Kempelen felt something he could not identify in certain terms, an uneasiness that devolved into confusion. That consecratory first night haunted him, how Franciscka had indifferently flushed his seed from her body, and their day-to-day, wordless existence resonated with a similar emptiness. She turned her cheek obediently for a goodbye kiss every morning, but he could sense her gazing off into the distance over his shoulder; she yielded nightly to his advances, but in an almost conciliatory way. Any attempt at communication was greeted with a mute, blank stare.

The answer Kempelen had been looking for still seemed to elude him, and he became preoccupied and began to neglect his duties as counsellor. His first project as a married man, a mechanical system meant to raise and lower the bridge into town, collapsed under the weight of its first crossing (two chickens drowned).

A day later, the empress sat him down at the chessboard and asked what was wrong.

"Something must have been amiss with my calculations," he offered.

"Oh, it's not just that, Wolfgang. What's the matter?"

Despondent, Kempelen dropped his pieces back into their box. "I can't play today," he said, then struggled to his feet and left the room. His limp seemed more pronounced than it had ever been; Maria Theresa watched him hobble away and realized something needed to be done. The empire depended on it.

A FEW NIGHTS LATER, Kempelen came home to discover Franciscka collapsed under the kitchen table, a half-drunk cup of cider puddling beneath her on the floor. Kempelen rushed to her side, knelt, and rolled his wife over — her lips were colourless, her body rigid, her brown eyes stared blankly heavenward.

The court coroner reported that Franciscka's heart had just stopped, like a watch smacked with a hammer. Kempelen's demands to perform a private autopsy were denied. Frustrated more than heartbroken, the counsellor sank into a deep depression, refusing to emerge from his home. After nearly a month of this self-imposed exile, Maria Theresa herself made the trip along the path through the woods to Kempelen's villa.

Skirts hitched, she banged on the door. "Wolfgang!"

No answer.

"Wolfgang, please, it's me. You've got to come out. The empire needs you."

Maria Theresa pressed her ear against the door. A cough. Then, muffled: "Send me away."

"Sorry?"

"Send me away from here. I don't care where. A place where I can make sense of things. A place where things make sense."

The empress paused. Something rose in her throat. Swallowing hard, Maria Theresa willed it away and spoke to the door. "As you wish, Wolfgang."

For the next dozen years Kempelen found himself shuttled all over the empire, arriving in locales where his brains were needed for problems agricultural, scientific — even judicial. In Transylvania, he concocted an ingenious pneumatic system for draining the region's flooded salt mines; in Banat, he undertook the role of detective and produced evidence to free a man wrongly convicted of murder.

During this time, Kempelen established a base back in his hometown of Pressburg. He found himself missing life in the capital but could decipher no concrete reason to return — after all, his services were in great demand elsewhere around the empire. He kept to himself, and loneliness haunted him. Without a worthy opponent, he began to build simple automated chess pieces with the gears and wheels of old watches: when prompted, they would walk across the chessboard to the appropriate square. It was an attempt, he knew, to make life of his own, to create something engaging beyond simple machinery.

Still, that life seemed hollow. Although the clockwork figures paraded around like little men, they were no real company, they provided no joy. At work, he performed his tasks methodically, without emotion, while everyone else celebrated his genius. Above all, when he thought about Franciscka's death he felt only curiosity — never sadness, and that seemed deeply wrong. It was clear, now, that he had never loved her — he had never loved anyone. He didn't know how to; he was a man trapped irrevocably in a realm of logic, distant from the enigmas of human emotion. Playing nightly chess games against himself, watching his automata march from one square to the next, the empire's prized counsellor felt the answers to life's greatest questions receding beyond his grasp.

IN 1769, KEMPELEN received word that the empress wanted him back in Vienna. "Come quickly," read the message, "this is a very urgent matter."

Fearing the collapse of the empire was at hand, Kempelen abandoned his work and made the trip back to the palace. Empress and counsellor met at their old spot in the gardens; she took Kempelen's hands in hers, seeming excited and flushed. It struck him, suddenly, that she might be in love with him, and that this rendezvous was designed to profess her adoration. That old sense of pride, long absent, swelled within him as he awaited her amorous confession.

"Wolfgang!" she exclaimed. "There is a French conjuror coming to Vienna. He was here last year, and the year before, and his tricks are baffling. The entire court was in an uproar. No one can figure out how he does it — rabbits from hats, scarves appearing from up shirtsleeves, people sawn in half. And then we thought of you!"

"That's why you ordered me here?"

"Yes! He's performing tonight. So you must come and

watch and then let us know how everything's done. Typical Frenchman, the bastard thinks he's got us fooled — but he has no idea that we'll have the cleverest man in all of Europe there tonight."

Kempelen gazed at the empress: a wild, expectant look filled her eyes. He bowed, defeated, and when he spoke, his voice was a thin, reedy whisper. "Pleased to be of service."

That evening the entire court gathered in the main ballroom. A thin, mincing man with an even thinner moustache performed some simple illusions, addressing the bewildered spectators in a Parisian accent rife with disdain. Kempelen, ire rising with each trick, muttered the fellow's secrets into Maria Theresa's ear while Francis Stephen whooped and applauded one seat over. After a finale that caused Kempelen to slap his own forehead in incredulity, the Frenchman bowed to a rousing ovation from all in attendance — excepting, naturally, the empress and her prize counsellor. When the applause receded, Kempelen stood and angrily addressed the crowd.

"This fellow is a fraud," he announced, his tone furious. "You people sicken me, how readily you allow yourselves to be fooled."

The magician spluttered and flapped his arms, his face reddening. Kempelen held up a finger. "Not only will I happily reveal how each of these illusions works to anyone who asks, but I am going to dedicate the next few months to creating something that doesn't need to dupe its audience with sleight of hand — something greater than human beings, something more clever, more cunning."

The Frenchman fled the room. A hush fell upon the crowd

as they waited, terrified, for whatever might come next. Kempelen looked down at Maria Theresa seated beside him. In his eyes was something she had never seen before: fire, passion. It frightened her. "Give me six months," he told the empress, and then limped out of the hall.

HAVANA, 1838

UPON ARRIVING IN Havana, Johann Maelzel had told the rest of the crew that he and his assistant, Schlumberger, had official business to attend to in Regla. After overseeing the unloading of the Turk and its automated brethren, the two men stole off into the night to a quiet bodega across the river recommended as "friendly" by an ageing queen back in New Orleans. With a single candle burning between them on the table and a cloud of mosquitoes whining through the air, they sat watching one another nurse their glasses of rum before Maelzel finally spoke.

"Christ, I never thought we'd get a moment alone."

Schlumberger glanced shyly at Maelzel before his gaze retreated to the floor. "Finally."

A local appeared at their table selling beaded necklaces. He stood there, a shirtless mulatto with a patchy beard, wares in hand, waiting patiently while Maelzel frowned and patted the pockets of his waistcoat. Schlumberger slapped at a mosquito on the nape of his neck. "Please, I'll get it, Johann."

The man pocketed the coins and wreathed Schlumberger. "¿Otras cosas?" asked the Cuban, winking at Maelzel, who shook his head, slumped in his chair, and waved the fellow away.

Schlumberger regarded Maelzel across the table and felt a pang of melancholy at what confronted him. Where was the charisma, the life, the energy of the great showman who had entranced crowds across Europe? Since coming to America, Schlumberger had struggled to avoid noticing his companion's steady decline in vivacity, but here it was: eyes sunken, hair dishevelled — the grey, dejected visage of a man beaten and broke. The thirty years that separated them were obvious.

"Don't worry," said Schlumberger, swatting at another mosquito, "you'll get back on top once this exhibition gets going. They loved you when we were here last."

"Oh, it's hardly just me, is it?" sighed Maelzel, pulling his hands sharply away as Schlumberger tried to take them in his. "I'm just who they see, parading around like some circus buffoon. You're the true genius behind our operation."

Schlumberger blushed. "I am only a pawn in the great Maelzel spectacle."

"Bah," said Maelzel, and disappeared behind his drink.

Schlumberger had found that lately he and his companion had taken to repeating conversations, and this one was familiar. He already knew what was coming next.

"You know old Kempelen never intended for a man to be inside, don't you?" Maelzel nodded at his own words, twisting his glass of rum absently round a ring of moisture on the table. "Imagine a machine that could play better than any man, Schlumberger! Imagine if he'd been able to do it. It must have eaten Kempelen alive. He was never able to make peace

with himself because of it and died a lonely, sad old man."
Maelzel drank, then continued. "And to think, seventy years
later, his failure is my biggest success."

Maelzel disappeared once more behind his glass of rum.
There were things Schlumberger wanted to say, but they
would have to wait until this whole tour was over and he and
Maelzel were back on American soil. Then Maelzel would be
finally able to pay off his many debts, and they could pack the
Turk up and get on with their lives.

Schlumberger lifted the beaded necklace and scratched
absently at the swelling mosquito bite on the back of his neck.
From across the table, Maelzel stared past him at some
indefinite place in the dark, lifted his glass again, and drained it.

AFTER FOUR DAYS of preparation, the exhibition began. On
opening night a huge crowd gathered to be dazzled by Maelzel
and his automata; many had to be turned away at the door for
lack of adequate seating. The show began with the famous
trumpet player playing the customary Handel — and, as per
the French-born Schlumberger's request, also a rondo of
Chopin's that left the crowd somewhat bemused.

Many of the locals and American expatriates in attendance
were especially interested in Maelzel's updated Conflagration
of Moscow, the original version of which hadn't made the trip
on his first visit to Cuba. Maelzel wheeled the complex diorama onstage. "The Conflagration," he announced to a round
of cheers, "of Moscow!"

After winding a crank to set the mechanism in motion, the
showman retreated backstage with Schlumberger. Squeezing

his secretary's knee as he sat down, Maelzel noticed that the young man looked flushed; sweat beaded his temples and along his upper lip. "All right?" asked Maelzel. Schlumberger nodded wanly, his gaze sinking to the floor.

The musical score to The Conflagration, composed by Maelzel's good friend Ludwig van Beethoven, began. Artificial daylight crept over the scene; mechanical peasants emerged from their miniature homes. The music grew in intensity, the movements accelerated, and when the first round of pyrotechnics flared up, the crowd yelped in shock and delight. Buildings toppled and bridges collapsed as Moscow's proud citizenry hurriedly razed the city to spite the invisible, encroaching Napoleonic army.

When the show concluded a few minutes later with a climactic rumble and a puff of smoke, the diorama lying in ruins, Maelzel bounded onstage to a roaring ovation from the audience. Schlumberger smiled weakly as Maelzel grandstanded about, playing to his fans, showing a hint of the old "prince of entertainers" who had taken Europe by storm over the last few decades. Still, there was desperation to it, as though this show could make or break his career — which, Schlumberger knew, was not far from the truth.

A succession of other displays of Maelzel's mechanical wizardry followed. By the time intermission finally came, Schlumberger's state had drastically declined. Backstage, meeting Maelzel to prepare the Turk, he collapsed, panting, drenched in sweat.

Maelzel laid a hand on Schlumberger's shoulder. "Jesus, you're looking rough."

"Thanks," said Schlumberger, struggling to his feet. "I'm sure it's just the heat."

"I've got just the thing." Maelzel produced a half-empty bottle of wine from a secret compartment. "Beaujolais."

Schlumberger watched him drink, but declined the bottle when it was offered him. Dabbing sweat from his brow with his handkerchief, he slumped back against the cabinet, shivering.

"We can cancel the show," Maelzel said, suddenly subdued, his hand on Schlumberger's shoulder, "if you're not feeling up to it."

"No, no. I'm okay. Let's try to get through two games."

Maelzel drained the last of the wine. With a quick look around, he leaned in and planted a kiss on the top of Schlumberger's head. "God, you're burning up."

"I'll be fine." Forcing a smile, he added, "The show must go on."

Schlumberger climbed into the cabinet while Maelzel lit the candles that allowed the Turk's operator to see in the dark. On the chessboard above, Maelzel positioned the pieces in the middle of each square so the magnets would line up with those below. Then he kneeled before the cabinet where Schlumberger sat curled behind his control panel. Gazing into those shadows, Maelzel thought of the show in Baltimore, after which the two of them had made love inside the Turk. It had been a cramped, goofy affair, and when they were finished, realizing they were locked in, they had been forced to kick the doors open from inside.

"And you're clear on how the new speaking contraption works?"

Schlumberger pressed a button. "Check," came a voice from the Turk. He pressed it again. "Checkmate," said the Turk.

Maelzel's smile quickly faded. "You okay?"

"Yes." Schlumberger's voice was faint and hollow-sounding.

Maelzel paused, then swung the doors closed, the click of the catches securing them in place. After a quick once-over, he rapped on the Turk's chessboard, waited, and then felt a flood of relief when a muffled knock finally came in reply. Maelzel wheeled the Turk onstage, where he was greeted with a burst of applause from the audience.

Although most in attendance had heard it before, Maelzel went through his usual spiel about "the amazing chess-playing Turk, the machine that has bested the greatest players in Europe," striding back and forth across the stage, all grand gestures and booming voice. The contraption itself was simple enough: seated behind a desk sat a wooden dummy in the flowing robe and sequined turban of an Ottoman emperor. On the desk itself were painted the checkered squares of a chessboard, over which loomed one of the Turk's hands; the other held a spindly, Oriental pipe. The front of the cabinet had two sets of doors. Maelzel strode up to these and flung one side open, revealing what appeared to be an empty cupboard. He waited until Schlumberger had time to shuffle over to the other side, and then did the same with the other doors, where a facade of utterly inoperative cogwheels and gears gave the impression that the Turk was, indeed, a functional machine.

"Who would like to try their hand at besting the mighty Turk?" demanded Maelzel.

The stands came alive with fluttering hands and cries. Maelzel pointed to a portly, elderly fellow in one of the front rows. Amid jeers from the gallery, he introduced himself as Paco, and at Maelzel's instructions he waddled over and took his seat on the other side of the chessboard.

"White or black?" asked Maelzel. Paco pointed to the black king, prompting more heckling from the audience. Maelzel cranked the mechanism, notifying Schlumberger that the game was about to begin.

The Turk made its opening move. Maelzel stood nearby, doing his best to provide illustrative commentary, in fact pre-occupied with the thought of his feverish companion huddled inside the cabinet. He grew more settled when it became obvi-ous that Schlumberger still had his wits about him: the Turk gave away a rook and a bishop, but Paco was a weak player, and unbeknownst to him Schlumberger was mounting a sub-tle attack based around both knights, the queen, and — much to Maelzel's glee — a rogue pawn that was stealthily making its way across the board.

As contestants tended to do, Paco quickly took to treating the Turk as a living thing, shaking his head when a turn took too long, wagging stolen pieces in its wooden face. The crowd divided into sides, with Paco's supporters mocking the Turk's every move, and vice versa.

After fifteen minutes or so Maelzel claimed to need to rewind the mechanism; the three turns of the crank he made were the sign for Schlumberger to wrap things up. A few moves later, the automaton called out, "Check," and all in attendance went wild. Paco, perspiring, sacrificed his rook, the Turk swung its remaining bishop across the board, released its grip, paused, and added, "Checkmate."

Once again the crowd erupted. An ironic chant of "Paco, Paco!" rose up while the old man cursed the Turk, pointing at it with a quivering sausage of a finger. Maelzel, glancing quickly at the board, was shocked to notice that the call had been premature: with one backward drop of his remaining knight, Paco's king would have been safe, forcing the Turk to cede the game. But before anyone could notice, Paco swept the pieces from the board, then stormed cursing out of the theatre, shaking his fists. Beneath the din that followed, Maelzel heard a cough from within the cabinet, followed by a long, plaintive groan.

IN SCHLUMBERGER'S hotel room, Maelzel hovered nearby while the doctor, a wiry American hidden behind a mess of grey beard, tended to his friend. The vomiting had finally subsided, but there was little to indicate that Schlumberger was doing any better; he lay helpless, emaciated and silent, like a bundle of twigs left for kindling.

The doctor turned and regarded Maelzel severely. "It's as I suspected. The infection's spread into his liver — that's why the skin appears jaundiced."

Maelzel breathed.

"Please, Mr. Maelzel," said the doctor, "if we can go into the other room."

In the adjoining room, Maelzel's own, the Turk sat glowering in the corner; the other automata lay piled around in various states of disarray, abandoned after opening night.

The doctor stroked his beard. "I have to tell you, Mr. Maelzel, that your friend might not make it through the night."

Maelzel nodded vacantly. He needed a drink.

"The fever is so far advanced there's little more we can do than wait." The doctor paused, staring at the Turk. "But if I may, Mr. Maelzel, could I ask you something?"

Maelzel shrugged. He was thinking, as he had been for days, of what might have happened had he allowed Schlumberger a night's rest — just one night of respite in the room, Maelzel spooning soup into his mouth. His thoughts were interrupted; the doctor was speaking.

"The Turk — has Mr. Schlumberger got anything to do with its operation? People are talking. They say he's actually inside, manipulating its arm on the chessboard. Since he's been ill, you haven't performed, and that first night, when in the middle of your show you claimed a mechanical malfunction, was the night you first contacted me."

The doctor paused, gazing at Maelzel, who in turn gazed past the louvred doors into Schlumberger's room. Then his face twisted into something ferocious. He turned to the doctor, breath whistling through his nostrils, eyes narrowed.

"Get out," he hissed.

"I didn't — " began the doctor, but stopped himself. Before him stood a man who, regardless of his secrets (and they were many, the doctor could see, and various), was ruined. The doctor collected his things, bowed quickly, and was gone.

Left alone, Maelzel pulled a bottle of wine from one of his many cases, uncorked it, and sucked back nearly half before making his way into Schlumberger's room. Lying down on the bed beside his companion, he felt the heat trapped in the sheets, saw the glassy, empty look in Schlumberger's eyes, could smell the sickly scent of rot and vomit from his mouth.

"Sorry, Johann," wheezed Schlumberger. "You will find someone else. There are many great chess players in America."

Maelzel shook his head. "Never, my friend. This is the end. No more illusions, no more secrets, no more hiding men in the bellies of machines."

Schlumberger coughed and something rattled deep inside him. His body bucked slightly off the bed and fell, shuddering. He settled back and closed his eyes. "I love you, Johann," he whispered, his voice papery and crackling.

"I'm sorry," said Maelzel. "You could have been a master, one of the great chess men of history. But I had to stuff you inside a box. What kind of love is that?"

But there was no reply. The mouth had gone slack. Maelzel leaned in, felt what he knew were Schlumberger's last breaths coming in short, dry gusts on his cheek. Quietly, gently, Maelzel laid his head on Schlumberger's chest, his ear against the dull throbbing of his companion's heart, and waited for it to stop.

MAELZEL STOOD swaying before the Turk, the pitching of the Louisiana-bound *Otis* amplifying his already compromised sense of balance. He gazed at its wooden face, paint starting to peel, turban unravelling. The only thing that still held life was its eyes, piercingly blue, burning with what always seemed to Maelzel something malicious, something evil. Perched behind its empty chessboard, the Turk sneered at him through the drooping points of its horsehair moustache.

Hollering came from above-decks from the ship's American crew, followed by a high-pitched Spanish reply — without doubt the handsome Cuban boy, Luis-Enrique, whom the ship had taken on before leaving Havana. Maelzel listened for more, but heard nothing further, just the gentle crash of waves against the hull, the mournful creaking of rigging and beams.

Turning away from the Turk, his vision swimming, Maelzel gazed around, trying to focus on the various other automata that packed the hold of the *Otis*: the Conflagration of Moscow, the Melodion, the Pyrrhic Fires, the Trumpeter, the Mechanical Theatre, the slack-rope dancer that Schlumberger had nicknamed "Guppy."

Schlumberger. Standing there in the dim light of the hold, yet another emptied bottle of wine dangling from his hand, Maelzel imagined that sheepish face, the shy grin, the slight stoop in his shoulders, likely aggravated by all that time hunched over inside the Turk — hours upon hours, curled up in there working the machine like a trained rat while Maelzel tromped about showboating to the crowds. A sour bubble of guilt and nausea rose in his throat.

As he vomited, the ship pitched and Maelzel was sent careering forward, bile and wine splashing down the front of his coat. The bottle flew from his hand and smashed on the floor, while Maelzel crashed into the cabinet, tumbled over, and landed face to face with the Turk. Maelzel could feel it mocking him. He closed his eyes; his head swirled and spun and danced. Spent, he collapsed finally onto the chessboard, arms splayed out, and lay there unmoving as the hull rocked with the undulating sea.

LUIS-ENRIQUE CASTILLO wasn't entirely sure what he'd been sent to the hold of the *Otis* to retrieve. The youngest son of a family of Cuban banana farmers, he'd sought work on board in order to make passage to America — although his English apparently still needed some work. It was impossible to decipher the Louisiana-born captain's orders. After a baffling sequence of instructions that rose in volume, but not clarity, and concluded with Luis-Enrique being slapped on the side of the head and pointed below-decks, he had slunk off, wondering if confusion would be all his life among Americans would entail.

Opening the door to the hold, initially Luis-Enrique thought he saw two men on either side of a chessboard, before realizing that one was a dummy; the other, slumped onto the desk, he recognized as the mysterious German who had been holed up in his cabin since departing Havana. From overheard snatches of conversation, Luis-Enrique had been able to glean that this Maelzel, some type of inventor-cum-impresario, had been driven mad by his own creations. Although now, as Luis-Enrique skirted a puddle of vomit and prodded the dead man with the toe of his boot, the cause of his tribulations was irrelevant.

As the bringer of the news to the rest of the ship, Luis-Enrique was assigned the disposal of the inventor's belongings. In Maelzel's sleeping quarters — littered with empty wine bottles, the stuffing of a mattress ripped to pieces, half-eaten meals, the shards of a shattered mirror — he discovered twelve gold doubloons, some paperwork documenting substantial debts and outstanding payments, a chessboard and set, complete but for one pawn, and a beaded necklace of the sort sold by male prostitutes in Regla.

Then there was the cargo that filled the hold. After mopping up the puddle of vomit, Luis-Enrique carted the strange machines out one by one, lining them up along the deck beside the dead man, now lashed to a stretcher and swaddled in a tarpaulin. The Turk, however, proved too large for him to move on his own, and none of the other crew seemed eager to lend a hand. Abandoning the frightening creature — Luis-Enrique found himself avoiding the piercing, accusatory stare of its sapphire blue eyes — he returned above-decks for the final send-off.

The funeral, a classic burial at sea, was attended by just under half the crew, many of whom chewed on cigars while the ship chaplain mumbled a cursory prayer. There was a half-hearted "Amen" before Maelzel's things were pitched overboard. The captain pointed at the corpse, then at Luis-Enrique, then down at the water.

Luis-Enrique lifted one end of the stretcher and, dragging its heavy cargo across the deck, wondered what sort of man this Maelzel had been, whom he was leaving behind. At the edge, with the body teetering over the sea, the boy paused. He felt something else needed to be said, but at that moment he felt a shove from behind. Stumbling, Luis-Enrique looked back, saw the captain grinning broadly, and only heard a splash from below as Maelzel hit the water and was carried off in the ship's wake.

PHILADELPHIA, 1854

"COME ON," said Mary, tugging at Silas's sleeve. "You promised you'd show me."

Silas faltered, looking up. The Chinese Museum loomed above them against the purple clouds of the night sky, a big, black box darkening a full block along Sansom Street between Eighth and Ninth. The lantern in his hand tempted him, but he knew it would only be safe to light inside.

"Come on," she said again, huskily, leaning close, her mouth at his ear.

Behind them the darkness was punctured by a single glowing street lamp at the far end of Sansom. Ahead another lit the corner at Ninth, but where they stood between the two lights was entirely in the shadow of the museum. It was as though this section of the street were removed from the rest of the city.

"If my father finds out about this, he'll kill me," mumbled Silas.

"You're twenty-five years old. And besides, you're not exactly the pride of the Mitchell family as is." The girl giggled and took off, dragging her sweetheart by the hand, her flowing skirts nearly tripping them both as they stole around to a door at the back of the museum. Panting, Silas produced his father's key-ring from his pocket. Mary held the lantern as he rifled through the keys jangling in his trembling hands.

"Hurry up," said Mary. "What if there are guards?"

"There's no guards — not yet, not until the exhibition opens tomorrow."

Mary pushed up against Silas, both her hands clutching his upper arm, squeezing. "I'm so excited. Do you really know how it works?"

Silas turned the key in the lock, there was an ominous click, and the door sprung open. "Okay," he said, glancing around. "Inside."

THE LANTERN THEY had brought splashed a pale yellow puddle before them, glinting off the glass cases that filled the museum, gridlike. The smell of burning kerosene hung heavy in the air, and beyond the lantern's feeble glow stretched darkness, eerie and silent, the vague shapes of statuettes and stuffed animals silhouetted against the walls. Through the windows, a half-moon like an upended china bowl appeared at intervals between the clouds.

"Where is it?" whispered Mary. The echo of her voice came hissing back at them.

"Downstairs. The door to the basement's just in the next room, to the right."

"This is so exciting!"

Silas, though, was not thinking about excitement. He was preoccupied with thoughts of his father noticing the keys missing and appearing in the laboratory to find Hammond alone and his son missing. Hammond was a good friend who would do his best to make some excuse — that the younger

Mitchell had left to hunt for snakes to extract venom, something diligent-sounding and plausible — but Silas knew that his father's innate sense of reason, coupled with a constant state of suspicion, would undoubtedly prevail.

Even half a world away, when Silas had been travelling around France, letters from Philadelphia had seemed to arrive almost immediately after another of the escapades he thought typical, if not expected, of a Grand Tour. Silas always opened mail from his father reluctantly, knowing it would comprise chidings and angry demands to return home, put his medical degree to some use and join the family practice, instead of wasting his time with frivolity overseas. Whether this was genuine, or merely an attempt to get Silas back so they could continue their private performances with the Turk, he was unsure. Regardless, when one of the letters, received after an evening out with some cancan ladies in Montmartre, concluded with the lament, "You are wanting in nearly all the qualities that go to make a success in medicine," Silas decided to return to Philadelphia — if only to prove his father wrong.

But here he was, trespassing in the Chinese Museum, now at the door leading to the basement, about to betray his father's trust yet again. And here was Mary, beautiful, brilliant Mary whom he loved, with her hand on his arm. "Down here?" she asked, wide-eyed.

Silas swung the lantern, light dancing across both their faces, shadows stretching out behind them. A sign on the door read Lower Hall Exhibits. "Down here."

As they descended, step by step, again Silas found himself thinking of his father, could hear the tone of disapproval if he were to discover his son sharing with a colleague's daughter his most prized possession. And not just any colleague's daughter: Mary's father, Dr. Alfred Elwyn, was an eccentric who opted, instead of practising medicine, to open hospices for the feeble-minded and chair societies dedicated to the welfare of animals. Silas knew that this time his punishment would not be limited to parental admonishments; now, considering the patriarch's condition and with the family practice at stake, disappointing his father would result in something far graver.

IN THE BASEMENT were cabinets full of Turk-related lore: articles in French, German, Italian, Spanish, and English detailing its conquests around Europe. Silas and Mary made their way slowly down the hall, shining their lamp over the exhibit. Here was a picture of its inventor, the Austrian Wolfgang von Kempelen, and a copy of the plans for the Turk's original design — all machinery, with no space for a man inside.

Another display was dedicated to the famed showman who brought the Turk to America, the German inventor Johann Maelzel. A brief biographical sketch was paired with a reconstruction of his Automaton Trumpeter, which played various tunes through the rhythmic pumping of a mechanical bellows. Maelzel was remembered in the exhibit as "a great entertainer who perished at sea of natural causes."

Nearby, among a collection of various relics, was a framed essay by Edgar Allan Poe exposing the secrets of the Turk. His guesses were close, noted Silas, reading in the lamplight, but certainly not the entire truth.

Then the wooden floor gave way to red carpet laid out in a long strip leading to the far end of the Lower Hall. This they followed in almost reverential silence, the lantern leading the way along, then up a short flight of stairs to a sort of proscenium before a high curtain.

And then there it was, perched squatly centre stage. It had been more than a year since Silas had seen the Turk, and in the shuddering yellow light it seemed even more menacing than he remembered: the eyes twinkled in an eerily lifelike way. He held the lantern as Mary crept forward.

"Oh, my," she said, standing before the cabinet, running her hand over the chessboard. "This really *is* remarkable, Silas. What was your father charging for demonstrations before he sold it to the museum?"

"Back when he had me working inside it was fifty cents or so to play, but I think after I left he offered private viewings for twice that." Silas resisted adding anything about the machine being worth more empty than it was with him inside. "He bought it for twenty-five dollars, so I'm sure he made the money back fairly quickly."

Mary circled around until she stood beside the seated figure. She reached out her hand to its face, but Silas called out, "Don't touch it!"

"Please, Silas. I'm not going to break it."

"Sorry. It's likely better not to leave evidence, is all."

"Evidence?" Mary giggled.

"Evidence. We were never here, remember?"

"Right." Mary stood staring into the light for a moment. The contrast of her beauty and the ugliness of the Turk struck Silas then. On her face was an expression of curiosity, intrigue, and a trace of fear — she seemed achingly human, vulnerable, but ready to be delighted. The Turk, meanwhile, glowered at him with a sneer of self-satisfaction and scorn. Silas felt ridiculous hating a machine, but he could summon no other emotion.

Mary tapped the cabinet. "Now, will you please show me how this thing works?"

Silas sighed. "Are you sure you want to know? Many people prefer to believe that it works on its own. Your father, for instance, left the room when we offered to explain it."

"That's my father. A dreamer."

"All right then."

Silas moved beside Mary and, kneeling down, placed the lantern on the floor so it illuminated the back of the cabinet. She crouched beside him, her hand on his back.

"Okay," said Silas. Flipping the catches he swung the back of the cabinet open and proceeded to demonstrate where he had sat and how the magnets below worked the pieces on the board above. He showed her the candle holders, the ventilation shaft, the sliding base that allowed him to move from one side to the other when the front doors were opened to display the interior, and the button to make it speak — which he pressed.

"Check," said the Turk, and Silas flinched.

That voice! Hearing it after so long tweaked and pulled at loose strings of memory until, finally, everything came tumbling back: the stifling smoke of the candles, the claustrophobia, the muffled wonder of Philadelphia's aristocracy as the automaton bested another of their rank. And the booming laugh of his father, championing the machine, mocking his peers in their defeat.

Silas paused, reeling, rocked on his heels, and landed with a thud on his back on the carpeted stage.

Mary was at his side, her hand against the side of his face. "Are you all right?"

Silas sighed. "I'm fine."

"Why are you lying down?" Mary stroked his cheek, smiled. "Is the tour over?"

He touched her hand, breathed. "You know, Mary, my father is dying."

"He's what?"

"Dying. And I am next in line to carry on his practice and work."

"Oh, no, Silas. That's so sad. I mean," she added hurriedly, "about your father. And the practice? This is something you'll be happy doing?"

Silas ran his fingers up Mary's arm to her elbow. She took his hand, adjusted her skirts, reclined, and lay down beside him, resting her head on his chest. Inches away, the lantern flickered, casting washes of amber light over them.

"Oh, it's fine. But I just feel that there's more to life than seeing patients and finding antidotes for snake venom. All his life my father has dedicated every day to science, to a pursuit of the truth, and look at him — the man knows his maths and equations, but he'd never understand the sort of truth you'd find in poetry or art. And look at his relationship with my mother. She's a wonderful woman, but he treats her like she doesn't even exist."

Silas thought about this. He looked up at the Turk, looming above them: from behind it was considerably less impressive, just some tatty old robes hanging limply off a brittle wooden skeleton. A machine, heartless and vacant, useless without a human hand to guide it.

Mary leaned in and kissed Silas, then — fully, deeply, on the mouth. He closed his eyes, felt her climb on top of him, skirts swishing and falling, heavy and enveloping his legs as well as hers, and he kissed her back, ran his hands from her neck down the sides of her body, along the curve of her hips, farther down.

As her mouth moved over his neck he reached as low as he could, grabbing handfuls of fabric, tugging upwards, hitching. The layers amazed him; there seemed enough material down there to outfit a small orchestra. He grabbed her hips and flipped her; Mary giggled, beneath him now, then nibbled at his earlobe, her breath coming heavier, and the skirts were finally nearing their end, he could feel garters somewhere beneath a petticoat and —

Silas paused, sniffing. A smell, a familiar smell, came wafting into his nostrils from nearby, something acrid and sour that he knew only to associate with danger, with emergency. He opened his eyes. The hall was bright around them; an orange glow bathed the room. Was it dawn already?

"Fire!" screamed Mary, flinging Silas off her. He rolled down the steps, his head smacking off each one as he went. Mary, meanwhile, scuttled backwards, crablike, away from where the lantern had tipped and spilled and flames were spreading hungrily up onto the curtains and along the carpet, toward the Turk. "Fire!" she screamed again.

At the bottom of the steps Silas stood, trying groggily to focus. His head hurt; his vision swam. Mary appeared at his side. "Silas, the lantern! We've knocked it over!"

Silas nodded — slowly, ponderously.

"Come on!"

He looked up at the Turk: flames a foot high, gathering intensity, fluttered around it on the stage. Smoke came billowing off the fire in waves, the curtains flapping and urging it on. Quickly the cabinet was alight, catching the Turk's garments. Silas stood, mouth agape. It was beautiful.

A hand slapped him across the face. Mary stood before him, shoulders heaving. "Silas, the museum is on fire, and we need to leave. Do you hear me? What's wrong with you?"

But Silas was entranced by the inferno eating away at the cabinet, crackling and alive, and he felt himself saying to Mary, "Yes." He heard himself tell her, "We need to leave," but even as she took his hand and tugged him back down the carpet toward the exit, he still watched over his shoulder, saw the turban unravel in a shower of sparks, the face paint melt, the pipe crumble into ash. As they made their way back into the stairwell, Silas caught one last glimpse of the Turk's eyes, blue and sparkling in the firelight, before Mary pulled him away.

OUTSIDE THE Chinese Museum, Silas and Mary collapsed choking on the back lawn, she on her knees, he right onto his stomach in the grass.

"Silas," she said, once her fits of coughing subsided, "we

have to run. The fire brigade will be here soon. They'll catch us and know we did it."

Silas sat up. He was smiling. "Let them come," he said. "We *did* do it."

Mary paused, then came over and smacked him again. "Don't be so foolish."

Behind them, smoke was beginning to waft out of the basement windows, but Silas just sat there, a grin on his face.

"Listen, you can go ahead and get caught, but if you think for a moment you're dragging me into this with you, forget it."

Silas looked up at her. "Mary, it's gone. It's over now."

"You're delirious. What are you smiling at? Get up!"

"Mary?" He pulled her down beside him. "I love you, Mary," he said.

"Silas, that's wonderful, but — "

"We can go, we'll go, but before we do, I just want you to know." She went to stand up, but he stopped her with a kiss, planted his lips on hers, both their faces smudged black with ash and smoke and joined together. Just as he released, an explosion came behind them as one of the basement windows was blown outwards. Glass came tinkling across the lawn, followed by the greedy roar of the fire inside.

Mary hauled Silas to his feet. "You okay now?"

"I'm okay," said Silas, wrapping an arm around her. They began to walk away, holding each other close. Behind them came another explosion; an orange glow stretched trembling across the lawn. Mary took Silas's hand and together they broke into a run. Very faintly, as they made their way off into the darkness, Silas was sure he heard a voice from deep amid the thunder of flames. It was a plaintive, desperate call. "Checkmate," said the voice, and then the roof of the museum came crashing down, a ball of flame rose into the sky, and all that was left was the rumble and hiss of the fire consuming the museum, devouring everything inside.

PET THERAPY

THE DAY EWING tried to bugger one of the goats, it went like this: Sujata Jain let Ewing outside and right away he started prowling around the pen, knuckles scraping the ground, breath whistling out through his nostrils, big simian head bobbing stealthily with each calculated step. There was something different about his movements, something dubious and predatory, and in that premonitory way in which animals can tell a storm is coming the goats staggered away from the lustful chimp, mewling. Before Sujata could intervene, Ewing scuttled over and mounted one of the poor creatures from behind and started humping away at its rear end.

It took a moment for Sujata to realize what was happening. For a moment, she stood watching, transfixed, before the screams of one of the younger patients — "The monkey's killing it!" — brought her to her senses. Rolling up her sleeves, Sujata rushed over, hauled the frenzied chimp to the ground, and then ushered him inside the playroom. By then the kids were hysterical and the dogs were howling and the goats huddled bleating in the corner of the pen, and a bewildered Sujata stood in the doorway, trying to figure out whom to console first.

Ewing, meanwhile, hammered off dutifully in the play-room. After ejaculating all over himself he waddled out back, where he sat, slumped in the corner of his cage, a white blanket pulled over his face, waiting to be locked in.

THE RAPE HAPPENED, a few days later the hospital's board of directors held an inquiry, and then, less than two weeks after that, Karel was hired as support staff — to "watch the horny chimp," as one senior official put it in the interview.

Sujata loved that horny chimp, though; she spent hours in meetings campaigning to keep him around. Karel's first day on the job, he walked into the Pet Therapy Ward and found her curled up on the floor with Ewing, stroking his furry back. Karel stood there for a moment, wondering if they shouldn't be left alone, before both woman and monkey looked up with the same curious expression on their faces.

"I'm Sue Jain," she said, standing up, extending her hand. Karel heard "Sue-Jane," which seemed impossible for this petite, chestnut-skinned South Asian; it was too Arkansas, too slapped together. "I'm in charge here."

Her palm felt greasy. "Hi, Sue-Jane. Karel. The new aide."

"I'm sure you've heard about Ewing." Sue-Jane nodded at the monkey sprawled between her feet. "You ever work with a bonobo before?"

"Bonobo? That's not a monkey?"

Sue-Jane's face crinkled. "You have much experience with animals?"

"Animals, no. Kids, plenty."

"Animals, no?"

"No. But I worked at a daycare for years. Like, before."

Sue-Jane stared at Karel for a moment, then reached down, took Ewing by the hand, and led him cautiously outside. "Judith needs feeding," she called over her shoulder. "She's the pig."

PET THERAPY operated under the premise that sick children would get well from being around animals, petting them, holding them to their ailing bodies. It was set up in the basement of the hospital in a room that had previously served as the morgue, now redecorated in a circus motif. Mobiles made by patients dangled from the ceiling: cardboard lions and clowns and big-top tents. Two picture windows looked out onto an outdoor animal pen that had been, at one point, a little patch of trees beside the hospital. A few stumps remained clustered around the perimeter of the yard, sawed off into flat, perfect stools. Immediately, Karel preferred to be outside with Ewing; the air in the playroom always seemed so still, almost oblivious to the life and action usually whirling around in it.

That first day, after a harried eight hours of vomiting dogs and vomiting children and a runaway Judith and a surprisingly docile Ewing, who hung around in the pen with the goats as if nothing had ever happened between them, Sue-Jane instructed Karel to join her for dinner. Had it been anyone else, Karel might have considered this a romantic invitation, but she seemed so pragmatic about it. Besides, the woman was forty or so, close to fifteen years Karel's senior.

Karel followed Sue-Jane in his Neon to an Indian restaurant near the hospital, one of those all-you-can-eat places with piped-in sitar music and statuettes of deities bronze and holy along the walls. Sue-Jane made straight for a table next to the buffet, nodding at the waiters as she breezed by. She slung her purse over the back of a chair, snatched up a plate, and stepped into line. Karel trailed closely behind.

"Hungry," she grunted.

They shuffled along, reaching out every now and then to slop curries onto their plates. "Not that one," Sue-Jane kept saying, steering Karel's hand away. "Take some of this."

Back at the table, their plates both heaped with identical, meatless meals, Sue-Jane sat down with a great, breathy exhalation and attacked her food.

"That's the stuff," she said. "Oh boy, that's the stuff."

Karel folded some eggplant into a piece of naan. "You a vegetarian?"

"Vegan."

"Oh yeah? No cheese, no eggs?"

Sue-Jane paused for a moment, her fork dripping. "Yes. Vegan."

"You find that hard?"

"Beg your pardon?"

"Sorry — I just, you know."

Sue-Jane shovelled a forkful of okra into her face. "Eat, eat."

Karel watched, marvelling at the silent tenacity, the icy resolve. He was used to meals with his parents hollering at each other across the table, occasionally roping him into diatribes on the decay of social values or the price of auto insurance. This absence of conversation now seemed wrong.

He opened his mouth to speak, and as he did Sue-Jane looked up, meeting his eyes. She gestured at his plate with her fork. Karel ate.

WHEN KAREL GOT back to the trailer that night, his cousin Wayne was out, presumably off playing pool at some nearby tavern — how he spent most of his free time. Wayne was only two years younger than Karel but looked about eighteen, with a Frida Kahlo moustache and the spindly arms and legs of a prototypical heavy-metal enthusiast. The day Karel moved in, he brought his cousin a case of beer as a thank-you gift. "Shit, dude — we're family," Wayne said, smacking Karel on the back hard enough to leave a mark. "I'll take the brews, but if you can't count on your family when the chips are down, what the fuck? Am I right?"

The trailer park sat on a hill that overlooked the town, twenty identical little hovels made of plastic and glass, wheels lifted off the ground by concrete blocks. The inside comprised one long, narrow room: the kitchen by the front door, a small living space that housed the TV; Wayne's waterbed was sectioned off by a curtain near the far wall. Karel slept on the couch.

Alone, the Indian meal a solid brick in his gut, Karel got out his laptop and spent a few hours on the Internet, looking up bonobos and relentlessly checking his email. Within the reams of spam promising him larger genitalia and smaller mortgage rates were two emails: one from the newspaper back home that Karel deleted without reading and another from his mother. This he opened with some trepidation.

Hi, Honey.

Just checking to see that things are working out. People here have been asking after you, if you're doing okay. Also, the lawyer dropped by with the paperwork for the counter-suit. We all think you should really consider it. Let me know and I'll send everything to you at Wayne's.

Love, Mom

Karel read the message again and considered a response. With a sigh, he tabbed over to the Trash icon and clicked. Then he made his way to the couch, lay down, and, after masturbating efficiently into a sock, fell asleep.

That night Karel dreamt he was at the end of a chain of monkeys, meticulously picking burrs and insects from the chimp in front of him. His own back was thick with fur and alive with crackling, crawling things; but while he slaved away, fingers sifting, hunting, flicking, no one offered to take their turn and groom him.

THE NEXT DAY, Sue-Jane and Karel hardly had a chance to talk: the craziness began at nine in the morning with the first patient appearing pale and wide-eyed at the Pet Therapy door and ended when the last of the children were collected by nurses at a quarter to five. Sue-Jane was occupied pretty much all day, regulating the petting of dogs or the feeding of goats — younger children had this tendency to drink from their bottles — or monitoring the handling of two chinchillas on loan from one of the hospital's more prominent donors.

Meanwhile, Karel kept a supervisory eye on Ewing.

Karel found it difficult to imagine the lustful urges that had possessed the chimp that one unfortunate afternoon. Ewing did his routine for any kids who ventured outside — hooting, throwing things, jumping up and down — all in a carefree, charming way that from his seat on a nearby stump warmed Karel to watch.

At one point, he got up to join in. Ewing was in the midst of turning somersaults around the pen, but when Karel came near he stood up and shuffled nervously over to the playroom door.

"Whoa," Karel said, trying to sound jokey. "Guess I'm not wanted here."

He went back to his spot on the stump, smiling stupidly. Minutes later, Ewing returned to entertaining the kids, who squealed and clapped with delight.

When Sue-Jane made an appearance outside at the end of the day, Ewing clambered over, leapt up into her arms, and clung there like a giant, sinewy spider. The kids circled around cheering and Sue-Jane laughed. When the bonobo's penis began to engorge, Sue-Jane dumped him on the ground, scolding him harshly. Ewing slumped away, while Karel observed quietly from his spot in the corner of the pen.

THURSDAY OF KAREL'S second week Sue-Jane announced at a few minutes to five that they would be dining together again. After stuffing themselves in relative silence they tottered out into the parking lot, located their respective automobiles, and went their separate ways.

Driving home, Karel wondered if these suppers together

weren't some sort of incentive set up by the hospital, part of Sue-Jane's job description. Or maybe they were friends? Karel felt himself figuring her out slowly, like a game of Clue, putting her together with little mental check marks, tick, tick, tick, hoping at some point it would all become clear — who, where, with what murderous implement: Sue-Jane.

THE FOLLOWING Wednesday produced another invite. As Sue-Jane's customary assault on her dinner began, Karel brought up one particularly sad-looking girl who had spent the entire afternoon trying to teach Jiva the macaw to say, "I love you." The girl had stood there, index finger reaching through the bars of the cage, coaxing, repeating in a parrot voice: "I love you! I love you! I love you!"

"Man, wasn't she sad?" Karel said. "I think she was in for a marrow transplant."

"You want to talk sad?" Sue-Jane wiped some chutney from her face with her sleeve. "In my religion we are in a period of suffering of twenty-one thousand years."

"I didn't know you were religious."

"Well, I'm doing my best."

"And how much longer do we have to go?"

"About eighteen thousand years."

"Only eighteen thousand? And after that?"

"Twenty-one thousand years of even worse suffering. All hope will be wiped from the earth."

"Oh, fun."

Sue-Jane had somehow fit a piece of potato the size of a child's fist into her mouth. She sat with her cheeks ballooned out like a squirrel's, looking unsure what she might do next. "So, what then," asked Karel, watching her, "after there's no more hope?"

Sue-Jane held up a finger and looked into her lap. Her jaw churned; she swallowed, gasping. "Rain for days and days, then everything is born again."

"And that'll happen when?"

"Forty thousand years. More or less."

"Oh, okay. I'll bake a cake." Sue-Jane shifted then, and Karel felt something — her knee or hand — brush his thigh. He looked at her and noticed, for the first time, the light dusting of fuzz that ringed her face. Leaning in, he lowered his voice to what he thought was an appropriately solemn tone. "So, if your entire life is just suffering, what's the point?"

"You do your best while you're here. You make your life worth living."

Karel felt it again, something warm against his leg. This time it stayed there. "By doing what? Like being good to others?"

"That's the idea."

"And what about yourself?"

Sue-Jane moved away. Whatever had been touching Karel was gone. She gestured at his plate with her fork. "Try the dhal, Karel. It's delicious."

THE FOLLOWING NIGHT, Sue-Jane said nothing to Karel, just nodded and was gone out the door, not even waiting to walk together out to the parking lot. Karel drove home through the city and out to the suburbs, pulled into the trailer park, and locked up the Neon with a robotic chirp. He stood for a moment in the dusk on the steps of Wayne's trailer, looking out over the glow of the city, all those homes producing all that light.

Inside, Karel heated up some dried pasta and store-bought sauce and ate with his computer on his lap, checking his email, erasing messages, writing to no one, scouring the Internet for bonobos, for porn, for whatever.

While he was online, a message appeared from his mother. This chilled Karel, the thought of them both in cyberspace at the same time — as if she might be spying on him, somehow.

Hi.

>Still no word from you. Are things okay? Please, Karel, remember that you can come home any time. You did nothing wrong. But your dad and I both really think that taking these people to court might give this whole ordeal some closure. Anyway, think about it, and write or call if you can.

>Love, Mom.

Karel trashed the message.

Well after Karel had gone to bed, Wayne came home and hovered over the couch, the smell of beer wafting from him and slowly filling the trailer.

"Hey, Kare," he said, prodding his cousin with his sneaker. "I got a date."

Karel rolled over and looked up at him. "Want me to sleep on the roof?"

"Not now, fucknut. Next week. You'd like her, she volunteers and recycles and whatnot."

"Cool. Can I come too?"

Wayne hiccupped, swayed, and hiccupped again. He pulled the curtains apart, collapsed on his waterbed with his shoes on. Within seconds he was snoring.

TO BEGIN KAREL'S fourth week as the Pet Therapy aide, he got in early, at about twenty to nine. Sue-Jane hadn't shown up yet, so Karel opened up a tin of food for Judith, pulled the cover off the parrot cage, fed the fish, checked on George and Martha, the gerbils, to make sure they hadn't eaten each other overnight, and let the dogs out for a pee. Then he made his way into the back room.

Ewing sat there, fingers laced through the bars of his cage. Karel crouched down and unlatched the door and Ewing came plodding past Karel and down the hallway, out to the playroom. Karel closed the cage and followed him.

Ewing perched on a stool by the window, presiding over the room like a judge. Karel squatted beside him and chanced putting a hand on the bonobo's back. Through the hair, thin and wispy, he could feel the tautness of muscle and, beneath that, the knobby cord of a spine. Ewing reached back, took Karel's hand in his, and held it up in front of his face as if he were trying to decide whether to eat it or read Karel his fortune.

Before he could do either the door opened and Sue-Jane entered the playroom. Ewing sprung off his stool and hopped about jabbering while she hung her coat.

Karel stood. "Hi," he said, waving.

Without looking at Karel, Sue-Jane swept Ewing up into her arms. "How's my baby?" she sang out, rubbing noses.

Soon after, the kids started filing in — the new ones tentative, the returnees going around and greeting the animals like divas at a cocktail party — and Karel took Ewing by the hand and moved outside. A crowd of young patients followed.

At five o'clock the nurses arrived and the kids dispersed, waving goodbye. Karel headed out back to lock the animals up for the night. When he returned to the playroom, Sue-Jane was gone. As he was turning off the lights, there was a knock on the door.

In the hallway stood a bald man in brown coveralls, holding a clipboard. Beside him was a dolly carrying a large wooden crate.

"Pet Therapy?" he asked, looking at his clipboard. A nametag embroidered on his pocket read *Angelo* and, underneath that, *Tropicarium Exotic Pets*. "We've got your delivery here."

"I'm sorry?"

"Are you . . ." Angelo's eyes narrowed. "Sujata?"

"Sue-Jane?"

"Maybe."

Angelo turned the clipboard around and showed Karel a name written at the top of a very official-looking form: *Sujata Jain*.

"Sujata Jain," said Karel. "Sue Jain."

"That's you?"

"No, no — but I'll sign. What have you got for us?"

Angelo looked at Karel sideways, grinned, then wheeled the dolly into the playroom. "You want to give me a hand here?"

Karel did his best to hold the crate steady as Angelo lowered the dolly. Together they slid it slowly onto the floor, Angelo coaxing, "Easy, easy." The thing must have weighed half a ton.

With the crate resting squarely on the floor Angelo produced a box cutter from his pocket, slashed at the bindings holding it closed, and pulled the walls down on all sides.

A few feet away, glinting in the fluorescent lights of the playroom, sat an oversized terrarium. And inside the terrarium, thick as a curb, wrapped and stacked upon itself, was a snake. Karel crouched down and stared into the two black, glistening eyes; his own reflection shimmered on the glass, a vague spectre of a face hovering around the snake's flat, angular head.

"Jesus — why didn't you say something?"

"Wouldn't have been a surprise then, would it?"

"What is that, a boa constrictor?"

"That, Sue Jain, is a reticulated python. Her name is Sally."

"Sally."

"She's twelve feet long, but she's young and might grow another six feet if you're lucky. But lately she's been refusing food. I think it's almost three months now that she hasn't eaten a thing. Maybe down here she'll get her appetite back."

"Well, let's hope." Karel couldn't take his eyes off the snake: it just sat there, a lethal coil of spangled, scaly muscle. "Angelo, that thing can't stay. This is a children's hospital."

"Relax, Sue. You keep her locked up and she'll be fine. Besides, kids love snakes."

"I'm sure there's been some sort of mistake?"

"Hey — I'm just the delivery guy. You got problems, talk to my boss." Angelo handed over a card. Karel crumpled it in his fist, still staring into the terrarium. He felt that if he were to slit the snake open the skin would peel back and reveal foam stuffing or a giant Slinky — never bones, never muscle, certainly nothing organic or alive.

Angelo passed along a booklet of care instructions, displayed how to open and close the lid, and offered additional advice that Karel didn't really hear. He plugged the terrarium into the wall and flicked on a heat lamp, lighting Sally up like a stove element. After checking that the lid was fastened tightly, Angelo headed out. Karel lingered in the room for a moment before shutting the lights off and locking up. The musty, burnt-cheese smell of animals filled the car as he made his way home to Wayne's trailer.

WAYNE WAS ON the phone. By the hushed tone of his voice, the unintelligible cooing, he was obviously talking to his new girlfriend. Karel tossed his keys on the kitchen table, poured himself a glass of juice, and sat down beside Wayne on the couch.

Wayne hung up and stood, fastening his belt. "Up to anything Wednesday, Kare?"

"Um." Karel swished some juice around in his mouth.

"Come to this thing with me and Maya."

"Maya? That's your lady's name?"

"It's some charity dinner. For the World Wildlife Fund, or whatever — hey, that's right up your alley, Dr. Doolittle. Here, I'll leave you an invite. Except you need a date."

"A date."

"Bring that broad you work with. She must like animals and whatnot."

"Sue-Jane?" Karel recalled Angelo's sheet. "Sue?"

"That's the one."

"And you really want me to go?"

"Shit, dude, I don't care." Wayne laid an envelope on the coffee table. "There are two tickets here if you want them. Come if you want, I don't give a fuck."

"This isn't the same WWF that's on TV on Monday nights — you know that, right?"

"Shut up, smartass. Maya volunteers for them."

Karel suddenly imagined Maya as a glam-rock groupie who liked kitty cats and blowing coke off guitar amps. "Tell you what, Wayne — I'll ask Sue about it tomorrow. If she's in, I'm in."

"Prime," said Wayne. He checked his watch again. "Listen, dude, I'm out of here." Then he was gone, leaving Karel alone with his juice. He drained the glass, produced his laptop from underneath the couch, and fired up the Internet. There was a new message from his mother: just a single line that Karel read quickly before trashing.

He closed his computer and rested his hands on the plastic lid. A slight buzz of warmth spread up from the machine into his palms. Karel sat there, thinking about the snake named Sally coiled in the dark basement home of Pet Therapy: silent, lethal, hungry.

TUESDAY MORNING Karel hurried to work, figuring there had to be somewhere they could stow Sally before any kids showed up. He could only guess how the board of directors might react to a patient getting swallowed.

When Karel arrived, Sue was dangling a frozen mouse by its tail into the terrarium, her hand perilously close to the python's head. The lid rested against the wall.

Sue sighed and stared at the snake. "She won't eat a thing."

"We're not keeping it, are we?"

"No, no," she said, straightening and patting Karel's arm. "They sent the wrong one. We were supposed to get two corn snakes. I don't know how this happened."

"But in the meantime?" Sue's hand held Karel at the elbow. He swayed a bit and felt the bulge of her hip against his thigh.

"In the meantime we should enjoy having Sally with us. Do you have any idea what one of these pythons costs? It's a real treat having an animal like this around."

"And the kids?"

Sue looked at Karel for a second, eyes scanning his face as though she were searching for something. The tiny hairs on her cheeks were orange in the light of the playroom. After a moment she let go of his arm and pulled away. "Oh, kids are always great too."

"No, no. Will it be safe? With the kids?"

"Listen, Karel, as long as no one climbs in there with it everything will be just fine. Even then she's so lethargic I doubt there'd be much danger. I think she's depressed."

They both looked at Sally, who had yet to move anything other than her eyelids.

"Maybe she's lonely," Karel offered.

Sue tossed the mouse into the terrarium. It bounced off Sally and landed on its back near her head. "Better get that lid back on before the patients arrive."

THAT MORNING KAREL stayed outside with the goats, dogs, Ewing, and one thin, jaundiced boy who had gone into hysterics over the snake and been relegated to the pen. In the playroom the rest of the kids huddled around the terrarium whispering and pointing at Sally. Sue got out the art supplies and soon the walls were plastered with drawings of a patterned spiral in repose.

Karel stationed himself between Ewing and the goats. The yellow boy poked for a while at a clump of dung with a stick, then threw his stick into the woods beyond the pen and, apparently having conquered his fears, wandered inside. The goats were eating plastic bags on the far side of the pen. Karel and Ewing stared at each other, neither quite sure what to do.

"So," said Karel, squatting.

Ewing shrieked.

Karel held up his hands. "Hey, I'm not going to hurt you."

Again Ewing yelped. His arms flapped at his sides like the wings of some desperate flightless bird. He yelped and flapped and started hopping in place, eyes wild and manic.

"Jesus," said Karel. "What's your problem?"

Ewing ducked past Karel and bounded up to the playroom door. He slapped his hands against the window and hooted until the door opened. Karel was left crouching in the hay and mud of the pen. The goats watched him, chewing.

AT FIVE, AFTER locking Sally up, Karel was ready to head out, but Sue intercepted him at the doorway. "My car's in the shop. Want to take me to dinner?"

"Yeah? I mean, no, I can't. I have this thing tonight. With my cousin."

"Oh yeah?"

"Yeah, I actually meant to ask you to come — it's just some charity dinner, or something."

"The SPCA benefit?"

"Maybe. I thought it was World Wildlife?"

"SPCA. I volunteer there sometimes." Sue looked intrigued. "You're going?"

"Well, yeah, I guess. I have tickets. Just have to go home first and grab them."

"Perfect. I'll be your date."

The inside of the Neon smelled like wet fur. Karel mentioned this to Sue as they pulled out of the parking lot, but she just laughed and said she didn't even notice that animals smelled different from people any more.

"So you've worked with animals for a long time?" Karel asked.

Sue smiled out the window and said, "Of course."

"Doing pet therapy?"

Her smile disappeared. "No."

"What, in a zoo or something?"

"Not a zoo." Sue looked at Karel, hesitating. "In a lab."

These three words were like a door closing shut on a private, secret room. Karel didn't say anything for a while, just kept driving. The sky was deepening into a sombre purple.

The car swallowed the yellow dividing line as it appeared on the road out of the dusk.

Karel broke the silence: "I was charged with abusing a child."

He could sense Sue stiffen in her seat. Karel breathed, signalling and turning the car off the main boulevard onto the quiet, dark road that wound up through the hills to the trailer park.

"At the daycare," he continued, "where I used to work. I was there for three years after finishing my ECE." He had to concentrate to keep his hands steady on the wheel. "Then one day my boss came up to me and she was like, 'There's been a complaint.'"

Sue watched him, waiting.

"It was — I don't know. It . . ." Karel breathed. "I just said, 'What?' That's all I could think, What? What? Like it couldn't be real. And I went home that night and my mom and dad were waiting with dinner on the table and I couldn't even look at them, let alone explain what had happened. I felt like I'd maybe even done it — that I might have blacked out for a bit and like sleepwalked my way into something. Or just been kidding around and maybe touched a kid in some way I shouldn't have, without realizing."

"Oh, Karel," said Sue. She reached out and took one of his hands from the steering wheel, cradled it in her lap. He looked over and then turned back to the road. Behind the looming shapes of oak trees identical duplexes slid by, some glowing from the inside, others just dark shadows in the dusk. Her fingers played over his; her thumb stroked his thumb.

"There was an inquiry. It turned up nothing but it went on for months. You live in a small town, everybody talks, and even when they figured out I hadn't done anything, I'd go around and people would still look at me like I was guilty."

Karel drove, his left hand clutching the wheel, his right in Sue's lap. She ran her nails over his knuckles. The sky was a deep bruise.

They turned another corner, headed up a private driveway, and arrived at the trailer park. Karel pulled the Neon in front of Wayne's trailer and sat there, the engine idling. "Looks like we're going to be a little late. Do you think it's a big deal?"

Sue stared out at the trailer. "You live in that thing with your cousin?"

"Yeah."

A chorus of crickets chirped away somewhere nearby.

Karel turned to Sue. "Do you want to see inside?"

In the trailer Karel poured them both glasses of juice. He flicked on the table lamp and a yellow splotch of light spread across the couch. They sat down together and Sue gazed around as if some detail might reveal the secret of the place.

Karel sucked back his juice and cupped the empty glass in both hands. "So, you volunteer over at the SPCA?"

"Saturdays," she said, staring at the curtain that hid Wayne's bed.

"You must be busy, Sujata." The name just came out. Karel felt strange, as though he'd crossed some unspoken boundary.

Sue lifted the glass of juice and sniffed it. In the lamplight, the fuzz on her face was golden. "What's your cousin like?"

"Wayne? Oh, he's all right."

"All right?"

"Well he's nice enough, but one of those people who lives totally for himself — 'in the now,' or whatever. Just look at this place. His whole world could up and roll away."

"Not like you."

"Well, no, that's not what I'm saying — that I'm better than him or anything."

"Right. So what are you like?"

"What do you mean?" Karel sat there, staring at the floor, pulling at some loose stitches on the couch with his free hand. "I'm looking for my own place."

Sujata sighed. "You know," she said, "we really ought to get another bonobo in for Ewing. A female."

"To mate?"

"No, no — to control him. Bonobo culture is dominated by the females. The males are pretty much at their mercy. They even dictate when and what to eat. Sex is used as a sort of regulatory device."

"But if we got Ewing a lady, he'd stop fucking the goats. Then you wouldn't need me at all."

Sujata smiled, considering. Outside, the crickets were still chirping.

Karel put a hand on her knee. Sujata slid her hand over his.

"I don't think Ewing even likes me," said Karel.

"Oh? Why's that?"

"I don't know. He's just weird, like he's scared of me or something."

"Hmm . . ." Sujata paused. "Maybe he's jealous."

They sat in silence, looking around, his hand on her knee, her hand on his hand. Karel's gaze wandered from the front door, over the kitchen, to the TV, and finally to the curtain. Behind it sat Wayne's waterbed, ready and waiting.

WHEN KAREL ARRIVED at Pet Therapy on Thursday morning, Sally lay coiled up in the same position, shimmering under the fluorescent lights. Sujata had already let the animals out and she was sitting with Ewing on a stump outside. The bonobo had his arms wrapped around her neck; both of them were gazing up at a solemn, overcast sky.

"God, I'm so tired," Karel said.

When Sujata spoke, it was less to Karel than to the clouds. "He's very clingy today."

Karel stood, wavering. He reached out to put a hand on Sujata's shoulder. Ewing hissed. "Jesus," said Karel, but Sujata just stood and carried the chimp past him into the playroom.

The kids showed up and flocked to the snake. Karel was left alone out in the pen with the goats, a golden retriever named Laika who was visiting for the day, and, eventually, Ewing, whom Sujata had ushered outside. He sat by the door with his arms folded, glaring at Karel.

"Oh, fuck you," Karel told him. Then, whispering, "We had sex, you know. Me and her."

Ewing buried his head in his chest.

"Stupid fucking monkey."

Karel sat down on one of the tree stumps, figuring a five-minute nap was all he needed; then he'd be fresh for the rest of the day. He looked inside, through the playroom window.

Sujata had opened the terrarium. The kids were crowding around, more intrigued than ever.

Karel closed his eyes. Soon he found himself tumbling down the dark tunnel of sleep. At its end a dream greeted him, something vague and palely lit. There were dim shapes crowding around what seemed some sort of waiting room, bumping into him as he tried to make his way up to the reception desk. There was no warmth to the bodies; the contact was like brushing up against things made of ice. From somewhere came the mournful sound of something crying.

Karel shuddered and the dream was gone. But the crying remained, now accompanied by frantic, desperate shrieks. He jumped to his feet and looked up to see Sujata hollering and smacking with a broom at something black and quivering. Underneath the black thing — Ewing! — was a bleating goat, legs buckling. Children spilled out of the door, gawking but silent.

Karel scrambled over to help Sujata. Together they tackled Ewing to the ground. The violated goat wobbled off to the corner of the pen, where its comrades huddled around in solidarity. The sobbing waned.

Sujata glared at Karel. "Get Ewing out of here."

Directing the bonobo's erection away from his body, Karel carried Ewing under one arm into the playroom and dumped him on the floor. Back outside, Karel stood by the door watching Sujata pace around the pen. She stopped beside the offended goat and put her hand on its head. The children sat expectantly on the stumps, startled but rapt. Above, the clouds hung heavy and grey with rain.

Sujata stroked the goat's face. Her tenderness, Karel realized, completely belied what had consumed her the night before: bent over on Wayne's waterbed, gasping, the flicker of something primal and hungry in her eyes as she watched Karel go to it over her shoulder. Afterwards she knelt on the floor draining into a T-shirt between her legs, the waterbed sloshing around as Karel stood to pull up his shorts. "Stay," he told her.

"I need to go," Sujata said, already dressing. "Give me a lift?"

The ride home had been silent.

Something wet splashed on Karel's hand. A single droplet of rain trickled along his thumb. Sujata was speaking. "Do you think we can forgive him?" she asked, and the children nodded, murmuring.

Something surged inside Karel. Then it was gone — they were talking about Ewing.

Sujata continued, her voice calm. The children listened in silence. Standing on the periphery, Karel felt himself fading from the scene, like smoke waved out through a kitchen window. Another drop of rain struck him on the face and dribbled down his cheek.

He slid quietly inside the playroom. He figured Ewing knew what he'd done wrong and should be waiting in his cage; it'd just be a matter of heading out back and locking the door. But his little metal cell was empty, the white blanket crumpled in the corner with no bonobo in sight.

Back in the playroom there was no sign of Ewing either, but Karel could sense — what? Something. His eyes took inventory of the room, processing it image by image. The mobiles, twirling in some imaginary wind. The birdcage where Jiva perched silent and still. Children's drawings abandoned on the floor. A scattering of paints and markers and crayons.

Then: the terrarium's wire lid, discarded nearby. The terrarium itself, open, winking with flashes of light. Inside it, Sally, brown and thick and suddenly very much alive, pulling and twisting behind the glass. The swish of her scales, the hiss of rain, and somewhere beneath it all the buzz of fluorescent lights. Karel stood, transfixed, watching. As Sally turned over, from within that scaly knot appeared the grey fingers of something almost human scratching against the inside of the glass.

Karel drifted forward until he was right at the terrarium, looking in. Later, he would realize that his thoughts weren't of heroism — what could he have done, anyway? Instead he was thinking of how it would feel to be caught in the grip of the snake. He watched as Sally curled one last time around Ewing, the length of her rippling forward, crushing his body and pulling the hand away, and thought how it seemed somehow comforting to die like that, embraced.

THE PAST COMPOSED

IN THE END, all the ruckus seems to be about a boy up Judy's tree. I stand there at the bottom, his backpack in my hand, looking up through leaves just starting to bleed the reds and browns of autumn. He's right near the top, this boy — a dark silhouette against the late afternoon sunlight, perched on a branch, shaking, terrified. Inside the house Judy's dogs are still going crazy.

"Hey there," I say, squinting.

"A squirrel chased me up here. I think it had rabies."

"Was it frothing at the mouth?"

"Frothing?"

"Yeah, like with foam coming out of its mouth."

The boy says nothing. The dogs have stopped barking, and the only sound is the dull, faraway hiss and hum of the city.

"You want to come down? I don't see any squirrels around."

He considers for a moment, evaluating the situation — or me, maybe. Then he swings down effortlessly, monkey-like, and lands with a dull thump on the lawn. His clothes seem to belong to someone years older: a Lacoste golf shirt and beige safari shorts, with a pair of blue socks pulled tightly up to his knees.

"All right?" I ask, and hand him his backpack. He's a funny little man, maybe eight or nine. There's something familiar, and vaguely cunning, about his face.

The boy stands there, scanning the front lawn, nervous. I look around too, then up at Judy's house, where I notice, wedged between a pink triangle and a MIDWIVES DELIVER! sticker, the Block Parent sign in the window.

"Oh," I say. "I'm Les. Do you want to come in?"

The boy eyes me, then the house. Eventually he nods and replies, "Okay."

I lead him inside, where the dogs greet us with an inquisitive sniff before letting us through to the kitchen. The boy edges by them, saying, "Good dogs," a gleam of terror in his eyes. I pour him a glass of milk and we both sit down at Judy's tiny kitchen table.

"Next time you get a squirrel after you," I say, "probably best not to go up a tree."

"I came to the door first, but there was no answer."

His glass of milk sits untouched on the chipped Formica tabletop. "You got a name?"

"Pico," he tells me, kicking at the chair with his heels. "Are you even a Block Parent?"

"No, no. That's the lady who owns the house. My sister, Judy."

"So who are you?"

"I live back there." I point out through the kitchen window at the shed in the backyard.

"What?" Pico snorts. "In that thing?"

I tap his glass with my fingernail. "Drink your milk, Pico."

BY THE TIME Judy gets home I am making dinner and Pico has left. He thanked me for the milk, then headed off down the street.

Judy appears in the kitchen, the dogs snuffling eagerly behind her. She slings her purse onto the table and sits down. "Fuck," she sighs. The dogs settle at her feet.

"I've got ratatouille happening here, Jude, and there's tabbouleh salad in the fridge."

"No meat? Pas de viande?" Judy, bless her, is trying to learn French.

"Sorry."

"Christ, Les," she huffs. "You're starting to make me feel like one of those crazy vegan dykes — living on nuts and fruits and berries like a goddamn squirrel."

I laugh and tell her about Pico.

"Pico? What is he, a Brazilian soccer player?"

"No," I say, stirring the ratatouille, recalling the boy's face. "He looks more like a mini–Richard Nixon."

Judy points at the classified ads I've left on the table.

"Any luck?" she asks.

"Nothing yet."

"Not that I want you gone. I mean, you're welcome here as long as you need to stay."

"I know, Jude," I tell her, sprinkling some salt into the pot. "Thanks a lot."

After dinner I head out into the backyard and work until dusk. The table I'm redoing right now is some cheap pine thing I picked up for forty dollars at a garage sale. But with the right stain, corners rounded off, and a good number of chips whittled out of the legs, it'll go for close to a grand in one of the antique stores uptown. I can just imagine some family huddled around it for supper — Mom in her apron doling out fat slices of meatloaf, Dad asking the kids about school, and this sturdy old table anchoring it all like the centrepiece to a Norman Rockwell painting.

Soon it's too dark to see much of anything, so I head inside my little cabin. Before I moved in at the end of the summer, Judy did a nice job fixing it up for me; she put down rugs and painted the wallpaper a quiet beige colour, even brought her fish tank out and set it up in the corner. It's an A-frame, this thing. Like a tent. At first it seemed claustrophobic, but it's turned out pretty cozy.

The fish are good to watch. There are three of them, all the same species, although what that would be, I have no idea. But there's something soothing about them, these shimmering, fluttering things, all silver glitter in the light of the tank.

We always talked about getting a cat, Rachel and me. But we figured we'd try fish first, and if they didn't die right away we'd chance it with a cat. But less than two months after we moved in together, before we'd even had a chance to go fish shopping, Rachel got pregnant.

At first having a baby seemed too big, too adult, too far removed from the safe little niche we'd carved for ourselves. But once we got talking to Judy, started considering her as our midwife, things began to take shape and make sense. At night, in bed together, Rachel and I would lie with our hands on her belly, talking about the future, how one day we'd look back on our apprehension and laugh. But I guess everyone constructs, at some point, these perfect versions of how things are going to be.

A WEEK OR SO later I'm in the backyard, down on my knees sanding the table legs, and Pico appears at the gate.

"Hola, Pico," I holler. "Come on in."

Pico reaches over the fence, flips the latch, and moves across the yard toward me, plucking an old seed dandelion from the grass on his way. Today is chillier; he's in a mauve turtleneck and a pair of pleated jeans. Pico leans up against the table, twirling the dandelion in his fingers. He lifts it to his mouth, sucks in a great mouthful of breath, and blows. The grey fluff catches a breeze and lifts scattering into the sky.

"Nice one," I say.

"How come dandelions aren't flowers?" Pico twirls the decapitated plant between his thumb and forefinger, then flicks it at the ground.

"Because they're weeds, Pico."

"But they look like flowers. When they're yellow."

"Well, that's their trick."

"Yeah?"

"Sure. They pretend to be flowers so you keep them around. But they're weeds."

"They look like flowers to me," says Pico, as if this settles it.

He starts walking around the table, running his fingers along the wood. Before I can warn him about splinters, he yelps and springs back like something's bitten him, his hand to his lips. Right away, I'm up, beside him. "You've got to watch that, Pico."

"Ouch," he says, wincing.

I guide him into the shed, where he sits down on the bed. I find some tweezers, and Pico puts his hand out, palm up, quivering.

I smile, the tweezers poised. "Trust me?"

Pico nods. I raise his hand up to the light, and there it is — a black grain of wood lodged into the skin. I slide the tweezers up to it, clamp down, and pull the splinter free. Pico bucks and yanks his hand away. But after a moment, he examines his finger and looks up at me in awe.

"Nothing to it," I tell him. But Pico has already turned his attention to my fish, the splinter apparently forgotten. He sits on my bed, regarding them with vague interest.

"Cool, huh?"

"Great," says Pico.

I struggle to think of some interesting fish fact, something remarkable and fascinating.

Pico beats me to it: "Did you know fish only have memories for five seconds?"

"Huh. I had no idea."

"They forget their whole lives every five seconds — then it's like they're new fish again."

"Or they think they are."

Pico gives me a funny look. "How come you're the only Block Parent on this street?"

"I'm not — really?"

"Yep. I went around looking for signs, and you're the only one."

"It's because we're the nicest."

"Can I feed your fish?" Pico asks, standing up.

"Sure." We trade places, and I settle into the groove he's left in my bedcovers. "The food's just there. But don't give them too much — "

Pico glances at me over his shoulder, already sprinkling the coloured flakes into the aquarium. "I know what I'm doing, Les."

On my bedside table is a deck of playing cards. I pick them up and try making a house, but the cards keep slipping off one another. Pico comes over, shaking his head.

"You've got to make triangles." He sits down beside me, takes two cards, and leans them against one another. He succeeds in building a few levels before the whole thing collapses.

"Hey, want to see a trick?" I ask.

"A card trick?"

"Sure. Just pick a card and tell me what pile it's in."

This is the only card trick I know, and it's a simple one: after three times through the same routine, the person's card is always the eleventh out of the pile. But I choose it with a flourish, throwing the cards around the room, and then walking around as if confused before pulling the right one up off the floor.

Pico claps. "Again," he commands. "Again!"

"Nope. Magicians never do the same trick twice in a row."

"Oh, come on."

"Sorry. Maybe some other time, Pico."

Pico looks at me carefully. "The kids at school call me Pee-Pee-Co, sometimes."

"That doesn't even make sense," I say. Here I am, sitting with this boy on my bed, this odd little fellow with the face of a diabolical American president. "You want to stay for dinner?"

Pico considers, tilting his head toward some indefinite place on the ceiling. "I'll have to call my nana," he says, nodding. "But I think it might be a good idea."

JUDY COMES HOME to Pico sitting on the floor of the kitchen, talking to the dogs. I've got a veggie moussaka in the oven, tomato and tarragon soup simmering on the stove, and a spinach salad tossed and ready for dressing on the counter.

"More bird food?" says Judy. She stoops down to greet Pico and his canine companions. "You must be Pico."

Pico looks up and grins. "I'm staying for dinner."

"Oh, you are now." Judy turns to me. "Did you check with his mom?"

"His nana," I tell her. But then I realize I haven't. I had stayed in the kitchen while Pico made the call from Judy's bedroom. Pico and I exchange a quick look, and then I turn to Judy. "I'm sure it's fine."

"She knows you're Block Parents," says Pico.

Judy shrugs, steps over Pico, and opens the fridge. "Don't we have any beer?"

"Beer?" I squeeze a wedge of lemon into a glass jar, add some olive oil, salt, pepper.

She slams the fridge door shut and then leans up against it. "What a day. I spend half my week wrist-deep in vaginas — you'd think I've got the best job in the world."

I frown and nod my head in the direction of Pico, but he seems oblivious, totally absorbed with trying to get the already prostrate dogs to lie down.

"Oh, shoot," she says, snorting. "Would you believe I've got another couple who are burying their placenta? Although at least these two aren't eating it. Man, these people. You'd think they'd just be happy if their kid comes out all right, it's not — "

She catches herself.

"Oh, fuck. Les — I'm sorry."

The room has changed. Even Pico is quiet. I shake up the jar of oil and lemon juice. I shake it, I keep shaking it, I stare out the window and I shake the jar, and all I can hear is the wet sound of the dressing sloshing around.

Judy is beside me. She has her hand on my arm. I stop.

"It's okay," I tell her.

"It's okay," she tells me.

We finish dinner by seven o'clock, so Judy and I ask Pico if he wants to come along while we take the dogs out for their evening walk. Before we ate, Judy had decided Pico needed to know I had a lisp when I was a kid, and he kept my sister in hysterics, calling me "Leth" and "Lethy" for the better part of the meal.

Everyone helps clear the table, and then we collect the dogs and head down to the creek behind Judy's house. We call it the creek, but it's basically dried up, just a gentle dribble through the ravine. The dogs love it, though; we let them off their leads and they go bounding and snarling into the woods.

The sun is just setting as the three of us make our way down along the path into the ravine. Judy's brought a flashlight, but she keeps it in her coat. "It's for when they poop," she tells Pico, and shows him the fistful of plastic bags in her pocket. His eyes widen.

Under the canopy of trees overhead, the light down here is dim — almost as if the ravine is hours ahead of the sunset. We unleash the dogs, who bolt, disappearing into the gloom. Judy and Pico follow them, but I move the other way, climbing over a mound of roots and earth, arriving in the dried-up creekbed. I kneel down, put my hand out, and I'm startled to feel water, icy and streaming urgently over my fingertips. But then I realize I can hear it, I probably could have all along — the happy, burbling sound of it barely above a whisper. I close my eyes, listening, my hand dangling in the thread of river.

Rachel and I went to an art exhibit once on one of our trips into the city. There was this room that you went into, and it was dark, totally black. When you entered, a single lightbulb turned on and lit up the room. And in this light you saw, written on one of the walls, text about guillotined criminals who were found to be able to communicate after their heads had been chopped off. Then, right as you read the last word, the lightbulb turned off, leaving you in darkness.

As we were coming out of the room, Rachel took my hand and whispered, "Man, that was spooky."

"Yeah," I said, but later I realized she was only talking about being left in the dark.

Out of the woods, one of the dogs comes trotting up to me and nuzzles its nose into my hand, then starts lapping at the creek. I smack its muscled haunches and the tail starts pumping. Judy and Pico are close, moving through the trees, their voices muffled. Then Pico starts calling, "Leth-eee! Leth-eee!" and Judy gets into it too, their voices ringing out in chorus. Judy turns on her flashlight — it swings through the darkness, sweeping the forest in a fat, white band. I hunker down, my arm around the dog, and wait for them to find me.

AUTUMN HAS FULLY arrived, the smoky, dusty smell of it thick in the air. The leaves are starting to fall, and in the mornings my breath appears in clouds as I putter around the backyard. I figure I'll get a space heater for the cabin once it gets really cold, but the big problem is that I don't know how much longer I'll be able to work outside. I had an indoor workshop at the old house, back when carpentry was only a hobby. It was odd moving, clearing out that room — with all my tools missing it became just an empty space in the basement, smelling vaguely of sawdust and leather. I'm sure Rachel's since turned it into the darkroom she used to talk about.

I don't see Pico for more than a week. Then one afternoon I'm out in the front yard doing the first rake of the season, and he wheels up on a bicycle.

"Les!" he yells. "Look at the bike my nana bought me."

He does a wobbly circle on the street. The bike is a throwback to a time well before Pico's birth — tassels dangle from the handlebars, and the seat curves up into a towering steel backrest. I give Pico the thumbs-up.

With some minor difficulties Pico dismounts, lowering the bike gingerly onto Judy's lawn. Today he is wearing a pink K-Way jacket about two sizes too big for him, blue sweatpants, and a pair of rubber boots. He runs up to me, and we both stand there for a minute, silent, breathing in the crisp autumn air.

"I'm not scared of squirrels any more," he says.

"Yeah?"

"I'm doing my science project on them. They bury their nuts in the fall, and then they find them later because they rub their feet on them and make them smell."

"Is that how it works?"

"Yep. People think they remember where they put them, but they don't. It's just the smell of their stinky feet." Pico starts giggling.

"Isn't that something else."

"You never showed me that card trick again."

"Help me bag these leaves, then we'll go in and I'll do it. But this is the last time."

In a drawer in the kitchen I find a pack of cards, and I deal them out on the table. Pico, eyes narrowed to slits, scrupulously watches my hands. Then I do my big theatrical bit at the end where the cards get tossed all over the room. I walk around for a few seconds in feigned indecision before snatching Pico's queen of spades off the floor.

"I saw you counting."

"No, way! This is a magic trick, it's all — "

"You counted the cards, Les, and mine was number eleven."

Pico gets down off his chair and silently collects all the cards scattered around the kitchen. I follow his lead and start to clear the table. "Well, now you know the trick at least."

Pico picks up the last card and hands me the deck, his face solemn. "Thanks, Les," he says. "I have to go home now."

And that's it. Pico abandons me in the kitchen. The front door wheezes open and a cool breeze floods into the kitchen, briefly, before the door slams closed. The house is silent. I look out through the kitchen window at the dining table sitting half refinished in the backyard. I head back there intending to do some work, but I can't figure out where to start. After hovering around the table for a while, I rearrange my tools, then head inside my cabin, and, leaving the light off, lie down on the bed. I look over at the fish, their aquarium glowing blue in the darkened room. Five seconds of memory. A lifetime composed of these five-second instalments, just flashes of existence, only to have them vanish, recede mercifully from you like an accident you'd drive by at night on a highway.

TWO WEEKS LATER, autumn is in full swing. Every morning I wake up to a backyard buried in leaves, which I dutifully clear away before starting my day's work. By the end of the after-noon the grass is already disappearing again, the lawn just green scraps under a patchy brown cover. I've finished the dining table with one last coat of mahogany stain; I'm keep-ing it under a tarp out back until I find a buyer. It looks about a hundred years older than it actually is.

Judy has convinced me to go to this thing with her this afternoon — that weird hippie couple intent on burying their baby's placenta. Judy, the deliverer of the baby, is the honorary guest. Last weekend we were down at the creek with the dogs and she told me all about it.

"I'd really like you to be there," Judy said. She sat down on an old mossy log and looked up at me. Nearby, the dogs were chasing each other through the trees, the patter of paws on fallen leaves fading as they ran farther and farther away.

"Who are these people?"

"Les, come on. You used to deal with parents like this all the time — you know, the kind that think they're bringing up their kids creatively but are just breeding weirdos? They're fun."

"Jude, I don't know."

"Think about it," she said.

When we got home I went right out into the backyard and sat down at the head of the dining table, the tarp ruffling in the wind. Judy stood at the kitchen window watching me. For a moment we locked eyes, and then she pulled away.

I'VE DECIDED TO wear a suit, a starchy navy thing I used to pull out for meetings or home visits back in my days of social work. In the cabin, I struggle to knot my tie, then head out to the front of the house to wait for my sister. A chill in the air hints at winter; the street is quiet, and still. The neighbours have their Halloween decorations up: front porches are framed with orange and black streamers, cardboard cutouts of witches and ghosts perch on lawns. Daylight is just starting to drain from the sky.

Some kid is weaving down the street on a bicycle, tracing these slow, arching parabolas from one curb to the other. The kid comes closer, closer — and then I recognize the bike, that retro frame, those tasselled handlebars, the banana seat. The pink jacket. And a gorilla mask.

"Hey!" I yell.

The kid slams on the brakes and looks over at me. The mask comes off, and underneath is the face of a girl. She's probably twelve, and Asian — maybe Vietnamese, maybe Cambodian.

"Hi," she says.

I walk over to her. My tie is choking me.

"Cool bike."

"It's from the centre," says the girl. "It's old. It's only a one-speed."

"The centre? You mean the Laughlin Centre?"

"It's the only bike they have."

"They got a bike."

"Yeah."

I point up to the sign in the window of Judy's house. "We're Block Parents, so if you ever get into any trouble . . ."

The girl is giving me a look that says, Can I go now?

I tell her to ride safe.

IN JUDY'S CAR we listen to one of her French-language tapes. She practises her verbs along with the voice on the tape while she drives.

"J'ai eu, tu as eu, il a eu, elle a eu," says Judy, and so forth. I sit staring out the window, playing absently with the power lock. "Try it, Les," Judy encourages me.

"J'ai! Eu!"

Judy grins. "Bravo, monsieur."

The woman on the tape continues to chatter away, but Judy seems to have lost interest. We pull up to a red light and sit idling while cars stream by in front of us. Out of nowhere, Judy does one of her snort-laughs. She covers her mouth with her hand, eyes twinkling.

"What's up?"

"I just remembered how when you were a kid, you used to tell Mom's friends that you could remember being born."

"What? Never."

"Yeah, always. You'd describe it to them and everything."

"Shut up." I'm laughing now too.

"Christ, Les. You were such an odd little guy."

We drive for a while in silence, then pull up in front of a grand old house, the front yard full of people. Judy cuts the engine and pats my knee. "Ready to bury some placenta?"

"Yep," I say, and we high-five.

Judy straightens her skirt. "Seriously, though — make me laugh and I'll kill you."

Not only am I the only guest wearing a suit, but there is a couple in matching muumuus and a woman with an owl perched on her shoulder. Music starts up, and everyone shuffles around until they've formed a delta with an open space in the middle. Judy and I retreat behind a tree. I look up through branches scrawling black and empty into the grey October sky.

The mother and father appear from somewhere, the mother carrying her newborn, the father toting a platter with what looks like a lump of meat heaped onto it. The placenta.

"Holy shit," I whisper, nudging my sister. "That thing's enormous."

Judy, the corners of her mouth twitching, does her best to ignore me.

The parents move into the empty space in the middle of everyone, where a sort of grave has been dug in the garden. Dirt lies heaped up around the hole in brown piles.

The mother steps forward and begins talking. I don't hear what she says. I am thinking, suddenly, of Pico, and considering what the three of us — me, Judy, and Pico — would look like together in this context. Maybe people would mistake us for a family. Sure: a father and mother, friends of the happy couple, and little Pico, who we might have brought on the way to his soccer game. We'd drive him there in our minivan, go sit with the other happy, proud parents along the sideline. Afterwards everyone would go out for ice cream; plans would be made for sleepovers and birthday parties and summer camps.

I look over at my sister and her expression has changed. She seems focused, solemn. There is applause, and Judy steps forward. She waves, then reaches back and, grabbing my hand, drags me up with her. The parents take turns embracing us. When the mother wraps her free arm around me, the baby, resting its head on her shoulder, regards me across her back: it's like we're sharing a secret.

The father lowers the platter into the hollow and hands Judy a small shovel. She casts me a quick glance over her shoulder, then steps forward and stabs the blade into the earth with a crisp, dry sound. Everyone is silent. Judy lifts a

shovelful of dirt and sprinkles it over the placenta, the patter-
ing sound of it landing below like the footsteps of a hundred
tiny feet.

WHEN THE CEREMONY is over, after the placenta is buried and
the last spade of earth patted down, we are all invited inside
for a reception. Judy seems to know everyone. She introduces
me to countless midwives and clients and former teachers, all
of them wanting to know what I do for a living. At one point, I
corner my sister and tell her I've had enough.

"Christ, I can't leave now," she whispers. "Can you stick it
out for another half-hour?"

"I'll walk — it's nice today."

She looks at me with this weird, sad smile. "Thanks for
coming, Les."

"Sure."

With that I leave my sister, I leave the party, I leave them
all behind and make my way outside. An earthy smell hangs
in the air and, beyond it, something cold and sharp and distant. On the front steps of the house, I survey the empty
front yard. A squirrel sits in the branches of one of the trees;
just as I notice it, the animal springs to life. It scrabbles
down the trunk, lunges, and lands silently on the grass. An
acorn appears from its mouth. The tiny paws claw at the
earth, then stuff the nut into the ground. The squirrel
straightens up. It turns, staring in my direction from two
black buttons in its face.

Something twitches inside me, and I have to grab the
railing to steady myself. I inhale, closing my eyes, and count

five seconds while my breath drains into the autumn dusk. When I open my eyes the squirrel has disappeared. The neighbourhood is silent, washed in dusty twilight. I let go of the railing and step down, one stair, then the next, and begin the walk home.

TIMBER ON THE WHEEL OF EVERYONE

AFTER HE EMERGED from the coma, when Timber explained to Janet his revelation that he and Lance Armstrong were polar opposites on the spectrum of humanity, he would pinpoint its genesis in a single moment: the front wheel of his bicycle smacking into the driver-side door of the navy blue coupe.

This had happened at the bottom of what Timber's son Neil and Neil's big weird friend from England, Rick, called Frog Hill. (Rick with the chapped lips that spread in a red clown mouth of flaking skin onto his face and who carried a cellphone, always; Frog Hill because in those sunny summer days post-chemo and pre-magpies Neil and Rick had found a frog in the woods and Rick had bullied Neil into launching it into the path of an oncoming truck, which had flattened the frog into a creamy green paste. Neil had come home for dinner and it had been two bites of spaghetti, a pause, a wave of guilt, and then vomit, everywhere, spraying and splashing like a fire hydrant in a film about Harlem.)

It went like this: Timber had been coasting down Frog Hill, all easy speed and carefree, no brakes, thinking of the successes of Operation Stoplight, thinking of Janet, whom he had not yet met but was sure he loved, thinking of The Neil

Kentridge X-Canada Tour for the Cure (the X denoting the word *cross* and nothing licentious) and thinking of these three very good things Timber spun his pedals backwards so something down there made that whizzing noise he enjoyed so much, and the pavement of Frog Hill zoomed by smooth and grey-black below, and gravity pulled him down, down, now at the bottom and the road starting to even out, flattening, and the sky above was a blue sheet slung arcing across the heavens — but then, wham! Here was a car door! With a crunch of metal the bike crumpled and so did he.

Timber lay panting, nuzzling the curb, no pain yet, vaguely aware that he was not dead. He could see the blurry shape of a head leaning gawking from the passenger-side window; equally blurry, the driver faltered half in and half out of her car. At that moment Timber's thoughts of Neil and Janet, of Operation Stoplight and X-Canada anything, and even his own life, still intact, were shattered by the image of Lance Armstrong, arms aloft as he crossed another finish line, champion, on the box of cereal that Neil enjoyed every morning.

When Timber thought of Lance Armstrong, Timber thought Hero. And when he considered himself, lying in the gutter, in relation to this Hero who had beaten cancer and won seven consecutive Tours de France, he thought Zero. He thought Fuck.

And then that final epiphany, materializing horrid and red like blood from a wound — like the blood that was now oozing through the torn knees of Timber's trousers, through the torn elbows of his shirt. All of humankind, Timber realized, existed on a spectrum, a wheel such as the one used to designate colours with opposites on either side: blue here and orange there, purple and yellow, red and green.

Here on the wheel was Mother Teresa, habit-clad and smiling and sickly thin and Good, and directly across from her sat a bristling, grumpy Hitler, Evil. And here was Evel Knievel and there was, what's his name, Super Dan? Mike? That guy, the one who always hurt himself: him. The Ex-Wife versus Janet. And on one side of the spectrum Timber saw Lance Armstrong, Hero, symbol of the triumph of the human spirit. And across from Lance Armstrong on this wheel, the Wheel of Everyone, Timber saw himself.

THAT MORNING, Timber had tried to ensure a normal routine. He and Neil sat at the kitchen table in Timber's rented duplex as they always did when Neil was in his father's custody. Timber slurped his chicory coffee substitute and grapefruit; Neil slurped his Tang and Lance Armstrong cereal drowned in 2%. It was Speech Day, and through breakfast Timber prompted Neil on his speech, which ended with the line, *And that's why Lance Armstrong is my hero.*

After only four run-throughs, Neil had it down. Timber reached across the table to proudly tousle his son's hair. It had grown back different after the chemo, curly and dark and fun to tousle — although Neil ducked away from his father's hand and chided him, Da-ad. Then Timber helped Neil don his ice-cream tub helmet for the wait outside for the school bus. Since starting the fifth grade, Neil preferred to do this alone: fine. Timber wanted to believe in the old adage about letting the loved bird out of the cage, free, or whatever, however it went, and so instead of joining his son at the foot of the drive-way, Timber watched from the den window.

In the trees the magpies were collecting, all glinting black eyes and fluttering wings. Neil stood below, oblivious — but safe in his ice-cream tub helmet, hopefully. The next day Neil had a track meet that Timber would miss, even though every weekend he had helped his son practise at the park: fetching and rolling back the softball, timing his laps around the soccer field, measuring his long jump in the sandbox, coaching and cheering him on through each event. But Timber recalled yelling, Batter up! when Neil had stepped to the start line for his 80-metre dash, and then realizing, Aw crap, he didn't know from sports, who was he kidding? And the way Neil faltered there at the other end of the field, he was likely thinking the same thing.

Watching his son wait for the bus, Timber tried to focus on The Neil Kentridge X-Canada Tour for the Cure, proof he could Just Do It as well as anyone. But then from nowhere, like a waft of sudden flatulence, the term *custody agreement* was upon him, and this conjured The Ex-Wife and The Ex-Wife's lawyer-slash-lover, Mr. Barry Parker, who together seemed negligent, did not appreciate the dangers facing young boys in town, especially young boys in remission — the magpies, for one, and also having reckless, cellphone-toting friends like British Rick. Who could a ten-year-old possibly need to call? But then the school bus arrived growling and took Neil away. It was time for Timber to head to work.

Timber's bicycle was the sort he imagined peasants riding in China: handlebars like the bow legs of a geriatric cowboy, horn wheezing with the tobacco-ravaged voice of the same cowboy's wife, three gears that sent the chain fumbling and clattering around each time they were adjusted, and a seat mounted on rusty springs that absorbed neither the shock from the road nor the weight of its cargo, Timber.

As he made his way down the driveway and out into the streets of the town, Timber thought proudly about how he was a *cyclist*, a word that to him conveyed something classy and nineteenth century and southern. Those other racy types who hogged the road in shorts of Lycra, aerodynamic helmets, gloves, pointed shoes clipped into pedals the size of tic tacs, Timber called *bikers*. The bikers' bikes were named Cliffjumper or Roadzilla and boasted hundreds of gears that slid digitally from one to the next. Instead of wheezy horns the bikers' bells chimed clear and true as ringtones; their seats were padded gel.

Mr. Barry Parker was a biker — a biker and a divorce lawyer and bonking The Ex-Wife. He had also replaced Neil's humble two-wheeler with a gleaming new twenty-one-speed featuring front and rear RockShox. Neil didn't even like mountain biking, Parker — what an idiot. But just as Timber thought this, in the pale light of the day's first sunshine as he emerged from his subdivision onto the major road through town, Barry Parker himself went rocketing by. Timber ducked his head.

If Neil were his son, thought Timber, would Mr. Barry Parker think of putting stickers on his ice-cream tub magpie helmet? Would he sand off the eyeholes for fear of sharp edges? Probably not. Instead Timber imagined Parker out in the garage oiling his hundreds of gears, waxing his frame, pumping his tires. And Neil would be alone, stabbing ragged holes into an ice-cream tub that the poor kid could barely see out of, and then retreating to the zillion-bit video-game system that his biker father had bought as a surrogate for love. Would Parker tell Neil stories of boyhood glory at bedtime? Would he ride his bike across the country for his cancer-survivor son? He wouldn't. Neil would feel neglected and sad.

Timber kept on, trundling round the bend at the strip mall with the office of Dr. Sloan, whose waiting room *Sports Illustrated* magazines had introduced Neil to Lance Armstrong in the first place. At the traffic lights the bikers were waiting as though they were the start line to a race. Parker balanced among them without putting his feet down, twisting his front wheel this way and that. They all knew one another, nodding, smiling and joking, admiring one another's bikerly accoutrements. Timber hung back, watching, hiding.

This was the point, waiting for the light to change, that Timber finally began to allow other thoughts to creep into consciousness. Operation Stoplight had begun six months ago, when Timber had been given a laptop, an email address (kittypuff@yahoo.ca), an identity (thirteen-year-old Tanya who loved emo but didn't like math), and an agenda: catch the sicko Ted Givens who was trolling emo chatrooms for young girls. They'd put him in touch via email with one of the other snares, a woman named Janet at sunshine_sara_xoxo@canada.com, whose assignment was similar. Timber and Janet were to discuss tactics and provide each other support when needed. And so their correspondence had begun.

But today was the day — for Tanya and Ted and Timber, at least. Janet was still working on Hassan Al-Taib, the sicko Sunshine Sara was trying to snare. Today Ted Givens thought he was meeting Tanya at four (after school) at the Mr. Submarine at the River Heights Shopping Centre. But instead of Tanya, Ted would meet a squad of police officers in riot gear hiding in the food-court bathrooms.

What did Timber feel? Pride? Janet had sent him an e-card proclaiming MY HERO!!! and then some JavaScript fireworks. He had replied that only when they had the sicko behind bars would there be occasion to celebrate. Oh, but Janet wasn't hearing it. He had done amazing work and was making the world a better place for everyone. She was so nice!

Of course it was Janet who had coached Timber through his messages about how *retarded* it was to have so much geography homework when geography was just colouring in maps, and how the seventh grade had been *waaaaaay easier*, or what colour panties he was wearing, or how, yeah, he believed that ted.givens@xxx.com did indeed have splendid genitalia. It had been tough, for sure. But Janet was a peach, a real peach.

Janet didn't know that Timber was into Barely Legals. Which was fine. Eighteen was fine. The law said so. But, still. There were times when Timber was enjoying the Barely Legals web site when he thought of Janet, and then he began to question if the girls were indeed eighteen as the site suggested. Any younger than eighteen and he'd be no better than Ted Givens. Some of them looked so young though. They were so pretty but so young. And then Timber would slam his laptop shut in a sweat and have to tuck his woody into his waistband and go outside for a walk.

Timber watched the crosswalk sign change from man to flashing hand.

When Timber had told Janet, in their first non-business-related email, that he was struggling to cook meals for Neil, she had sent him recipes for spaghetti sauce and meatloaf. The meatloaf had seemed complicated, but the spaghetti sauce, until Neil had vomited it everywhere, was exquisite. Then there were her messages, sometimes two or three a day: funny, caring, sad, conflicted. Timber and Janet began to share what they were telling their respective sickos, the humiliating, disgusting things. But it was okay. It was for a good cause, maybe the best cause of all. Nothing they told the sickos was real.

Over Instant Messenger Timber told Janet everything — about his work, about his son, about his life. And Janet did the same: she was divorced too, but with no kids. She had a dog named Barney and joked about her weight, although Timber hated that. *Who cares?* he wrote. Also Janet liked reading and Frisbee.

Timber was supportive, and Janet was supportive, and it was really great. Meanwhile, the Barely Legals were bookmarked on Timber's browser and at 5:01 p.m., right after signing off with Janet, he'd hit the page for the daily update. His favourite Barely Legals were Grace and Sari. Once Grace and Sari had done a shoot together and Timber had for a while archived the images in a folder on his computer named Taxes 2003, and then one day panicked and deleted them and obliterated any trace of anything and stayed off the site entirely for five whole days.

After six months, Timber had got to know Ted Givens nearly as well as Janet, almost felt sorry for him, certainly felt sorry for his wife, his two teenaged sons, his ailing, rheumatic mother. Jail would not be kind to a man with designs on bonking a thirteen-year-old, real or not. Jail might even, as retribution, do some bonking of Ted Givens of its own.

But Ted Givens was a sicko, and Timber was doing the right thing, he knew — a heroic thing, according to Janet, a thing of glory. Still, it remained a silent, secret sort of glory; even when Ted Givens would be revealed by the press, cowering under a hoisted suit jacket on his way to trial, the man who had unearthed this scurrilous creature, mastermind Timber B. Kentridge, would remain anonymous. No one would ever know about him, or Janet, or any of the other snares of Operation Stoplight scattered around the province; little would be made of their tireless crusade of e-deception for the greater good. Besides, would he want people knowing about the things he had written as a thirteen-year-old girl to seduce Ted Givens? And what if his own appetites were somehow leaked, despite how many times he cleared his Internet history and deleted every cookie in sight. He couldn't imagine Neil finding out about all that flesh and fluid. Or Janet.

But look, the light was green and the cars were moving and the bikers were off like shrapnel. Timber eased off the curb and, wobbling slightly, made his way forward. He was halfway to work. The morning sun shone down palely from above. A few magpies went flapping across the sky.

What would Neil be doing, right now, at school? Acing a test. Or gazing out the window of his classroom and thinking suddenly and for reasons beyond him, cosmic reasons, of his dad. Timber figured he would call Neil from wherever he ended up the following evening, the first stop on the Tour for the Cure — Quebec, maybe, if he could make it that far — and surprise him. Neil would get off the phone and tell his mother, Dad's biking across the country! And The Ex-Wife, in the den of Barry Parker's yuppie condominium, everything mono-chrome and sterile, would look at Neil radiating pride and affection, and all The Ex-Wife could say would be, Wow. Lost in this fantasy, Timber went pedalling through a yellow light, and a car turning left had to swerve not to hit him. Timber waved: Wopes!

Safely on the other side of the intersection, Timber thought again of Janet, shut away in an office just like his, alone at her computer. Even before knowing about the Tour for the Cure, before Timber had sent her a PDF downloaded from MapQuest with his route plotted out and a spreadsheet of potential sponsors, she had commended him as *a real hero* — but Janet threw that word around a tad too liberally. She said that the snares of Operation Stoplight were all heroes. He wanted to believe her. They were in this together, this business of busting sickos, and also maybe Timber was in love with Janet a little bit.

Was Timber a coward? He had been a single man for only eight months. Dating so early would be a mistake, said the advice column in the local paper, "Ask a Woman," which The Ex-Wife herself penned and had been the reason they'd met in the first place, ten years prior, after Timber had emailed her asking why no one dates good guys any more and she had — perhaps rather unprofessionally, in hindsight — written back to suggest *going for coffee,* claiming to be tired of dating bad boys and wanting to settle down. Coffee!

Timber had not been able to drink coffee since the divorce, but he *had* emailed "Ask a Woman" from a phony address, and "Ask a Woman" had published the letter with the suggestion of waiting a bit longer before jumping back into the throes of courtship. But hadn't The Ex-Wife moved on even more quickly, bonking Mr. Barry Parker while still married? Her moving on had been pre-emptive. If computers could reduce everything to zeros and ones, why wasn't life so easy? Zero, zero, one, zero, one, one: plug something in, get something out, an answer, simple. Timber slowed at a Stop sign, sat there contemplating this while a pickup went by in front of him, the goateed driver inexplicably giving him the finger.

Well, thought Timber as he pushed off, maybe when he came back, victorious, he could track Janet down — like, physically. He'd find her IP address somehow and locate her with a blip on a GPS that meant: Janet. He would go to where the blip was and fling the door to her office open and announce, I'm back! Oh, god, she would say and she would be beautiful, not too thin, healthy, with her T-shirt bulging slightly where her bra strap carved a channel through the skin of her back, and she would tell him, I've been watching you on TV. Timber would shrug: It was nothing for a father who loved his son. Janet would say, Now everyone knows what a hero you are, and Timber would shrug again. They would lock eyes and Timber would take Janet in his arms and hold her close: Hello, Janet, at last. Or, better: Move into my duplex with me, Janet, let's make a life together, I love you.

Or maybe he could just call her sometime. Either way.

Regardless, here Timber felt a longing to be — what? Someone else. Someone who shone beyond the Internet, in the real world. Who was that famous hero-slash-romantic, that Spaniard? Don Quixote? Yes, no, but Don Quixote was someone else entirely, wasn't he, and goddammit wasn't Timber always getting these things wrong, people, history, facts, idioms, things that every other human being in the universe seemed to know innately and which time and time again caused him to hang his head in shame. Timber pedalled faster, harder, pumping his legs and whizzing through the rush-hour streets at a speed that seemed breakneck.

He should have called her before, sometime — Janet. There had been a chance once, when she had hinted at wanting to hear his voice and messenged him her cell number. But Timber said maybe that wasn't such a good idea. Something about professionalism or something. Oh, but wasn't that just his way, Timber thought as he signalled and made the turnoff toward Frog Hill, tiptoeing through life. When Neil had been sick The Ex-Wife had remained a pillar of strength, rational, while Timber trembled and wept nightly in the kitchen, collected Neil's hair in Ziplocs as it fell out in clumps around the house.

Ahead loomed Frog Hill, steep. By now Timber's legs were pumping, the wheels turned, the bike creaked and rattled, the sky was blue, the sun shone down. He wasn't pedalling: he was stomping his feet. Starting tomorrow, he was going to ride his bike across the country. TV stations would get word of his plan and follow him along and at the end of every day they'd ask, Wow, how do you keep going? and Timber would look right into the camera, imagine all those people at home waiting for him to give their lives meaning or direction or something, anything — and Neil, held captive in the condominium of Mr. Barry Parker, his curly little head silhouetted against the glow of Parker's hi-def TV, knowing that his dad was looking at *him*, that this was all for *him* — and Timber would shake his head slowly. Keep going? he would scoff and tell the world about Neil, about what a trooper his son had been, how he was the real hero. Not Timber. Timber was just doing what any good, loving dad would do.

As he crested the hill Timber wanted Neil to know that everything was for him: the magpie helmet, the cycling, the purging of sickos, maybe bringing lovely, sweet, smart, generous and voluptuous Janet into the family but not as a replacement mother, regardless of how vastly superior she was to the original in every way. Even so, Janet would be good about it. She would be like a nice aunt whom Neil would grow to love and she and Timber would only bonk when Neil was at his mom's — kids don't need to hear that — and their bonking would be tender and soft and Janet would be kind even if Timber sploodged early on her tummy. And he'd never look at Barely Legals again.

There had been nothing Timber could do while Neil shuttled bravely in and out of the hospital; he could only watch as every week the doctors pumped his son full of chemicals to burn away the black dregs of cancer in his body. But that was then! Here he was sailing down Frog Hill with the breeze blasting his face, hair rippling, on his way to what he knew would be one last, final question typed and sent to Ted Givens, a question that suddenly struck him as delightfully ironic after the number of times he had answered it himself: *What are you wearing today?* And then he would forward this information to the office of Operation Stoplight, who would inform their squad to look out for a middle-aged man in a black turtleneck and Dockers, or whatever, and when the fellow came sauntering into the Mr. Submarine they would nab him, pin him down at gunpoint, and just like that the world would be a better place.

And tomorrow! Tomorrow would be the beginning of something special — a man and his bicycle, nothing flashy, just pure love and honour and dedication. Timber would even wear a Lance Armstrong bracelet. The Neil Kentridge X-Canada Tour for the Cure, Operation Stoplight, Janet, they all became a harmonized hum in his brain, and thinking of these three very good things Timber spun his pedals backwards so something down there made that whizzing noise he enjoyed so much, and the pavement of Frog Hill zoomed by smooth and grey-black below, and gravity pulled him down, down, now at the bottom and the road starting to even out, flattening, and the sky above was a blue sheet slung arcing across the heavens.

TIMBER WAS AWARE of a woman upon him, blubbering, with a run in her support hose. Another pair of legs stuffed into high-tops came shuffling into view, and from above them came a voice Timber recognized, a boy's British accent thick with phlegm: Cor, that's Neil's dad. The woman knelt down, reaching out but not quite touching Timber, hesitant, as though he might scald or infect her on contact.

Are you, she managed, all right?

The boy was mumbling something else now, something about Frog Hill, something about Timber being just like the frog and the coupe just like the truck, and now he was fumbling with a cellphone, flipping it open, the burble of it coming to life.

The woman stood, smoothed her skirt, looked anxiously up and down the empty street. Timber closed his eyes. What was he supposed to be doing? There was a task, today, right now, that he was neglecting. He tried to think of what it was, what he could ask or tell these people, but only the most banal question seemed to come to mind. He thought he'd try it anyway, and whispered, What are you wearing?

The woman looked down sharply at him.

Was this right? He couldn't think of anything else, so he willed his eyelids open and repeated, slowly, What. Are. You. Wear. Ing.

What are you wearing, Mum. He wants to know. Go on, tell him.

What am I wearing? the boy's mother repeated, her gaze tracing down over her power suit, noticing for the first time the run in her nylons, then down to the man splayed across the pavement, one leg at a funny angle, and bleeding.

Timber whispered it again, What are you wearing?

Almost before it was out, the woman was backing away and hissed, Get in the car, at her son, and she gave him a shove and there was a quick tapping of footsteps and doors slamming and Timber waited for the revving of an engine and a car speeding away. But it never came. He looked up and there in the front seat sat Rick on his cellphone and his mom had her head in her hands. Was she weeping? Why?

Timber's body felt strange and cold, and here was the pain, coming in surges from his toes to the tips of his fingers. Everything throbbed in time with his pulse. He closed his eyes and here appeared Lance Armstrong. And here also was Neil, standing between his hero and his father, a great wheel around them. The boy gazed back and forth between the two men.

Timber wanted to say, Come this way, son, but when he opened his mouth to speak nothing came out; he felt like a fish wordlessly blubbing away as it bobbed about its tank. Lance Armstrong stood beaming. Neil looked confused. But then Timber realized that it wasn't a wheel at all, but a web, and Lance Armstrong held the opposite end of the same flimsy strand of silken line as Timber, and Neil balanced precariously in the middle, tightrope-style, and they were working together to keep the boy from falling.

And it wasn't just Lance Armstrong either — all around the web people materialized, holding on, keeping Neil up: The Ex-Wife held a piece, eyes fierce; dressed in his scrubs, there was Dr. Sloan, clutching on as though for dear life; Mr. Barry Parker was lending a hand, steadying his thread in two hands, looking resolute and focused. Grace and Sari were there too, fully clothed. Even Ted Givens stood nearby, doing his best despite himself.

From somewhere in the real world came a sound of birds cawing, twittering, and the swoosh of flapping wings, and suddenly beneath the web in Timber's mind's eye sprung up a thick, dark forest of towering trees, and in the branches of these trees were magpies, stretching their wings, roosting.

Lance Armstrong looked frightened! Lance Armstrong didn't know what to do; he looked as though he might drop his side of the web and send Neil plummeting into the woods and the waiting magpies. This was Timber's moment, and Timber had helmets, ice-cream tubs, with holes cut for eyes. He held out a tub to Neil, while the magpies began to emerge from the woods, rising like a handful of soot flung up from the treetops below.

In the real world Timber thought he heard a siren, the far-away scream of it, maybe coming closer. But he willed the real world away, and Janet was with them now, Janet with a tub of pralines 'n' cream on her head beside him. Neil was moving across the web, reaching for his own tub decorated with stickers of all sorts, gleaming, and Janet's body was warm and soft, a breast against Timber's arm, and Lance Armstrong and everyone else were fading, fading, while the magpies circled up squawking all around them.

Everyone was gone then. There they were: Timber, Janet, and Neil. They huddled together in their helmets. Through the eyeholes everything looked black. The magpies were wing to wing, moving in. No light shone through. Timber held Janet close and Janet held Neil close and with their bodies clinging to one another Timber felt deep within all that suffocating fear a little flicker of something. Maybe they would be all right. Timber wrapped his arms around Janet and Neil, drawing them in, their helmets knocking together.

Looking out, it seemed as though the magpies ceased to close in. Everywhere was still black, but Timber felt more like he was standing in a room suddenly plunged into darkness, with the walls of the room at once disappearing and seemingly speeding outwards, and with it the room, yes, the room became as endless and infinite and terrifying and wonderful as the universe.

RESPITE

ON SATURDAY evenings the writer named Womack takes a break from his novel and looks after the boy. He goes to the boy's house in the suburbs, far from where Womack lives among the other writers and artists in the city. It is winter and he rides out to the suburbs on his bicycle, wheels up slickly in the slush on the street and chains his bicycle to the fence that pens in the yard, then comes into the house, shivering and wet.

The boy is twelve, and dying of a degenerative illness. He can no longer see, hear, walk, or speak, although there are times when he laughs. This laugh is a cackle, a shriek. If Womack were to describe the laugh in his novel it would become *a sudden bolt of blue lightning over an empty, black sea.* Womack is a writer of prose, but fancies himself something of a poet also. Womack has studied writing in university and wants his novel to be something new, something fresh and free of cliché; these days he hears clichés even in speech and cringes.

Saturdays are the same, almost without variation: Womack arrives and the boy's mother, Sylvia, is waiting in the den, standing over her son in his wheelchair. She offers thanks and passes the boy off to Womack and disappears into her bedroom, and Womack then hoists the boy out of his wheelchair and props him up against his body and carries him around the house, and the boy moans. The boy moans and moves his legs as if he were walking, but he is not; the boy's legs hang limply from his body, dragging on the floor. Like this Womack manoeuvres the boy, slowly, step, step, step, from room to room around the house.

THE WRITER Womack used to live with a woman named Adriane whom he had that autumn begun to introduce to people as his partner, as though they were business associates or cops. The word arrived into his vocabulary at a party that was both Halloween party and stag-and-doe party for friends of Womack's, friends named Mike and Cheryl who would be married a week before Christmas. In the hallway, Womack's arm draped over Adriane's shoulder, a woman dressed as Fidel Castro introduced another woman, also dressed as Fidel Castro, as her partner, and Womack repeated the word in reference to Adriane. At this, like a child escaping the embrace of a foul-breathed and bearded aunt, Adriane slid out from underneath his arm, nodded at the Castros, and sipped her drink. Later, she confronted him in the kitchen.

Partner? she asked. The kimono of her geisha outfit shimmered and swished.

Sure, Womack told her. His costume was Hockey Player: helmet, gloves, stick. That's what people say now, he said.

Straight people?

Sure.

For the rest of the evening, Adriane adopted a Texan accent when addressing Womack — Yee-haw! Fetch me another drink, pardner! Even so, the new label made Womack feel modern and serious. Gone was the term girlfriend, used for those who had filled that role since his early teens. Now he had a partner. This was heavy stuff.

At midnight Womack and Adriane came home to the place that they had moved into together that July, their place that was not quite loft and not quite studio, their place where a wall divided two long, high-ceilinged rooms in defiance of architectural categorization. You entered the apartment to a kitchen and dining space; through an arched doorway was a living area with a couch and a stereo and the desk with the computer where Womack wrote his novel. At the back of the room, behind drawn curtains, sat their bed. This area they called the bedroom, even though it was not technically a room at all.

Adriane, who worked the next day, went straight to bed. Womack ditched the helmet, gloves, and stick in a closet, sat down at his desk in his uncomfortable chair, turned on his computer, and began typing. The uncomfortable chair had wheels and the floor was warped, slightly. At one point, when Womack's typing relented and he let go of the keyboard, the desk released him gliding into the room until he stopped with a bump against the window on the far wall.

Sitting there under the window, the computer glowing across the room, he could hear Adriane's breathing from behind the curtains. This is what their weekdays had become: dinner or the occasional outing, Adriane falling asleep hours before him, then up early the next morning and off to the counselling centre. Womack would sleep until noon, get up, drink too much coffee, and eventually make it to the computer, to his novel.

In the summer, when they had moved in together, they had bought tropical houseplants and named them: Hangy, the bushy one dangling from the ceiling above the dining table; Jules Fern, whose leafy tendrils spread out over the couch; and, guarding the bedroom, sombre and violet: Jacques Laplante. Back then, Adriane would arrive home and it would be sex, first thing, almost before she was even in the door. Her clothes would come off and so would Womack's and they would romp for a while on the bed, if they made it that far, and afterwards have a nice meal wearing only housecoats and slippers. Then there might be more sex and snacks made in the toaster oven, gobbled dripping cheese over the sink, and finally, clinging to each other in bed: Goodnight Adriane, I love you, and, Goodnight Womack, me too, and Adriane would go in bleary-eyed to work the next morning.

Now this, every night: Womack wide awake at his computer and Adriane asleep behind the curtains. This was the life of couples, he assumed, of partners — functional, pragmatic, a pattern established and repeated with someone who found it mutually tolerable. Womack thought of his parents, marching together through their marriage like soldiers in a military parade. Partners. Life.

But Womack was writing a novel, and he was doing good work. He had written more than one hundred pages. The words were coming. Sentences spilled into paragraphs spilled into chapters, while on the periphery Adriane came in and out of the apartment like the mechanical bird in a windup clock.

AT THE HOUSE where Womack volunteers, there are two other children, the boy's sister and brother: Jessica and Andrew. They are younger, nine and six, and often play The Game of Life on the den floor while Womack carries their dying older brother around nearby. Womack and the boy step over the two children and their board game, which it seems only Jessica understands and wins convincingly every time, and Womack says, Excuse us, and watches as Jessica takes advantage of the distraction to steal three five-hundred-dollar bills and a husband from the box. Nice characterization, notes Womack.

ONE COLD EVENING a week into November, Adriane came home from yoga class, which she had recently taken up and went to twice a week straight from work. Womack was at the stove, making dinner. Outside, the first snow of the season came sifting down like wet flour from the clouds. It lit briefly on the streets before melting into the grey puddle that soaked the city.

Adriane hung her coat and came into the kitchen. Through the doorway to the other room drifted the sound of the stereo in the next room, playing music. Ah, there's a good Womack, she said, nodding. My little housewife. Her face was pink; icy droplets had collected in her hair and eyelashes.

Womack laughed, stirring a creamy sauce. How were The Youth today?

The Youth were troubled, said Adriane. She pulled the Dictaphone she used for interviews from her pocket, placed it on the kitchen table.

Any good stories?

Adriane snorted, shaking her head. This again, she said.

Oh, come on, said Womack. Who am I going to tell?

Adriane started rifling through the stack of mail on the dining table. Hangy drooped down from above, lush and green. What did you do all day?

What do you think?

She fingered Hangy's foliage. Did you water the plants?

I watered them like a week ago. They're fine.

And the RSVP to Mike and Cheryl about the wedding?

Oh, come on, Ade. They know we're coming.

She held up an envelope. How about the phone bill?

Oh, shoot. Womack stopped stirring.

Adriane looked up. You're kidding, right?

I got busy.

Busy doing what? You were home all day!

Home, working. The spoon stood erect in the coagulating sauce. It's not like I'm just sitting around picking my ass.

I guess if you ever called anyone, you'd probably care if the phone got disconnected.

Was this a fight? wondered Womack. Were they fighting?

Adriane looked at him, the look of an executive evaluating an employee at a time of cutbacks and layoffs. Womack wore the cut-off sweatpants and T-shirt he had gone to bed in the night before. Adriane reached out and pocketed the

Dictaphone, then spoke before he could: When was the last time you went outside?

Two nights ago. I picked up sushi, remember?

During the day. For more than errands.

Ade, this is what I do. I'm writing a book.

A novel, she corrected him, smirking.

You go to work with The Youth, I work at home. Okay?

Adriane said nothing. Womack returned to his sauce, which had developed a rubbery skin he now began to churn back in. After a minute, Adriane stood, moved to the front door, and put on her coat.

Where are you going? asked Womack.

To the ATM, said Adriane. She held up the envelope. To pay the phone bill.

WHAT THE BOY likes is doors. He and Womack stop in front of a closed door in the house, a bedroom or a closet, and the boy takes Womack's hand in his and places it on the doorknob, and Womack opens the door and the boy laughs. When Womack closes the door the boy moans and takes Womack's hand again and places it on the doorknob, and this continues until the boy becomes restless, and then they move to a new door in the house. Womack watches the boy delight in the doors and thinks to himself, I should be able to use this as a metaphor for something.

A FEW DAYS later, Adriane came home from yoga and Womack was wearing a shirt and tie. Dinner was on the table: meatloaf and green beans and rice. She disappeared into the den, turned off the music that was playing, then re-emerged in the kitchen.

What's the occasion? asked Adriane. You look like a dad.

No occasion, said Womack. But thank you.

They sat and ate.

How was yoga? he asked.

Good. You should come some time.

Ha! Womack nearly choked on a green bean. Yoga! God, like one of those New Age creeps in a unitard and a ponytail, some white guy named Starfire or Ravi. No thanks.

Adriane looked at him, opened her mouth to say something, but seemed to reconsider and instead filled it with meatloaf.

I've been thinking, said Womack, chewing.

Oh yeah?

Yeah. I've been thinking about maybe volunteering somewhere. You know, getting out and doing something, getting involved. In the community. With people.

Adriane took a sip of water, put the glass back down, waited.

Maybe something with kids, Womack said.

That's a great idea, said Adriane. Womack detected something in her voice, though: hesitancy, maybe. Doubt?

After dinner, Adriane washed the dishes while Womack retreated to his computer. He took off his tie and typed and deleted and typed some more. Adriane did paperwork at the dining table, the murmur of voices playing from the Dictaphone as she made her transcriptions. Eventually she came into the den, rubbing her eyes, tape recorder in hand.

I'm pooped, she told Womack. Stood there while he stared at the computer screen.

He looked up. Sure, he said. I'm just going to finish this bit, okay?

Adriane turned and disappeared between the curtains. Womack could hear the whisper of clothes coming off and pajamas going on. And then the bedroom light clicking off and the bedside lamp clicking on. He typed these two sentences into his computer.

I'll come kiss you goodnight, Womack called, cutting and pasting the pajama line into another section of his novel. Let me know when you're in bed.

Another click, extinguishing the glow of the bedside lamp. The rustle of sheets. A pillow being fluffed. Silence.

Womack read the section over, then pushed away from the desk on his wheelie chair. Behind the curtains, Adriane lay in bed with her back to him, facing the wall. Womack slid under the covers and put a hand on her back. He felt a tremor in her body. She was masturbating.

Mind if I join you? asked Womack.

Suit yourself, said Adriane, her hand at work between her legs.

Womack reached into his pants and began to coax himself into arousal. Beside him, Adriane's breath came in gasps. After a few minutes, just as Womack was growing hard, she went limp.

Did you finish? he asked.

I'm tired, she said.

Oh.

Outside the snow had become the hiss of light rain.

Okay, said Womack. Sure. Well, goodnight. He leaned in and planted a kiss on the back of Adriane's head. She tensed, slightly.

Everything all right? he asked.

I'm tired, Womack.

Womack lay there, propped up on one elbow, staring at Adriane's back. Eventually, he got up, ducked between the curtains, and sat back down at his computer. He typed *volunteering* into an Internet search and, with a licorice-scented marker and a stack of Post-It notes, began taking stock of his options.

AFTER AN HOUR or so of Womack carrying the boy around the house, it is time for the boy's supper. This supper is puréed and usually cauliflower. Sylvia emerges from the bedroom looking half asleep, heats up the boy's supper in the microwave, and gives it to Womack to feed to her son. At this time she also gets out some leftovers from the week and heats them on the stove for herself and Jessica and Andrew. When everything is ready, everyone sits down at the table: mother and two children at one end, Womack and the boy at the other.

A WEEK AFTER submitting his online application, Womack was registered with The Fountain Group, an organization that paired its volunteers with families in need of respite care. The family assigned to Womack was named Dunn; their address was included, and a telephone number if Womack wished to call and introduce himself before he visited their home. He did not.

His first Saturday, Womack woke up early. Adriane was sleeping in; it was her day off. Although Womack was not scheduled to be out at the family's home until four that afternoon, he paced around the apartment, wondering what to wear, eating breakfast, then brunch, then a giant toasted sandwich at a few minutes past noon. He felt nauseous and bloated. It was the first day he had not turned his computer on in months.

From Womack's apartment to the Dunns' house took just under a half-hour by bicycle. He rode along the major avenues and boulevards of the city that narrowed into the thin, tree-lined streets of the suburbs. The trees were leafless. The streets were black with melted snow. Womack pulled up to a squat bungalow with a cracked driveway and a lawn littered with children's toys: Tonka trucks and hula hoops and a few upended sand pails. This was the place.

Inside, Womack met first Sylvia, then Jessica and Andrew, who both stared for a moment at Womack's outstretched hand before bounding off giggling down the hallway — and then, finally, sitting in the kitchen in his wheelchair and moaning, the boy. Womack approached him as one might a lion escaped from its cage: at a crouch, whispering. Sylvia stood behind the chair and secured the boy's head in an upright position. Saliva dribbled from the corner of his mouth, strung to his shoulder in gooey threads. The boy's eyes were milky and gazed blankly in the direction of, but not at, Womack.

Hello, whispered Womack.

The boy moaned.

He likes to have his face touched, said the boy's mother. She cupped his ears, demonstrating. The boy laughed, a sudden burst like the crack of a cannon. Womack jumped. He composed himself, squatted beside the boy in his wheelchair, and, looking up at the mother, replaced her hands with his own. The boy shook his head free and moaned. Womack stood.

He just needs to get to know you, explained Sylvia.

The rest of the evening Womack spent at a distance observing the boy's routine: Sylvia fed her son, bathed him, eventually put him to bed. He admired her ease with the boy, the mechanical, almost instinctive acts of jeans being pulled off and a diaper being folded on, pajamas, and then the tenderness of her leaning over and stroking his face while he lay in bed and Womack stood in the doorway, dimming the lights. Motherhood, noted Womack. In the front hall, handing Womack his coat, she told him the following week he would be on his own, and did he feel comfortable doing it all himself?

Womack said, Sure, nodding a bit too vigorously.

When Womack got home, Adriane sat at the kitchen table before an offering of Styrofoam tubs. The Dictaphone sat nearby atop a pile of manila folders. She was reading a book —a travel guide: *Southeast Asia on a Shoestring*.

Planning a trip? Womack asked, taking his place at the table.

I wish. Adriane stood and began peeling lids off containers, revealing noodles, barbecue pork, and cashew chicken. Sitting back down, she added, I mean, I wish I could afford it.

Sure.

Anyway, I ordered Chinese. She gestured at the food. I didn't feel like cooking.

Fair enough, said Womack. He pulled apart a pair of chopsticks. Looks good.

While they ate, Womack detailed his afternoon spent with the boy. Adriane responded with single words muffled by mouthfuls of food: Yeah? Really? Uh-huh.

He's more . . . he's sicker than I thought he would be. Like, he can't really do anything for himself. It'll be me doing pretty much everything — feeding him, giving him a bath, changing his diaper.

Adriane looked up. Like his mother does every day?

Oh, she's amazing. Can you imagine? You should see her with him.

Womack didn't know what else to say. What were the words for this? He could only think of clichés — *the power of the human spirit*, stuff like that. Adriane went back to her meal, chopsticks gathering, plucking. They ate silently, methodically, and when the Styrofoam containers had been emptied, Womack put down his chopsticks and looked across the table at Adriane, this woman he had lived with for five months, his partner. She was leaning over the last few scraps of chow mein, eyes on her travel guide.

So, he said, crumpling the empty food containers one by one under his palm, like a tough guy with beer cans. Southeast Asia.

Yep, she said.

Sounds fun.

Adriane speared a piece of pork with her chopstick, lifted it up, bit down, and sucked the meat into her mouth. Something to read, she said.

Just something to read?

Sure. She rolled her eyes. God, listen to me — *sure* — I'm starting to even talk the same as you.

Womack ignored this. Well, why not the newspaper? Why not a book? I've got lots of books. He could hear the crescendo of his own voice. You want to borrow a book?

A *novel*?

Womack paused. When he spoke, his tone was quiet, low, but something uneasy rippled through his voice: What, exactly, is that supposed to mean?

Oh, you know, big writer. You and your *novel*. She slurped a noodle into her mouth. It whacked against her cheek on the way in, leaving a brown stripe across her face. Am I in there? Is there a bitchy girlfriend character? Is she always nagging the hero to take out the garbage and pay the bills?

Since when do you care about my writing? said Womack, aware, immediately, of his own earnestness.

Adriane stared at him, chewing. The saucy stripe lay like a wound across her cheek. *Since when do you care about my writing?* she mimicked, standing, carrying her plate behind the kitchen counter, where she slid it among the dirty dishes piled in the sink. This is my day off, she told him. I have to deal with bull-shit all week. I want to have my weekends to relax, not get into these stupid arguments about nothing.

Womack looked away. On the table before him, splayed open to a page titled "When to Go," sat the travel guide.

Womack imagined Adriane surfing on a ratty shoelace along the river from *Apocalypse Now*, heads on spikes lining the shores, bullets whizzing through the air. All around, crumpled Styrofoam tubs sat like ruined sandcastles. Womack placed his hands over his ears, tightly. There was a dull echo inside his skull: the empty, hollow rumble of a stalled train.

FEEDING THE BOY is easy; he eats mechanically, unquestioningly. Womack sits the boy in his wheelchair and scoops spoonfuls of puréed food into the boy's mouth, and the boy swallows. At the opposite end of the table sit the boy's mother and brother and sister with their plates of leftovers, but they are in a different world, apart. While Womack feeds the boy, Andrew shovels mashed potatoes and corn at his face, spilling most of it on the floor; Jessica eats demurely, telling stories about which boys at school she dislikes this week; Sylvia takes it all in, nodding, smiling, pushing her food around, hardly eating. Womack feels invisible, as if he were watching their meal through a two-way mirror — collecting evidence for a trial, a detective, or a spy.

IN THE MIDDLE of December, Womack surprised Adriane with dinner reservations at a Vietnamese restaurant. Adriane smiled at this. Encouraged, Womack kissed her on the cheek and took her hand in his as they walked down the street.

At the restaurant, a woman in a Santa hat seated them at a table for two and handed over menus they struggled to read in the dim light. Womack, squinting, made a few suggestions — What about number twenty-three? Or sixteen, the shrimp?

— before the waitress arrived and Adriane ordered a bowl of soup.

Soup? said Womack. He looked apologetically to the waitress. Why don't we share a couple things?

I'm not that hungry, said Adriane. She gazed around the restaurant, up at the walls decorated with posters and maps of Vietnam, at the shelves of ornaments by the door. A few booths over, a couple were drinking with their arms entwined.

Womack decided on the shrimp dish for himself, plus a half-litre of house wine for the two of them, to share.

The waitress left, smiling. Womack looked at Adriane, then over at the romancing couple, then back at her. He rolled his eyes.

What's wrong with that? she asked.

Nothing, said Womack. Just a little cheesy.

They were silent until the food and wine arrived, and even then, their meal was only punctuated by Womack asking, How's your soup? to which Adriane responded, Good, how's your shrimp? to which Womack responded, Good, and then Adriane slurped her soup and Womack chewed his shrimp, which were not good at all but overcooked and rubbery, and when the meal was over Adriane put it on her Visa and they left the restaurant and walked home, Womack behind Adriane, single file.

Back in the apartment Adriane went directly to bed, and Womack, tipsy from all the wine he'd drunk alone, sat at his desk with the computer monitor off, staring at the blank screen.

WHEN HE IS full, the boy moans. Womack excuses himself from the table with the boy's dishes, rinses them in the sink, stacks them in the dishwasher, and then wheels the boy into his bedroom. Womack sits on the bed and tells the boy, You need to digest your food. The boy moans and rocks slightly in his wheelchair. Womack looks out the window of the boy's room, at the sun setting or the children's swing set in the backyard, and thinks about the novel he is writing. He has wanted for some time for this boy to become a character — someone tragic, his novel lacks pathos — but how to write about a dying child without resorting to sentimentality, to cliché?

THAT THURSDAY, two days before Mike and Cheryl's wedding, Adriane announced to Womack that she would only be able to make it to the reception.

There's this Hot Yoga class starting on Saturday afternoons, she told him over a dinner of fish sticks and peas. If I don't go to the first one, they won't let me sign up.

Hot Yoga? said Womack, stabbing at a single pea with his fork. Ade, these are two of my best friends.

Really? When was the last time you talked to them? Halloween?

Whoa, said Womack. The pea rolled away; he put down his fork.

I'll be there for the reception — that's what matters. They won't even notice me missing at the ceremony. And you know how I feel about church and religion and all that.

I've cancelled volunteering for the day, Ade. You don't

think you could just do your Hot Yoga some other time? He looked at her. What the fuck is Hot Yoga, anyway?

Sorry, she said, and reached across the table, unexpectedly, to squeeze Womack's hand. He felt something like warmth at this contact and hated himself for that.

At the wedding ceremony Womack sat at the end of a pew in the back of the church, the space beside him conspicuously empty. When Cheryl came up the aisle he turned with everyone else, beaming, trying to catch her eye. She stared ahead, some strange mix of terror and joy on her face, and walked deliberately through the middle of the congregation as though she were trying to ignore everyone there.

After the vows and photos and everything else, and the two hundred–person congregation had shifted to the community centre across town, Womack found his seat at a table with strangers, right near the front of the reception hall. The folded card on his plate read *Womack + Guest*. The room began to fill, and Womack kept asking the woman on the other side of the empty chair between them what time it was, before, finally, just as the head groomsman was about to give his speech, Adriane came breezing in. She was dressed in black pants and a black sweater, and her hair was still wet from the shower.

Thanks for showing up, whispered Womack as she sat down.

Adriane shook out her napkin and laid it across her lap. That was some *hot* yoga.

Right, said Womack, and pulled away.

The speeches began. They were long. Adriane sat there,

her back to the stage, staring into space. Womack drank a few glasses of wine and began to feel disappointed that he hadn't been asked to speak. He would have been good. He was a writer, for fuck's sake.

Then the speeches were over and Cheryl was standing up at the front with a big white bouquet, back to the crowd, and a cluster of women were gathered jostling at the front of the hall. The deejay got on the microphone and everyone joined in the countdown, and at Zero! Cheryl launched the bouquet upwards over her head, and even before it landed, Womack could trace the trajectory, could see in horror that it was coming toward his table. When it smacked down on Adriane's plate he could only stare into all those flowers, the ivory gloss of them. He was aware vaguely of Adriane saying something like, Oh, fucking fantastic, and felt nothing when they got home later and her first move was to the kitchen, where she stuffed the entire bouquet into the trash underneath the sink.

AFTER THE BOY digests dinner it is time for his bath, and Womack fills the tub and strips the boy down and lifts him up and eases him into the water, which Womack takes great care to ensure is the right temperature. The water sloshes around and Womack struggles for a simile to describe it to himself in his head, but the boy is floundering about in the water and needs calming, so Womack abandons similes and instead attempts to soothe the boy by putting his hands over the boy's ears. The boy's thrashing subsides; he sinks down into the water with Womack's hands on his face, smiling, laughing. Then Womack sponges the boy down and shampoos his hair, and when the boy is pink and rosy and clean, Womack lifts him out of the tub and towels him off.

TWO WEEKS BEFORE Christmas Womack decided to buy a turkey. At the supermarket he scooped one from the deep freeze and brought it home on his bicycle in his backpack. When Adriane came home that evening from yoga, after she turned off his music and reappeared in the kitchen, Womack opened up the refrigerator door and displayed it to her, proudly, as if it were something he himself had constructed or laid.

Better keep it in the freezer, said Adriane.

Yeah?

Well, it's not going to keep in there forever.

Doesn't it look delicious?

Adriane eyed the turkey, a pinkish lump nestled between the milk and pickles. It looks like a dead bird, she said.

Womack slammed the fridge door. For fuck's sake, Ade.

What? She was laughing at him.

Can you get excited about anything?

A turkey? You want me to get excited about a turkey?

Well, something.

Adriane shook her head and went into the den. Womack followed her and stood in the doorway, watching her remove the Dictaphone from her pocket, place it softly on the coffee table, then pick up *Southeast Asia on a Shoestring* and start reading.

So when are we going? he asked.

Adriane laughed, turning the page. You think you could afford it?

Womack faltered. He could feel what was coming, knew it from so many bad TV shows, the script of The Couple's Fight.

What is this? he asked her finally.

What is what?

This. You. Never home. And when you are, acting like I don't exist — not talking, disappearing into that book, going to bed.

Don't you ever get tired of just sitting around? There was something tired and pleading in Adriane's eyes. Womack did his best not to read it as pity.

You want to take a vacation? he demanded. Take a vacation. Go. I'm not stopping you. I'll lend you an extra shoe-string if you want.

Oh, put it in your novel, writer. Adriane sighed, closed the book, and flopped back on the couch. She was silent. Womack was silent. Then there was a loud click from the Dictaphone. They both looked down at it sitting almost guiltily on the coffee table.

What the hell? he asked, moving across the room.

Adriane stood. Don't, she said.

But Womack was already there, the recorder in his hand, hitting the Eject button, popping the cassette out of the recorder. What's this? You're taping our conversations?

Adriane was reaching toward him, a nervous expression on her face.

Give that to me.

Womack slid the cassette back into the Dictaphone, hit Rewind for a few seconds, then Play.

From the speaker, his own voice — tinny, but audible: *Can you get excited about anything?*

And then Adriane's: *A turkey? You want me to get excited about a turkey?*

His, more incredulous and desperate than he remembered: *Well, something.*

And so on, their voices, back and forth. Finally, Adriane's, *Oh, put in your nov—* was cut off, and the tape began to whine before snapping to a stop.

Womack stood for a moment, silent, gazing at the Dictaphone in his hand as if it might speak up and offer an explanation. Adriane sat down on the couch.

How long have you been doing this? Womack asked, his back to her.

Adriane said nothing.

He rewound the cassette, farther this time, letting the counter wind backwards a few hundred digits. He pressed Play.

Here he was: *I guess so, yeah.* This was followed by hiss, the odd clank of something metallic. Chewing. Womack watched the wheels of the cassette turn, waiting. Then, himself again: *So, Southeast Asia.*

Yep, she said.

Sounds fun.

A pause. Her: *Something to read.*

Just something to read?

Womack hit Stop. Christ, he said. You're messed up, you know that? He took the cassette out of the recorder, turned it over in his hands.

There was a sigh from the couch, but Womack refused to

look over. He wiggled his finger into the empty space at the base of the cassette, hooked it under the tape, and began pulling, pulling — not angrily, but purposefully, the wheels spinning, however many of their recorded arguments unravelling into piles of glistening black ribbon at his feet.

AFTER BATHING THE boy, Womack has to get a diaper on him, which is always a struggle. With one hand Womack lifts the boy's legs and holds them together at the ankles, knees bent, while with the other he hoists up the boy's backside and attempts to wedge the diaper underneath. Occasionally the diaper ends up the wrong way on, but by then Womack is often so exhausted he says, Fuck it, to himself, and pulls the boy's pajamas on over the backward diaper and gives him some pills. The boy might at this point again be moaning. Womack does the hands-on-the-ears thing. It has become a reflex. The boy grins, gurgling, cooing. With his hands cupped over the boy's ears, Womack looks down at him, at the boy lying on the bed in his pajamas, something like delight on his face, and he tries not to think the expected thoughts of fortune and misfortune, chance and fate.

TWO NIGHTS AFTER the incident with the Dictaphone, Womack and Adriane had another argument that, with Adriane in bed and him sitting before his computer, filled Womack with shame and embarrassment. He recalled himself screaming things like, Will you think of someone other than yourself, for once? and Adriane crying and screaming back, When was the last time we did anything fun?

As Womack sat there, from behind the curtains in the bedroom came the light whistle of a snore, the creak of bed-springs as Adriane turned in her sleep. Womack pictured her, wrapped in the covers — but the image included him, lying next to her, staring into her face as she slept. A hard knot rose in his throat. Womack sighed deeply, rose from the uncomfortable chair, pushed through the curtains, and stood looking down at Adriane, her eyes closed, mouth half open, hair splayed across the pillow.

Hey, he said.

A pasty, smacking sound from her mouth.

He sat down on the bed, reached out, and prodded her with his fingertips. Hey.

Adriane rolled over. What time is it?

Ade, this isn't right. Us sleeping in the same bed.

What? She sat up.

Us, like this. I can't do it, act like nothing's wrong, lie down next to you. I can't sleep like that. Like, physically, I can't sleep.

Okay?

So maybe one of us should sleep on the couch. Like we could take turns, or whatever.

Look at you, she said. Her mouth was a crescent-shaped shadow in the dark.

Me?

Making decisions. I'm impressed.

What are you talking about?

I'm talking about you, actually doing something for a change. Not just sitting back and watching and then going to your computer and typing it all down.

I'm sorry?

You know, it's too bad you wrecked that tape I was making. I was planning on playing it back for you, so you could actually hear yourself. Like, for real, instead of the version you make up in your head.

What would you know about that?

Listen, she said, kicking the covers off. I think one of us sleeping on the couch is a great idea. And I volunteer myself. Seriously. No problem. The bed's all yours.

And then she ducked through the curtains and was gone. Womack looked down at the S-shaped indentation her body had imprinted on the mattress. Lying down, curling his own body to fill the shape, he could smell Adriane's hair on the pillow. He pulled the sheets around him and cocooned himself within the heat she had left behind.

WOMACK'S LAST TASK before he puts the boy to bed is to give him water. This is not as simple as running the tap into a cup and tipping it down the boy's throat; while puréed foods are not a problem, the boy chokes on liquids. Drinking is a complicated, almost medical procedure. The boy has been outfitted with a sort of valve above his belly button. It looks to Womack like a valve you might find on a pair of children's water wings: a little tube that juts out of the boy's stomach and a stopper on a flexible hinge that plugs and unplugs the opening of the tube. In the corner of the bedroom, Womack sits the boy down in his wheelchair, lifts his shirt to expose the valve, and attaches a tube connected to an IV bag hanging from the ceiling. Water from the bag drips along the tube and directly into the boy's stomach. Womack sits back, waiting, and watches the boy drink.

ONE OF THE last nights before Adriane moved out, Womack came home from volunteering and she was sleeping in the bed, the curtains open. The blankets on the couch were still there, crumpled in a woolly ball from where she had kicked them that morning. It was early, barely nine o'clock. Womack stood between the open curtains, looking down on her lying there, listening for the whistle of her breath. There was silence. Womack knew she was awake.

Hey, he said, getting into bed.

There was no reply, but Womack could feel her shifting, moving closer.

Hey, he said again.

Adriane turned over. Womack reached out and put his hand to her face, felt the wetness of tears on her cheek.

Just sleeping, right? said Adriane. No fooling around.

Womack nodded, avoided saying anything about old time's sake.

He slid one arm underneath her neck, another around her back, his thigh between her legs. Their faces were close. Her breath was salty and hot.

I miss you, he said.

Adriane sniffed.

He kissed her, then, felt her lips against his, but the kiss felt only like a gesture: a handshake, a nod, a wave goodbye. Then she turned and he curled tightly into her back and closed his eyes. After a few minutes like this, he felt her body relax as she fell asleep. Her breath came in deep, restful sighs.

Womack lay there, the tickle of Adriane's hair against his face. Sleepless minutes became an hour. An hour became two. He was hot. He kicked the covers off. Another hour passed. Womack thought, Sleep, sleep. He tried to match his breathing to hers. Eventually, he rolled away, releasing her, and sat up. Legs dangling off the bed, Womack looked at Adriane over his shoulder. Her face.

In the kitchen Womack filled a mug with milk and put it in the microwave, which whirred to life and cast a yellow glow in the dark kitchen. He leaned back on the counter in front of the refrigerator, smiled, then reached forward, opening the freezer. A cold blast of air, and there was the turkey, surrounded by ice-cube trays and TV dinners and Tupperware.

In the den, Womack sat down with his warm milk on the uncomfortable chair and turned on his computer. He sipped at the milk while things booted up, thinking of the turkey in the freezer: a last sad attempt at domesticity, futile and abandoned and collecting the white fur of frost.

When the computer was ready, he opened up the file on the desktop that was his novel and sat there, reading it over, rolling slightly this way and that. He leaned back. The milk was done. He let the cup rest in his lap, stretched out his legs, and the next morning when Adriane woke, she found him asleep in the chair underneath the window, the computer's screensaver whirling around on the other side of the room.

ON THE BOY'S bed are a harness and guardrail to prevent him from rolling out over the course of the night. These Womack once forgot to put in place; he realized the following morning and promptly called the boy's mother to make sure the boy had not cracked his skull open over the course of the night. The boy had not. Sylvia explained that every night after Womack leaves the house, she checks on her son and kisses him goodnight.

NOW IT IS the last Saturday before Christmas. Next week the family has told Womack to take the day off. A holiday. But today Womack is scheduled to head out there on his bicycle, to go through his routine with the boy of opening doors and supper and bathtime and bedtime.

In his place that he now inhabits alone, in his place that is not quite loft and not quite apartment, his place that contains just under half as much furniture and two tropical house-plants fewer than it did a few weeks prior, Womack gets ready for his day of volunteering. He eats a sensible lunch of a bowl of soup, a bagel, and an apple. The coffee maker is gone, so instead Womack makes a cup of tea, which he sips while he edits a draft of his novel, not yet complete but still printed out and lying in two stacks on the kitchen table. He works with a blue pen on the stack of paper to his right. The completed pages he turns over and adds to the stack to his left. If he were honest with himself, he would admit that he cannot write any-thing new; the editing gives him something to do.

When it is time to leave, Womack finishes the page he is working on, stands, puts on his coat and hat and gloves, checks for the key to his bike lock in his pocket. At the door on his way out, he pauses for a moment, looking back across the kitchen, at the refrigerator, at the freezer.

At the family's house Sylvia is waiting, as always, with her son in his wheelchair, but this time the other children are decorating a Christmas tree in the corner of the room. Andrew is hanging ornaments with methodical symmetry; Jessica is wrapping the branches in silver tinsel. A blue macaroni angel looms above. Womack removes his coat and hat and gloves, lowers his backpack to the ground.

What's in the bag? asks the boy's mother.

Ah, says Womack. A little present.

He opens the zipper, and, shaking the backpack a bit, produces the turkey.

A turkey, says Sylvia. Beside her, the boy begins to moan.

I thought we could maybe have it tonight, says Womack, cradling it like an infant, adding, Together.

That's very kind of you, says Sylvia, but I think it's still frozen. It'll take at least a day to thaw before we can even think about cooking it.

Womack wavers at this, feeling vulnerable and foolish.

Hastily, Sylvia holds out her hands for the turkey. But if you're not going to eat it, we'd love to keep it for another time.

Womack smiles. The boy moans. Okay, says Womack.

The rest of the afternoon is spent predictably: the walking about, the doors, supper, the boy's bath. Womack lies the boy down on his bed, lifts the boy's legs up in the air, does his best to get the diaper on. Next: pajamas. Outside the December sky glows a dull orange. Womack closes the blinds of the boy's bedroom, pulls back the covers, starts to lift the latches on the guardrail to secure it alongside the mattress.

When the boy is safely in bed, Womack's duties will be over for the evening. He will cross the hall and knock on Sylvia's bedroom door. He will hear the click of the lock and the door will open and Sylvia will smile a tired sort of smile and say, Thank you, Martin, Merry Christmas, and Martin Womack will say, No problem, Merry Christmas to you too. He will say, See you in two weeks, Sylvia, and Sylvia will say, Yes.

But tonight, Womack realizes, in the den Jessica and Andrew will not be packing up The Game of Life, Jessica having won again, her little car packed with the blue and pink pegs of a successful family, her bank account bursting, her assets bountiful. They will have finished decorating the tree. They might be watching a movie, a Christmas movie, the tree blinking coloured lights from the corner of the room. Goodbye, Womack will whisper, as he puts on his coat. Jessica will say, Your turkey's in the fridge, not turning from the movie, and Andrew will wave and grin.

And so Womack will leave the family. He will head outside and unchain his bicycle and hop up onto it and push off and begin to pedal his way home, where his half-written novel waits for him on his kitchen table. The bicycle will cut down the darkened streets of the suburbs, heading toward the city and the novel. The streets will be black and wet with melted snow and spangled golden with streetlights, and riding back home along them, through the winter night, will tonight feel to Womack a little bit like falling.

WHEN JACQUES COUSTEAU GAVE PABLO PICASSO A PIECE OF BLACK CORAL

ON ONE OF their many dives in the Red Sea, Jacques Cousteau and his crew excavated a piece of rare black coral from the reefs off the shores of the Sudan. Months later, Cousteau sat with Pablo Picasso on the whitewashed balcony of the painter's villa in Cannes, drinking wine of an inconsequential vintage and gazing out over the Mediterranean.

"I've brought you something," Cousteau said, reaching into his satchel and producing the coral. He handed it to his friend. "The Saudis use it to make prayer beads."

Picasso nodded, turning the coral over in his hands. It was a small branch from one of the great underwater trees, brownish and knobby. Beneath the villa, the sea crashed frothing against the seawall.

"It took one of our men over an hour to saw it off." Cousteau smiled. "He came up covered in coral mucus. Two days to wash himself clean."

Picasso nodded again. He ran his thumb over the coral's rough terrain, cataloging its crevices and ridges by touch. Then, with a jerky motion, the painter tossed the coral into the air, caught it, and dropped it into the pocket of his baggy velvet trousers, where it became a vague lump in the soft fabric. Picasso raised his glass to Cousteau. "Thank you," he said, and swallowed the wine in a single gulp.

INSIDE, COUSTEAU moved from room to room admiring the art that filled the villa: paintings piled on floors, drawings pinned to walls, sculptures clumped in corners. He stopped before a sketch of Picasso's mural at the UNESCO building in Paris. In its centre was what looked like a spindly blue man, falling downwards, arms flailing over his head.

Picasso slid up beside Cousteau and placed a hand on the explorer's shoulder. Cousteau pointed to the man in the picture. "What's he meant to be doing?"

"You know," Picasso said, "art critics have written extensively about that figure. Some say it is the fall of Icarus. Others that it is Lucifer being cast from heaven."

"So?" said Cousteau, still staring at the drawing.

"Don't tell anybody, Jacques." Here Picasso leaned in closer, his mouth almost touching Cousteau's ear, the wine sweet and lemony on his breath. He whispered, "I was just trying to paint a diver."

WHEN IT WAS time for Cousteau to leave, Picasso walked with him down the stone stairs of the villa. With one arm he held the door open for Cousteau as he stepped outside onto the street. Picasso's other hand remained buried deep in the pocket of his trousers.

"Sorry to run, Pablito," said Cousteau, "but I'm playing truant from my crew."

Picasso laughed. "Back to discovering lost worlds," he said.

"And you, back to inventing new ones." Cousteau reached out to shake hands.

Picasso hastily removed his hand from his pocket. In it, a rusty, mottled husk, sat the piece of black coral. He paused for a moment, locking eyes with his friend. Then, before either could speak, Picasso slapped his hand into Cousteau's, clasping the coral between their palms. Cousteau felt it there, the sharp sting of its knobs and spines. Picasso pumped his arm vigorously, crushing the coral into Cousteau's hand. Then he pulled away.

"Take care, Jacques," Picasso said, grinning. He dropped the coral into his pocket, waved, and closed the door.

Cousteau was left standing on the street, the midday sun slicing down and carving shadows from the rooftops, the thunder of surf in the distance. His palm still stung. Turning his hand over, looking down, Cousteau saw what had been etched there: a pattern of holes and furrows and puckered wrinkles, carved deep and pink into his skin.

ACKNOWLEDGEMENTS

"The Film We Made About Dads" was first published online at sweetfancymoses.com, and subsequently in *Maisonneuve* magazine.

"Pushing Oceans In and Pulling Oceans Out" was first published in *Prism International* as "Pulling Oceans In and Pushing Oceans Out."

The postcard described in "Dizzy When You Look Down In" is real and very exciting.

"The Love Life of the Automaton Turk" could not have been written without Mark Sussman's essay, "Performing the Intelligent Machine: Deception and Enchantment in the Life of the Automaton Chess Player," published in *The Drama Review* and *The Turk: The Life and Times of the Famous Eighteenth-Century Chess-Playing Machine* by Tom Standage.

"The Past Composed" was first published in *Grain* and subsequently in *The Journey Prize Stories 16*. The art exhibit described in this story is an installation by Douglas Gordon called "30 Second Text."

"Respite" was first published in *Malahat Review* and subsequently in *The Journey Prize Stories 18*. The Fountain Group is based on Le Phare, a non-profit organization that provides respite care to families with terminally ill children in Montreal. Please donate money to them.

"When Jacques Cousteau Gave Pablo Picasso a Piece of Black Coral" was first published in *Prairie Fire* and borrows heavily from Cousteau's excellent book *The Living Sea*.

I'd like to express special gratitude to the Ontario Arts Council and the Toronto Arts Council for financial assistance.

There are many, many people who deserve credit for their various roles in helping turn a file on my computer into this book. Thanks to each and every one of you, very much, for all your help and support.

ABOUT THE AUTHOR

Photo: Jason Borners

PASHA MALLA was born in St. John's, Newfoundland, grew up in London, Ontario, and now lives in Toronto, Ontario. He has written regularly for *McSweeney's*, has had multiple stories nominated for the Pushcart and Journey prizes, and has contributed to CBC Radio's "Definitely Not the Opera." He is currently working on a novel to be published by Anansi in 2010.

Printed in the United States
by Baker & Taylor Publisher Services